Challenged

The Awakened Series: Book Two

Kenneth Creech

Other books by Kenneth Creech:

Awakened
The Awakened Series: Book One

Challenged
By Kenneth Creech
Published by Kenneth Creech

Copyright © 2022, by Kenneth Creech
All rights reserved.

Dedication:

To everyone who believed I might, even when I didn't know I could.

Beginnings

Excerpt from
<u>The Awakened History</u>:
Romulus and Remus
April 771 BC:

Their feet sunk into the mud as they pressed on through the dense grasses. The sun beat down on them, relentless in the midday sky as if it were personally watching over their journey through the wilderness to ensure they didn't make another mistake. The two men had been traveling up and down the Tiber for three days, looking for the contents of the woven basket that held the twins. So far, there had been no signs of anything they could bring back with them. Cnaeusis had already reported the deaths to his master, but neither he nor Felix was positive, they had died, and certainty was the only thing that mattered. Amulius had been clear that their death was the only acceptable outcome; the twins could not be allowed to survive into adulthood. Failure to kill them surely meant that Felix and Cnaeusis would take their place in the afterlife, and Cnaeusis was not eager to leave his life behind.

As they left a particularly thick patch of tall grasses, Felix spotted what looked like the overturned basket washed up on the shore. Both he and Cnaeusis ran to the basket but found it empty, with no sign of the twins. Surrounding the basket, they found paw prints left in the mud, which led to the river's edge and away again, but it was impossible to tell whether the animal and the basket had been in the area at the same time. They decided to follow the prints as far as they could to find out whether the animal had completed the job they had not.

Felix pointed to a change in the tracks. "It looks like it was dragging something here." He knelt and touched the faint marks that began after a few hundred yards. "It was carrying something in its mouth; the drag marks split the paw prints." Cnaeusis bent down, examining the line in the dirt. He had always been a servant and had not learned how to track animals, so the lines meant nothing to him. But he trusted what Felix told him because the Gods blessed him with luck, something Cnaeusis hoped would rub off on him.

"We proceed then, and we may yet save ourselves, Felix!" Cnaeusis' mood was beginning to lift. Since he had lied to Amulius, he could not eat or sleep, which was a fast way to die in Alba Longa. Now that they seemed to have found out the twins were likely dead, Cnaeusis could feel his hunger returning as keenly as he felt the overwhelming need to sleep. The two continued in silence, Felix tracking and Cnaeusis daydreaming about a good night's sleep. He was so far into his imagination that he did not notice when Felix stopped abruptly and plowed right into him.

Both men fell face-first into the dirt, and when Cnaeusis looked up, he could see what had caused Felix to stop so suddenly. Right next to his left hand was the most recent print from the animal, but this print had five toes, a heel, and a long arch that connected them all. The animal prints had disappeared entirely, and in their place were two very human-looking feet. As the realization of what they had been tracking settled over both men, a faint cry filled the air. It was coming from a large fig tree just ahead of them.

They scrambled to their feet and crept toward the tree, their knives ready. Felix took the lead and walked around the side of the tree toward the sound. Cnaeusis followed at a distance, which allowed him to see the surprise that overtook Felix's face before he disappeared behind the tree and out of Cnaeusis' view. He could hear Felix's cries of pain, which froze him in place until the sounds stopped. As he circled behind the tree, he saw the last remnants of a woman's human body before she became a wolf.

Cnaeusis ran toward the wolf, his knife held high in the air, and tried to plunge it into her body before she could bite him. The people in the Alba Longa spoke in whispers about the shifters, but Cnaeusis, as a royal servant, felt he was above the superstition. However, it was hard for him to deny the animal staring him down now, and the intelligence in her eyes was apparent. She jumped out of the way of his knife and advanced on him slowly. She moved to his left to get him away from the protection of the tree where Felix's body laid, motionless. As he backed away from the beast, Cnaeusis heard twin cries a few feet away from where he had been standing. The wolf had moved him away from his target, and while he was distracted, she attacked him.

He used his knife to stab and cut her where he could, but her attack was so violent that he lost his grip on the blade, and she tossed it away with her nose. The wolf watched as he struggled to breathe until she seemed satisfied that he was no longer a threat, and then turned and walked back toward the tree where the twins were hidden. Before he died, Cnaeusis saw the young woman appear again with the twins, Romulus and Remus, still carefully wrapped in their blankets and safe in her arms.

Challenged
Part One

Chapter One
Present Day

"Caleb, we've got a problem!" Adam burst into my bedroom while I tried to cling to the final minutes of sleep before I knew I had to get up.

Dread immediately filled me, and I jumped out of bed. "What? Oh, God! What happened? Hang on. I'm almost ready!" I tripped over my dirty clothes piled up next to the bed, random shoes, and some books I'd been reading. "One second!" I grabbed the first shirt my hand touched and pulled it over my head. I was pretty sure it was on backward, but this was no time to worry about my appearance. It took me another minute to get dressed, and then I ran past Adam toward the front door of Lorelai's house, where I was still staying. I'd hoped to be back in my apartment by now, but it hadn't yet been a week since I had awakened, and no one was taking any chances.

I stood by the door and waited for Adam to come down the hall after me. I went back to my room to get him when he didn't. He sat on the edge of my bed calmly, with a smirk on his face. I looked down at myself; sure enough, my shirt was on backward and inside out. Even after I fixed it, he still didn't budge, and the slight smile never left his face. I wanted to smack him in his adorable dimple.

Instead, I yelled at him. "What?!"

"We're out of milk, and I really wanted cereal for breakfast."

I shot him a glare that could maim as I tried to process what he'd just told me. "You want *what?*"

Now that my anxiety level was relatively normal, I had difficulty functioning.

His smile grew with his reply. "I wanted cereal for breakfast, but now we have to go out for food instead. Fortunately, you look ready to go."

I tried to protest, but he walked past me and touched my arm as he did.

"I'll drive."

He continued down the hall, and an intense desire for a ham and egg burrito hit me. He'd pushed his hunger into my mind when he touched my arm. The last time I'd tried that on him, an attempt to make him fall in love with me ended with me going insane for a cheeseburger. You can only make people want things they might typically want on their own, a technicality I hadn't known at the time. He still hadn't told me exactly how it worked, and so far, it only led to me eating when he was hungry.

"Damn it, Adam! I told you to stop doing that to me. You're going to mess up my normal eating schedule." He was already out the door and wouldn't have cared even if he had heard me. My sleep schedule hadn't changed since I'd been fired from my overnight job at the hotel, and everyone was trying to get me to spend more time awake during the day. Adam was the only one who still found it funny to watch me run around like a crazy person. He took advantage of my extreme level of anxiety anytime he could, to mess with me. There was no way he'd let me go back to bed now, and my stomach began to make a strange keening noise, so I followed him out to his car.

"Just so you know, I hate you." I buckled myself into my seat and then crossed my arms in front of me.

"Oh good," he said, his face calm, though I could tell he was hiding a smirk. "That should keep you from ogling me while we eat breakfast." He winked at me, and I couldn't keep my laughter from filling the car.

"I don't ogle," I said. "I merely appreciate." My cheeks flushed red, as we sped off down the driveway and toward breakfast. "Anyway, I have Gabriel now. I don't have to ogle or appreciate anyone else anymore." I thought about what I'd just said and rolled my eyes a little. "Well, you know what I mean."

He just laughed at me, as he took the turns at 60 miles an hour.

"I do. Speaking of Gabriel, where has he been? I thought you two would be connected at the hip now that you're officially together." Adam had a strange way of talking about my relationship with Gabriel. It sometimes sounded like jealousy, but he had Megan, and she rarely stopped talking about how hot he was.

"He's with his mom right now. He wanted to show the new pack members that he is still one of them, even if they are all now part of us." I got confused when I tried to talk about the packs because there was only one now, but days ago, we'd been ready to kill each other. There was still a feeling of us versus them, but Gabriel and I had done our best to bridge the divide and create a singular group identity.

"That's understandable. From what I've seen, you both seem to be handling the stress that awakening early thrust into your lives well." His compliment seemed sincere, which was a nice change. I was about to respond when I caught a glimpse of my shoes. One was black and dressy. The other was a white tennis shoe. Proof that I was still not great under pressure, even when I was in control of my body and mind.

"Yeah, thanks. So why did you drag me out of bed at…" I glanced at the clock on the dashboard, "10:15 in the morning?" It still felt early to me, but from the appearance of his dimple, I could tell that he was holding back a laugh and likely didn't feel bad for me.

"We need to discuss some issues that have to be addressed soon. I thought it would be good if you had some knowledge of what was waiting for you before anything happened."

He pulled into the parking lot of a small Mexican restaurant and turned off the car before looking at me.

"I know I'm not officially in any position to tell you how to do things, but I want you to know that you can come to me with questions, and I will be there for you."

His serious expression surprised me, given how he'd been acting. I nodded and tried to swallow down the nerves that had started to creep up from my chest.

I grabbed his forearm, looking into his eyes as I did. "Thank you, Adam. I appreciate your willingness to help us through this transition, you have been a great support, and I know I speak for both of us when I say…let's eat!" I smiled, let go of his arm, and then ran to the restaurant before he could figure out what I'd done.

"Caleb!"

"Payback's a bitch isn't it?"

I laughed and went inside to order a meat-filled burrito just to mess with him. He ended up ordering the same despite my best suggestive efforts, which meant he didn't normally eat egg whites and steamed veggies. No surprise there. I would figure out the whole suggestive touch thing someday. Being one of the "most powerful" Alphas ever had to count for something, right?

When our food arrived, we sat in silence, our mouths too full to carry on the conversation without losing pieces of our burritos. Once we finished, Adam put on his serious face, and I knew I'd better get ready to pay attention.

"Your mother asked me to get you up to speed because very soon, she will officially step down as the Alpha of our pack, and you and Gabriel will need to take over. You'll be responsible for handling the disagreements that you're already dealing with, but you will also oversee everything else, as well. The pack has a bank account that we all have to contribute to, and you'll take over as the signers on that account."

I checked to make sure he was about to laugh at me for falling for another joke before interrupting him. "Are you messing with me? I barely have my own bank account, how the heck am I supposed to manage other people's money?"

"That's easy, you just let it accumulate, and hope we don't have to use it."

"Oh great! Now you've jinxed it, and I'm gonna mess the whole thing up." I had already begun to try to figure out how I could get out of this responsibility, but Adam was determined to continue.

"I'm sure you'll do just fine. In addition to the bank account, you also lead any pack-related meetings and events, which means you need to learn our traditions, and you're responsible for the training of the newly awakened." I could handle the meeting stuff, but the training wasn't something I felt qualified to do on my own. Then I remembered that Lorelai had recruited Adam and Carlos to train me. Thinking about Carlos caused my stomach to clench, and I had to focus on something else so I could breathe.

"I can delegate some of that stuff, right?" Adam began to move around in his seat and crack his knuckles, then nodded. "So I could get you to do the training then? You're good at that stuff…you and Brent, maybe? He'd be interested in helping out right?"

His smile finally broke through, and the knuckle popping stopped. "We could do the training. I know Brent would be willing to help, but you may want to consider adding a woman to help so everyone has as much knowledge as possible."

I raised my eyebrows at his suggestion, but smiled when his expression remained earnest. I was happy to include a woman in training and remembered some of the ones that had fought against me when Carlos was in charge. I was surprised that Adam wanted to share the responsibility with anyone, even Brent. His suggestion of adding a third trainer seemed out of place to me.

"It'd be a good way to incorporate some of the new members and help the rest of them feel more comfortable if they knew someone who was helping out."

"I have to say that I'm pretty impressed with you Adam. You're welcoming the new members a lot faster than I thought you would; being willing to train with them is even more amazing."

"Are you kidding? I want to see what they can do!" The fire was back in his eyes, and they began to glow slightly. Leave it to him to make a diplomatic gesture, based solely on a desire to fight.

"I'll talk to Gabriel later and find out who in the new group might be interested, and the five of us can sit down sometime and discuss what the best approach would be. Will you bring it up to Brent and make sure he's interested?"

"I'll send him a text right now, but I can pretty much guarantee that he'll want to help with training. It's something we talked about when we were going through it at your age." He snatched my hat from my head, messed up my hair, and then put the hat back on over my eyes.

I fixed my hat and glared at him again.

"On second thought, maybe Brent and Gabriel's pick can handle training on their own."

I got up and threw my trash away before walking out to the car. I could hear Adam following behind me, but it wasn't until we got to the car that he attacked.

"You wouldn't dare!" He grabbed me around the waist and started tickling my sides and stomach. I laughed so hard I had to gasp for air before he finally relented, and I agreed to let him help with training. He smiled as he walked around the car to the driver's side and got in. I wasn't sure what just happened, but I didn't think I would tell Gabriel about it, just in case.

Chapter Two

We got back to Lorelai's house quickly, and I left Adam to his own devices while I went to call Gabriel. We hadn't seen each other much since we'd awakened, and I hoped that would change soon. I missed the days of seeing him at work, carrying luggage or running back to his post after parking a car. I always tried to catch his eye or find a way to talk to him, which usually ended in me muttering something unintelligible. Now that we were officially together, it felt like some of the excitement had already begun to disappear. I shook my head to try to clear the negative thoughts away, and instead focused on how excited I would be when we finally got together again tonight.

I dialed his number and lay back on my bed while I waited for him to answer. After a couple of rings, he answered, and the happiness in his voice was unmistakable. My doubts seemed to float away the moment he said, "Hey! I was thinking about you!"

I smiled and settled down further into my comforter.

"Oh really? Good things I hope." I laughed.

"Of course! I was thinking about heading to quit my job at the hotel now that things have calmed down enough for me to do it. Do you want to come?"

He'd promised me he would quit after I told him I was fired. At the time, I didn't know that he had only taken the job because his old alpha had made him. Now that she was dead, and I was gone, he said it didn't make any sense for him to stay. It made me feel good that, even though he didn't have to quit, he was going to because I was not there. I chose to ignore the fact that he was also not being forced to stay anymore. Who cared about details?

"Are you sure about this? It is a paycheck. Giving up the one you have for no reason may make it harder to find another one."

He didn't pause to think about it. "I'm not staying. Without you peeking over at me every few minutes I don't think I'd have any fun."

I was caught off-guard and struggled with a reply.

Beginning to laugh at my silence, he went on, "I thought it was cute that you didn't think I could see you even though the glass was transparent."

That got me laughing, too. "I was just making sure you were doing your job correctly."

I could feel my cheeks blush, and was glad he couldn't see my face at the moment. "Besides, I've seen how other people look at you. I don't think you would have any issues getting attention without me around to stare at you."

"I liked that you couldn't take your eyes off me." He said it so quietly that I almost didn't hear him.

I wasn't sure how to respond, so I pretended that I hadn't heard.

"Can you pick me up? I'm still without a car right now." I slapped my forehead. *Why was I the least smooth person in the world?*

"No problem; I'll be there in a few hours if that's okay, I have some errands to run first." I agreed, and we hung up.

I'm such an idiot! I rolled over and buried my face in my pillow. Soon enough, I could feel myself drifting back to sleep, which seemed better than thinking about my idiocy.

I'd barely fallen asleep when the darkness closed in on me. This time I didn't run because I knew there was no escape. Instead of being afraid, I remembered it was how I changed shape. In my dream, my body took on all kinds of forms, not just the wolf I'd become recently. Suddenly everything stopped, and a mirror materialized in the distance. When I looked in the mirror I was surprised to see that it wasn't my reflection looking back. It was the same shape and had the same hair, but my eyes weren't the bright blue they should have been, and I looked older somehow. When I tried to get a closer look, the mirror disappeared, and I could feel myself shifting. Unable to maintain a shape longer than a few seconds, I started to panic. My eyes snapped open, and I realized I'd been dreaming. Sweat covered my body, and I was now wrapped up in my sheets.

I checked the time on my phone and realized it was almost 2:00 pm and I'd slept for over two hours. After shaking off the dream and forgetting about the face that looked back at me from the mirror, I realized I still hadn't showered, and I was wearing dirty clothes and two different types of shoes. It was one thing for Adam to see me like that, but I wanted to look as good as possible around Gabriel. I turned on my shower and stripped down, making sure to put all the dirty clothes in the hamper so I wouldn't wear them again.

Just before I climbed into the steam filled shower, I caught a glimpse of my reflection in the mirror and realized I looked a little different. I'd packed on a little more muscle, which I attributed to fight training. I had also started to get a bit more color in my face and arms. Not having to work the night shift meant I could be out in the sun occasionally. The changes looked good in my opinion, and hopefully, Gabriel thought so too.

Twenty minutes later, I was squeaky clean and dry. I was combing my hair when I heard a knock on the bedroom door and Gabriel walked into the room. As soon as I saw him a huge smile spread across my face, and I couldn't stop it no matter how hard I tried.

His face lit up just as much, and he came into the bathroom to give me a hug. I inhaled his now familiar scent of chocolate, and something wild, which I found out was his inner wolf. "Mmm."

"What?" He pulled back and looked at me, his brows furrowed. I was a couple inches taller than his six-foot frame, so we fit perfectly together when we hugged. His hair, which was now a mixture of dark brown with streaks of maroon tickled my cheek, which caused me to laugh a little and made him even more curious. "What's so funny?" He squeezed me tightly.

The blush that spread across my face helped to erase my grin.

"Nothing, I'm just happy to see you." I turned around then and hoped to avoid making an even bigger fool of myself. "Let me finish doing my hair really quickly, and then I will be ready to go."

I grabbed a brush off the sink and ran it through my dark hair quickly, the hair started to fall into place without much effort. I picked out matching shoes and some socks, and we were out the door.

Gabriel opened the passenger door for me, and I just stood there for a minute, thinking he was going to grab an old fast-food bag or some other item he'd left there. Instead, he looked at me and waited until I figured out that he had opened it for me and got in the car I'd never had anyone open a door for me before; unless I counted the time Adam had carried me over his shoulder before he threw me into his car-- which I didn't.

Gabriel reached out and took my hand in his own. I waited for the shock that used to accompany our touches, but it was noticeably absent. Instead, I felt the warmth spread from his hand into mine, which felt nice. For some reason, my heart started to race, and when I looked down at our hands, mine had begun to shift into a midnight black paw.

"Oh, what the hell!?" I pulled my paw away from Gabriel before the change could travel further up my arm. He started to laugh uncomfortably, and I joined him, nervousness fueling my laughter.

"That's not the most convenient thing to ever happen to me."

His laughter filled the car and helped me to relax. Before long we had forgotten the awkwardness from earlier and moved on to an easy conversation. I filled him in on my talk this morning with Adam and his suggestion that we find someone from Gabriel's half of the pack to help train the young.

"I have the perfect person in mind. She was part of our old alpha's core group. You've met her, at the hotel." I tried to think about all the women I had seen over the past few months at work, and then the realization of who he meant hit me, and I freaked out.

"You had better be shitting me right now," I said. The face of the woman who had accompanied the old alpha and Dominic the first night I realized I was in danger was burned into my memory. Her 'smile' that was just teeth and the sense of fear that she and the others instilled in me was hard to shake. "Isn't there anyone who hasn't threatened my life that you can think of?"

"What do you mean? They weren't supposed to threaten you; they were only there to see if you were the son of Lorelai. Did she say anything to you?"

I thought back on that night, "Well, technically no. But Dominic came back after and tried to scare…well, he didn't try, he succeeded in scaring me. And then he killed Karen, who came to protect me."

Gabriel looked at me out of the corner of his eye, continuing to drive toward downtown.

"But Tanya had nothing to do with that, and she's the best fighter in my pack now that Dominic and our old alpha are dead. I think she'd be a great asset to the whole pack."

It was hard to argue an emotional point against someone using logic. I knew this was supposed to signify that we were all together as one pack, so I agreed.

"Tanya, it is then. I'll tell Adam when we get back to the house."

Gabriel smiled at me. "You won't regret it, I promise." As he said it, he leaned over and kissed me. "What else do we need to do for the pack? It feels like there should be some big event to bring us all together," he tapped his fingers against the steering wheel.

I thought about it and realized I didn't know much about the pack's day-to-day activities. When I found out I was an Awakened, I was around some of the pack members, but it wasn't until the attacks that everyone else came together.

"What was your pack like before they tried to take over this area? Did you all get together all the time? Were there weekly pack meetings or group runs or something?"

He looked at me like I was crazy, then realized I was completely serious, and he started to laugh at me again. I was getting tired of this response; I had no idea what it was like to be raised with other Awakened.

"No, none of that stuff. But my mom and I were sent to live out here when I was young to keep track of your pack. The rest didn't come to California until recently, so I'm unsure what they did before getting here. Once they arrived, though, we rarely got together as a whole pack. The alpha and her core group would make decisions, which got passed down through the ranks until everyone knew what was happening."

"So, we don't have a good reason to get everyone together for official pack stuff, then?"

"Not as far as I know…but we could call a meeting and make sure everyone is there. We're the new alphas, after all."

The idea of forcing anyone to do anything sounded ridiculous, but I was willing to try it.

"Okay, we can talk to my mom about how to get the message out to my half, and you can talk to yours about spreading it to your half. All that's left is for us to decide what we want to say at this meeting."

We talked about it for the last few minutes of our trip downtown but put it on hold when we pulled into a parking spot near the hotel. Gabriel had typed up an official resignation letter that he planned to leave for Robert, so I decided there was nothing wrong with walking in with him. I could tell that my presence was not as unnoticed as I'd hoped it would be. My old co-workers from the front desk saw me and immediately started to gossip.

"There he is…I can't believe he said a homeless guy attacked him. I mean, really? What an idiot!"

"I know, right?! Like a homeless guy would come into the hotel. And now I have to cover his shift until Robert finds someone else. He deserved to get fired." Then a guest approached the desk, and they had to stop their chatter and work.

My increased hearing ability came in handy but left me feeling a little sick. I'd never said a homeless guy came into the hotel, but I did tell Robert I was attacked. Somehow that news made its rounds and turned into something too ridiculous to believe. I was glad to be out of this place and never had to worry about running into these people again.

"Mmmm, look at his fine ass."

"It's too bad he has to stay outside all day with those losers."

The voices from the front desk attendants caught my attention again as their gossip continued. I could tell they weren't talking about me, but when I saw them looking at Gabriel, I just about lost my composure. They were practically drooling over him as he waited for the door to the back to open so he could leave his letter for Robert. They smiled at him every time he looked over in their direction. The door finally opened, and when he disappeared through it, they turned their attention back out to the front, where they caught me looking at them.

"Oh god, he's looking at us again," one of them said to the other. Trying to tune them out, I quickly looked away, listening to cars driving past outside instead. I was still concentrating on the traffic when Gabriel returned, so I jumped a little when he reached out and touched my shoulder.

I looked up and smiled at him. "Sorry about that. I was lost in my head. You ready?"

"Yep, I'm officially a free man now. Well, when it comes to work anyway," he said. He smiled at me and started to walk toward the sliding glass doors to leave. I could feel the eyes from the front desk on him, so I decided to do something a little out of character for me. I grabbed his arm and pulled him into a kiss in the middle of the lobby. I heard gasps all around us, but the two from the front desk made me smile.

"I'm so proud of you." I put my arm around his waist as we walked out. Before we were completely out of sight, I waved goodbye to the hateful pair still watching us leave. The look on their faces made the public kissing worthwhile, and my smile from earlier returned.

Chapter Three

On the way home, we decided to stop and get a late lunch, which my stomach appreciated. I didn't like to talk about the pack while it was just the two of us. I was always afraid I would make the wrong suggestion or mess something up without someone else to keep me in line, and I didn't want it to have to be Gabriel. But I realized I would have to do so before long, so I sucked it up. It felt strange to attempt to speak with any authority on a subject I knew nothing about. I decided to wait until we got back to the car, which also helped to protect our conversation from prying ears.

The trip to Lorelai's house passed faster than I'd hoped. I never seemed to run into traffic when I wanted to go slowly; it only happened when I had places to be. The short drive was enough time to determine what we planned to do to get everyone together. We'd decided that even though everyone needed to come, we would try to make it as enjoyable as possible. I assumed we could throw together some food and drinks for a gathering and announce the changes we implemented once everyone arrived.

Gabriel was confident he could get everyone from his side of the pack, and I knew Lorelai could get everyone on our side. I wasn't sure they'd come running when I called, but I hoped that would change after the gathering. We agreed that we would make it clear that we were one united pack, and, as a result, Gabriel and I had to stop referring to the pack as his side and my side. It meant I would have to learn a few new names and faces, but fortunately, Gabriel was there to help. He mentioned that we should create a small group of advisors from the group to help us keep everything in order, and I thought it was a great idea. I nominated Lorelai and Olivia, and he selected two men he knew, Lucas and Kevin. That gave us people within the pack that could help with any problems as they arose or act as an ear for thoughts and concerns from the pack beyond our own.

Finally, I told him I was still trying to figure out how to shift forms, and I was still waiting for someone to bother to teach me.

"But you changed during the fight in the arena? And you changed back as soon as the fight ended. How do you not know how to do it?"

His face was scrunched up, and his head was cocked to the side as he looked at me. It made me laugh and helped me feel more at ease about my lack of knowledge.

"You did that. I didn't know what was happening. I got angry, and I started to cramp up. Then, when we were done fighting, you touched me again, and I was suddenly myself. I didn't think about changing or anything like that, so I haven't been able to do it since. Except for that whole paw thing earlier." Realizing I'd shifted my hand into a paw without trying was strange.

"Aw, poor you," he laughed at me and squeezed my thigh just above the knee, which caused me to squirm in my seat.

I pushed his hand away but held onto it once he let go of my leg.

"Not all of us grew up with people around to help us figure this out. Some of us are busy playing catch up, jerk." His laughter grew louder at my rebuttal. He was still laughing as we pulled into the driveway but stopped long enough to kiss me.

"Do you want to come inside for a little while?" We hadn't had much downtime together lately, and I wanted nothing more than to decompress with Gabriel by my side.

He looked at my lips and smiled, leaning close enough that I thought he would kiss me again, but he stopped just before our lips met. "I'd better get home. I told my mom I'd help plan the party, so she didn't have to do it alone. Rain check?" He closed the distance between us, but I'd looked down when he'd said he couldn't stay, so he kissed my forehead gently.

"I understand," I did my best not to let my smile fade. "Maybe another time," I offered before climbing out of the car and heading inside.

I tried not to dwell on my disappointment too long since I had things to get in order if we were getting the pack together soon. I walked into Lorelai's house and searched for her to run our ideas by her before approaching Olivia. Fortunately, I didn't have to search for long; she was in the living room watching television.

"Can I talk to you?" I asked. I stood just outside the circle of seats in the living room and clasped my hands together to avoid fidgeting.

She looked up and smiled at me before turning the television off. "Of course. What's on your mind?" She patted the seat next to her on the couch, and I plopped down and smiled back nervously.

"I'd like to talk to you about my plans for the pack and what Gabriel and I have decided. I wanted your opinion and to see how you thought everyone else might react." My heart began to race for some reason, and I felt uncomfortable talking to her about our plans for the pack.

Her smile got even wider, which helped calm me down a little. "I would love to hear your ideas."

I knew she would be supportive even if she had to be critical, so I took a deep breath and began. "We'd like to have a party here and invite the entire pack. Everyone can meet and interact without the danger of attack. We're one pack now, and we want to ensure everyone acts accordingly."

"I think that's a great idea. I'd be happy to host everyone here, but we may need to think about space issues. We could probably have everyone outside in the backyard if you don't think they'd mind."

I glanced out at the spacious patio and the beautifully manicured lawn beyond it, which had polished cement pathways leading out to a large gazebo.

"I'm sure we could make it work."

I smiled at her, thankful that she was willing to open her home to the other pack members. I hoped it sent the right message to everyone without us having to say too much about it. "At the party, we want to implement some new rules for the pack as well. To make sure they know we are taking our roles as alphas seriously, and that we are working to bring us all together."

"It looks like you have put some thought into this Caleb, I'm very impressed." I squirmed at her compliment, a little uncomfortable because of her praise then smiled but didn't say anything.

"Gabriel and I are both young and inexperienced when it comes to some of the rules and expectations of the Awakened. I'm especially unprepared because I don't even know how to shift yet, so we'd like to name people to act as advisors for us. A pack council, to be our eyes and ears in the larger pack."

She nodded her head, but her eyes had a faraway look in them, which suggested her mind was not in the room anymore.

"Lorelai?"

She snapped back to attention, and I could see the light fill her eyes again as she came back. "Sorry about that, I was just thinking about the actual Council, and what will happen to you there."

I swallowed past my fear and continued with my original thought.

"That's another reason we want to have our council here in the pack. Gabriel and I will have the added responsibility of the other Council, as well as our pack. Knowing there is someone we trust in charge here will help us stay focused on what we need to accomplish there." I tried to force my voice to sound more confident than I was, but any thought of taking over a group of Alphas was intimidating especially since none of them had been below someone else since they became an alpha.

I looked her in the eyes when I said the last bit of what I wanted to discuss with her.

"We'd like to have you be one of the members of the council. People already know and trust you because you were their alpha, and between the two groups, you are the only one with experience. Your insight and opinion will help Gabriel and me become better leaders and will help others get used to this transition quickly." *I hope.*

"I'd be honored Caleb. But I want you to know that I believe in you and Gabriel. I know you both possess the power to be great leaders, or you would not have awakened early. Together, you two will be an unstoppable force. I know it." The glow of pride was back in her gaze, and I tried to meet her look head on without feeling unworthy of it. She was right of course; together we had beaten Carlos and awakened earlier than almost anyone else in our known history. That had to mean something.

Over the next few minutes, we discussed details of the event and the food options. We decided to ask everyone to bring something to the party so they could all have a say in things. I was happy to relieve myself of that burden and hoped everyone would be excited about getting together.

When the party planning was over, I called Olivia and explained the pack council to her as well. She was quiet until I asked her to be on the council. It sounded like she might have dropped the phone, and when she picked it up, I could tell that she was crying. It made me a little concerned until she started to laugh excitedly and agreed to take on that role for the pack.

I'd only told a few people about our thoughts for the pack, but already it seemed like there was support for the changes we had planned. I could only hope that everyone else would be as enthusiastic about the changes. As I walked back to my bedroom, my phone started to ring, and when I fished it out of my pocket, the name on the caller ID made my heart skip a beat.

"Hey! How are you? How have you been? How was your trip?" The questions spilled out of my mouth faster than my parents could respond, but I had missed them so much and worried about them since I had to send them away on their impromptu vacation.

My dad was the first to respond.

"It was great, thank you again for the tickets. We had a great time, and it was nice to get away, just the two of us, for a while." I could hear the smile in his voice, and it made all my worry seem worthwhile. "How have you been?"

I thought about what I should tell them and decided to stick as close to the truth as possible.

"I've been all right. Some not-so-great things have happened lately, but I'm trying to look on the bright side.

Speaking of which, I met someone recently, and we've started dating."

"Tell us about him." My mom spoke up then, always interested in the ups and downs of my love life.

"His name is Gabriel. He's super cute and nice. I think you guys are going to love him!" I smiled, glad that I was able to share this happiness with them. "We met at work before I got fired…"

"You got fired?!" My dad was back.

Whoops. I forgot that I hadn't already shared that bit of information with them.

"Yeah, it's a long story, but like I said, everything happens for a reason, and I'm going to start looking for something else soon." I couldn't tell them that Lorelai had already offered to cover my bills since it was pack business that got me fired.

"Well, I'm sorry to hear that. Do you need us to put some money into your account this month for your rent?"

"No, I'm fine. I got a severance package from the hotel when they let me go, so I have enough to get by for a little while." I hated lying to them, but what they didn't know couldn't hurt them right? Especially since my bills were being covered, just not by the hotel.

"Okay well, let me know if you need anything, you know we are happy to help out."

"I know Dad, thank you." We talked for another fifteen minutes or so before I could tell they were out of things to say. "I'm glad you made it home safely and glad to hear you had fun on your trip! You'll have to e-mail me pictures so I can look at everything you did."

"Will do. We love you, and we'll talk to you soon."

"I love you both too, and I'm sure I'll talk to you soon!" I was determined to talk to Lorelai about being able to tell my parents about being Awakened, but I figured it could wait until after the party. I pushed the thought from my mind and got to work on the rest of the plan.

I called Gabriel and found out that Lucas and Kevin had agreed to be on the pack council and that Tanya had accepted her role as a trainer. We decided to have the party the following weekend so we could move forward with everything as quickly as possible. After about ten more minutes, we had everything laid out for the night of the event. All we had to do now was invite everyone and put our plans into action.

Chapter Four

That night, I had the nightmare again, the darkness closed in around me, and just like before, I stayed still because I knew I couldn't outrun it. I could feel my body shift into something new, and when I looked down, black fur covered my newly formed front paws as my muscles bunched and stretched under the skin. Then my body changed shape again, and colors exploded around me, and I could see plants and bushes around me that hadn't been there a second ago.

I took a tentative step toward them and realized I was still on four legs, but the black fur had become a rich brown color, and my pads had somehow changed into hooves. The sensation was utterly foreign. I could imagine that I had fingers, but when I stepped on the soft earth beneath my hooves, I couldn't feel the individual leaves anymore. I had an awareness of the leaf litter as it contrasted with the dirt and the occasional small rock, but that was all. There was something sweet that I couldn't quite identify in the air. I could tell it came from the bushes in front of me, and when I looked, I realized I could differentiate color between the leaves and the berries. I walked toward the berries and reached out for them with my tongue, but before I could pull one free, my body shifted again. I was back in total blackness again, and I couldn't tell what was around me, but I could feel my whole body again, so I knew I was back to normal.

Behind me, there was a small amount of light somewhere in the darkness, and when I looked, I could see the mirror that had been in my dream earlier. I walked toward it; afraid the face that looked back at me wouldn't be my own. When I reached the mirror, I was glad to see my reflection, but there was another face on top of mine that became clearer the longer I looked. The eyes were darker than my own, but our faces had similarities. They had the same jaw, same hair color, and same intensity in the eyes.

The mouth on the other face started to move, and I took a step back, afraid of what would happen if I got too close. In the reflection, I could see the darkness close in again, and somehow, I knew I was about to wake up. The other face repeated his message, but I couldn't understand the words because I wasn't a skilled lip reader. However, I managed to make out one word before I woke up. He'd said the word 'son.'

***

My body jolted into an upright position, and I gasped for air. Even though I hadn't run from the darkness, I found it impossible to breathe when it closed in around me. Once I was awake, it was no longer a problem, and I was able to relax again. I thought about the dream and what it could possibly mean. It was different now that I had awakened, but I didn't know what had changed. Now all of a sudden, I shifted in my dreams from one shape to another, which I knew I couldn't do.

I continued to try to figure out what it meant, and why the face in the mirror had said, 'son.' I couldn't tell if it had been the end of another word, or if he'd said the word 'son.' Then I realized why the face looked so familiar, and I felt like an idiot. My birth father was the face in the mirror! He tried to tell me something, and I had to figure out what. Then, a memory from the past popped into my head. The night Adam rescued me from my car accident he told me that he knew about my nightmares. I'd meant to ask him about it, but other things came up, and I never got a chance, and then I'd forgotten all about it. If he knew about my dreams, it stood to reason that he might know what they had tried to tell me.

He still worked nights as a bouncer, so I hoped he'd be able to take my call. I dialed his number and waited; he picked up after three rings, but I could hear the loud music from the bar, so I knew he would probably have issues hearing me.

"Hey, can you talk?" I tried to yell over the noise but then realized it was late, and I would wake up Lorelai if I continued to do that.

"Is everything okay?" He didn't raise his voice, but I realized I was still able to hear him over the music in the background.

"Yes, everything is fine. I just had some questions to ask you." I lowered my voice then. If I could hear him, he could probably hear me too.

"Sure, go ahead." I heard him talking to other people; I assumed they were at the door, so I gave it a second before I continued.

"How did you know about my nightmares?"

"Huh?" Maybe I was wrong about him being able to hear me over the music. I tried again but spoke a little louder.

"How did you know I had nightmares?"

"Everyone has nightmares; you'll have to be more specific." I could tell he was trying to listen to me, but he also had to do his job. I thought about just trying again later, but I decided to try one more time before I gave up.

"That night you pulled me from my car, you said you knew about my nightmares." I hoped he remembered, or this whole thing would have been a waste of time and I wouldn't be any closer to figuring out what the heck had happened.

"Oh, *that* nightmare," he said. "We all get that one; it's an Awakened thing. It's how we figure out how to change." He said it so nonchalantly that I thought I might have misunderstood him. *Everyone had the same dream?*

"What do you mean it's how we learn to change? What does the dream have to do with shifting?" I was excited because I may have just stumbled on the answer to one of my biggest problems of the moment, shifting.

"When you changed during your fight, you lost all of your senses right?"

He didn't wait for my response and continued to speak as though he already knew the answer.

"Your body is changing, so for a little while, you don't have any senses until the change is over. You can feel your body shifting, but your eyes, ears, nose, and mouth are all changing, so you can't use any of them to experience the world around you. In essence, it seems like darkness is cutting off all your senses. The dream is a collective thing we all share; it helps prepare us for that experience, so it isn't as scary when it happens the first time."

Everything started to click into place for me, and I remembered that night in the arena, and for a few seconds, it had felt like my dream had come to life. When I came out of it, I was a wolf, but I never really thought about what happened to my human body as everything shifted around. I felt a lot better, knowing that the dream was expected and I wasn't the only one who experienced them.

"When do they stop?"

"Pretty soon after you change. You don't need to know what the awakening process is like anymore because you have already been through it, so you go back to dreaming about normal things…well, normal for you."

"Whatever. Thanks for the information. I started to think I had gone crazy, especially since other things started to happen during the dream." I could see the face from the mirror in my mind, and I tried again to figure out what it said, but I still had no idea.

"Sounds like it's already starting to be taken over by other ideas and thoughts in your mind. Don't worry about it. It should stop in the next few days. The more you change, the faster the dream fades and…." As he tried to continue, I heard a deafening commotion and a lot of screaming and yelling from his end of the phone. "Caleb, I have to go, a fight just broke out inside!" He clicked off the line before I could say goodbye, but I figured the fight was more important than my goodbye.

I rolled over and checked my phone for any missed e-mails or other messages, but there were no notifications to be seen. My boredom seemed to overwhelm me, much like my dreams had. I tried to read but couldn't quiet my mind long enough to get really into the book. I didn't have a television in my room and didn't want to use the one in the living room in case it woke Lorelai. Stuck with my thoughts, I decided to try to figure out how to shift form since no one had told me how to do it yet. There didn't seem to be any risk, so I stared at my hand and willed it to change into a paw.

I concentrated as hard as I could, imagining my fingers were short stubby pads and envisioned fur that had sprouted all over as my nails extended. I did that for fifteen minutes, hoping my body would change. Still, nothing happened. Frustration with myself for being unable to do something so simple and natural to everyone else burned inside my chest. *It happened so quickly with Gabriel.*

As my anger increased, I could feel my concentration sharpen, and my sight improved, which made the room appear brighter. I remembered the day in the shower I'd first seen my paw, I had been angry at Adam for what he'd said to me, and the anger had caused my hand to change.

Holding onto that same anger, I recalled the humiliation from that day and the feelings that led me to change. I focused that energy and directed it toward my hand. It didn't take long before the soft, black fur sprouted from the back of my hand. It moved down over my fingers, which had become pads with sharp nails attached to the ends. In my excitement, my concentration faltered, and as quickly as it had started, the change began to reverse itself. Within moments my hand was back to normal, and my disappointment consumed me. Motivated by that small victory, I immediately tried again.

It was easier to do the second time around, and I could change both hands and arms into front legs with paws before my concentration gave out again. I was mesmerized by the change back to my normal body and laughed as dark fur seemed to get sucked up by my skin and thick pads stretched and straightened into my fingers once more.

Enthralled by my progress, I decided to try to change my whole body to see how far I could get. I thought back to when I was bullied and beaten up in high school by other students. I imagined those situations to experience the emotions I felt during those encounters and piled all of those feelings into my attempt at shifting. Surprisingly, the change happened almost instantly, and I felt the world shrink around me as my senses were cut off. Moments later, the world seemed to explode outward again, but this time everything was brighter and clearer, except the colors, which had become muted and sometimes challenging to tell apart.

Taking a look down at myself, I found my whole body was covered in fur, shimmering in the low light of my bedroom. *It worked! I did it.* Heart pounding, I almost expected the break in focus to cause me to go back to my human form. Moments passed, and nothing felt different, so I glanced down myself again, only to see that my paws were still where my hands would have been. If I crossed my eyes, I could see the tip of my long muzzle and feel the sharp teeth in my mouth with my tongue. I was so happy to be a wolf that I started to jump up and down, which was a strange sensation in my wolf body.

Now that I'd changed, I wanted to do more than sit in my room, so I pulled the handle of my bedroom door down and then nudged it open with my snout. The house seemed entirely new for me in this form, and I could sense things I hadn't noticed before: the varnish on the wood floor and even imperfections from wear and tear. The smell of food from the kitchen had my stomach rumbling, so I headed to see what, if anything, I could find to eat. Unfortunately, with my new body, I couldn't open the refrigerator door, and even though it smelled good, I wasn't hungry enough to knock over the trashcan and eat actual garbage.

I padded to the back door and the rather large dog door next to it. I passed through it into the world outside. The night unveiled itself to me, the stars were brighter than I'd ever seen them, and the light from the moon high overhead made it seem like it was daylight outside. The smell of the apple trees was almost overwhelming even though they weren't blossoming anymore. My ears were sensitive enough that I could hear the distant traffic from the freeway, the occasional sound of birds settling on branches, and rodents scurrying through their underground burrows. Taking a deep breath in, I began to sprint toward the fence at the back of the property. My claws dug into the soft ground beneath me, and when I neared the fence, I sailed over it without hesitation. The burn in my haunches from the leap was exhilarating.

I raced over the ground until my lungs screamed for a break. I had never felt so alive in my life, and even though my body ached slightly from the exertion, nothing had ever made me feel more free or alive.

Chapter Five

When I finished my exploration of the land around Lorelai's home, I realized I didn't know how to change back. I'd already lost my focus and stopped concentrating on my anger hours ago, and I was still in my wolf form. *Maybe if I relax, it'll just happen?* My mind wandered as I returned to the house to settle into my bed; exhaustion weighed down every extremity of my body. Sneaking back in through the large dog door in the wall, my paws quietly carried me back to my bedroom, where I leaped onto the bed and fell asleep in a heap of fur on top of the covers.

I was surprised that my body was back to normal the following day. I still had no idea how to do it on my own, but at least I was myself again. I rolled over and realized I didn't feel sore despite all the running I'd done the previous night. *I can't believe I never have to worry about muscle fatigue or spraining an ankle, or breaking a bone. Not that I've done that in the past, but this still feels like a win.*

I got dressed as quickly as I could, and when I went out to the kitchen, I found Lorelai eating a bagel and waiting for me to join her.

"Good morning, Caleb," she said. "How did you sleep?" There was something in her tone that seemed off somehow.

"Fine, thanks. How about you?"

"I slept well, thank you for asking, but it was what I woke up to that was an issue for me this morning." Her eyes were narrowed at me, and her arms were crossed tightly across her chest. I couldn't figure out what I had done that might have made her mad.

"I'm sorry to hear that." I was at a loss and didn't know how to respond.

"Would you perhaps like to explain this to me?" She stepped aside, and from the living room, through the kitchen, and partially back down the hall toward my bedroom, was a trail of muddy paw prints I'd somehow completely missed on my way into the kitchen. *So much for improved vision if I was this oblivious.*

My eyes widened, and my face flushed.

"Oh no! I'm so sorry! I didn't even think about the mess!" There was a small pond behind the house that I'd stumbled upon. While jumping in it to catch some fish— which I failed at—I got covered in mud. I had enjoyed myself so much that I didn't think about tracking anything inside. Something about her stance told me Lorelai wouldn't care how much fun I had in the pond.

"You should be sorry." She shook her head, and her voice was low, which made me feel even worse. "You went out running last night and didn't wake me up to see if I wanted to come along?" She raised her voice so I'd look at her, but now she was smiling. The change in her mood was so abrupt that I had a hard time following it.

"Huh?" I was bewildered and speechless.

"Next time, wake me up; I would love to run with you. I always thought it was something we would do together when you finally came back to me." Her smile was wide enough that I knew she wasn't upset about the mud.

"I'm sorry. I didn't want to wake you, so I tried to keep quiet."

"Well, now you know for next time. Don't forget to clean up this mess as punishment for leaving me behind." She grabbed her bagel and messed up my hair as she walked past me.

I smiled at her and begrudgingly agreed; it was my mess. "Before you go, can I ask you a strange question?"

"Of course; what is it?"

"Well, I had a strange dream last night where I was surrounded by darkness and shifted into my wolf, but I think I might have become a deer or something after that because I had hooves." I looked up at Lorelai's face to gauge her reaction, but her expression was blank. "Then I changed into myself again, and my face became my father's. Like, my birth father, I mean."

Lorelai's face remained emotionless, but some of the color seemed to drain away. "How did you know it was him?"

"I happened to be looking in a mirror at the time," I responded, hoping I didn't sound as crazy as I felt. "It's happened to me before, but I didn't recognize him until last night. It's like I'm looking at myself in the mirror, and then suddenly, he's looking back at me."

I pictured the dream in my mind again as I told her about it and saw his lips moving slowly, making it easier to see the shapes they made.

"I think he may have called me 'son.'" I didn't want to bring up a painful memory for Lorelai, but I needed to know if this was part of the normal Awakened process, like Adam said.

"Well, maybe it's just your way of connecting with him, and you're doing it in a way that makes you feel comfortable. You didn't know him, so it must be hard to imagine what he would be like in person." She smiled at me warmly and continued, "You have seen his face, however, and I see so much of him in you already; it makes sense that you would see the same thing."

"What about the whole deer thing? Adam said the dreams would start to fade and change, and he thought the new things I saw were proof of that, but they feel the same to me." I didn't share that they terrified me and made me panic and break out in a cold sweat, no matter how seemingly benign.

"I wouldn't worry too much about it. I'm sure Adam is probably right. You're working through the end of your dreams, and they're taking on new images along the way."

I sighed and smiled at her, hopeful that she was right. "Okay, thank you for listening. I appreciate it."

"Anytime." She smiled at me again and left the room, leaving me alone with my thoughts. I decided I didn't want to think about the dream anymore, so I called Gabriel to see what he was doing.

He answered on the first ring. "Hey Caleb, I was just going to call you."

"Oh yeah?"

"Yeah. My mom and I were discussing the party, and what may need to be done, so we figured we'd come over early to help you and Lorelai get ready."

"That's so thoughtful of you. Thank you! This is why I love y…" My mouth got carried away with me, and my brain only had enough time to stop at the end of what I was about to say. "I mean, uh…that's why I love how you think." I took a deep breath and hoped he'd let my slip-up go.

"Oh…yeah, thanks."

That didn't sound awkward at all.

"Of course." I tried to make my voice sound easy and unaffected, so I sounded happy. I would have slapped myself around at that point if I could have. "We make a good team, I think." I tried to backpedal but felt so weird that it was difficult to act normal now.

"Uh, anyway, I was thinking about going running later. Do you want to come along?"

"Running, like for exercise?"

"No, like running for fun. As wolves." I figured if Lorelai enjoyed it, then Gabriel might too, and it would give us something to do that wouldn't require talking.

"Yeah, that sounds like fun. Do you want to come here, or should I meet you out there?"

I was happy he'd accepted my olive branch in wolf's clothing, so I figured I'd make it as easy for him as possible.

"I can come to you; I just have to ask to borrow the car. Give me a second."

I went to Lorelai's office and knocked softly on the door before cracking it open. She spun around and looked at me but was on the phone, so I mouthed my question, using my hands to pretend to drive to illustrate my question. She laughed quietly but agreed, so I mouthed my thanks and closed the door.

"Okay, shouldn't be an issue. I can be there in about twenty minutes if you can be ready by then?"

"Yep, no problem…it's not like I have to do my hair or get dressed up," he sighed. The sarcasm in his voice made it hard to tell if he was joking or upset about not having enough time. But I chose to take him at his word.

"Good call; I'll head out then and see you soon!" We hung up, and I grabbed the keys out of the junk drawer in the kitchen, where Lorelai kept her spare set. I was glad to be behind the wheel of a car again. It felt like it had been years, even though my car had been blown up less than two months earlier. Rolling the windows down, I enjoyed the chilling air whipping through the car. As fall descended to winter, the cold air across my face and arms may have previously deterred me from going for a run, but not now. I cranked up the radio and sang along with anything I recognized until I got to Gabriel's house.

I was nervous about shifting again because I had only been able to do it twice. He'd been the one to help me through it the first time, so I tried to force my self-doubt away. I focused on the fact that this would be the first time we would change together without our lives being in danger. I still didn't understand why we'd been able to shift early, but I had a feeling that it had something to do with our connection and that electricity that was a near-constant companion. *Why had it gone away now that we'd awakened? Was it a normal part of the process, or had there been something special about us? What did it mean now that it seemed to have faded away?* I pushed the questions out of my mind, knocked on the front door, and smiled when the door opened. I kept the smile in place when I realized it was Gabriel's mom at the door, not him.

"Hello, is Gabriel available?" I suddenly felt like a ten-year-old asking if the neighbor kid could come out and play.

"Hi Caleb, yes he's here, come on inside." She smiled, and when I stepped across the threshold of her door, she dropped her head a little, exposing her neck to me. I knew why she was doing it, and I appreciated the gesture of solidarity, but I wrapped my arms around her in a hug instead, pretending that I hadn't seen her sign of submission. I could tell from her reaction that she was somewhat surprised by my behavior, but she did her best not to let it show. She moved back when I let her go a second later and turned toward the rest of the house.

"I'll go get him if you want to have a seat in the living room." She pointed me in the direction of the room and then disappeared quickly.

A few seconds later, Gabriel plopped beside me on the couch, smiling at me.

"What?" I asked.

"My mom told me that you hugged her…."

"Should I not have?" I hadn't considered that she might be one of those who didn't like being touched by others. I should have asked before assuming that a hug was okay.

"No, it was great. She likes you a lot more now."

"That's a plus!" I reached over and took his hand in my own. "So, are you ready to go running?"

He jumped up and led me toward the back door.

"Definitely! Let's do it." He let go of my hand and began changing into a black wolf that was my twin. I was so caught up in watching his transition that I forgot to shift my body. When I realized, he was done and sat watching me, waiting.

I focused on the same memories that had helped me shift the night before. Gabriel leaned over and touched me with his nose, and I could feel the change begin, and I relaxed into the darkness until I emerged a wolf.

Chapter Six

The world took on its now familiar difference as I stretched my limbs and prepared for our run. There were so many new things I couldn't understand in my human body that I could as a wolf that it didn't matter. I could experience the world around me through my nose in a way that didn't make sense when I wasn't a wolf. In this form, the smells were so strong that it was like getting a glimpse of the parts of the world I couldn't see with my eyes. Gabriel seemed to notice it as well, and his head swiveled back and forth, his ears flicking forward and backward as he tracked different sounds surrounding us.

I took advantage of his lapse in attention and pounced on him, pinning him quickly to the ground. I laughed in my mind.

Gotcha! I let him up quickly but kept my eyes on him in case he tried to retaliate.

Oh, it's on. Let's do this!

I could tell he was ready for a match, and since we had both Awakened early, it was hard to tell which of us would become more powerful. I tended to think it would be him because he had grown up with the expectation of changing, and I was still figuring it all out. He ran at me and reared up on his hind legs, allowing him to push me backward toward the house's back door.

Once outside, I was able to hold my ground and jostled to get into a good position so I could get the scruff of his neck in my mouth. I clamped down just long enough to get the rest of my body ready to run, and then I let go and took off. I could hear him recover and chase after me, so I darted through a gap in the fence and ran out into the front yard of his house. I thought back to the time I spent crouched behind the bushes across the street while I waited for him to be released from his captors. Obviously, the reality of the situation was a little more complicated than what I thought at the time, but I decided not to focus on the past. I could hear Gabriel closing in on me, and I sped up until I reached the bushes where I'd hidden with Adam.

I leaped over the bushes, surprised by the ease of the move and my uncanny ability to land without falling on my face. I slowed down a little at that point and let Gabriel catch up to me. When he did, we continued running side by side, our breathing matching the other and our strides aligning quickly, as though we had been doing this for years. We ran for another ten minutes before I had to take a break and find something to drink. Even though I was panting like crazy, I was still able to communicate effectively with my body language.

Even though Gabriel was always able to understand me in this form, I still had no clue how it all worked. I thought about what I wanted to say, and my body reacted as though it had been a wolf my whole life. Similarly, when Gabriel made noises or moved in specific ways, I knew what he was saying without hearing the words. He ended up taking the lead and brought us to a low-lying area where rainwater had collected from a recent storm. It was cool and soothed my dry throat. I tried not to think about what was possibly in the water that I was lapping up from the ground and hoped that my iron stomach would be able to handle anything I might have ingested.

After quenching my thirst, we strolled back toward his house. Before too long, we ran into a couple of joggers who noticed us right away. From a distance, I could see them backing away, which triggered something inside me that made me want to hunt them down. I clamped down on that feeling and tried to avert my eyes. The urge to chase was hard to swallow, however, so I took off running in the opposite direction, hoping some distance would make it easier to concentrate on something other than hunting. I could hear Gabriel running just behind me, so I kept moving, pushing myself faster as we ran to get away from the joggers. I could see his street coming up in the distance, so I began to slow a little to avoid running in front of an oncoming car, or smack dab into another person.

Gabriel nudged me forward and continued across the main road and down his cul-de-sac into his backyard. I followed close behind and finally began to relax once we weren't out in the open. It hit me then that I still didn't know how to change back into a human on command. I had tried the previous night but ended up falling asleep and waking up human. I assumed that meant I just had to relax, but I already felt relaxed, and nothing was happening. I started to panic at that point, my fear level ramped up again, and I worried that if I kept this up, I would never shift back. Slowly, I got my breathing under control and took a few steps closer to the door to look at myself again. Behind me, I saw Gabriel was shifting back to his usual self, and when he was done, he walked up to me, his hand held out in front of him.

His mouth moved, and sound came out, but I had no idea what he was saying to me. I felt like I was trapped in a foreign country, where I didn't speak the language, and no one could communicate with me. Fortunately, when Gabriel reached out and ran his hand down my neck, I could feel the change beginning. The skin under my fur began to ripple and move as my body reshaped itself from a wolf into a teenaged boy. I felt the muscles reshape themselves and the bones shortened in my arms, legs, hands, and feet. The result was an overwhelming urge to pop every joint in my body, but then the shift moved up to my head and my vision went dark again.

When it cleared, I looked to make sure everything was back to normal, wiggled my fingers and toes, and smiled. Then I looked up at Gabriel, who was watching from a safe distance.

"What?"

"Are you okay?" His head was cocked to the side, and I could see that he was breathing hard. "You took off running all of a sudden and I had a hard time trying to keep up."

"Sorry about that. It was hard for me to ignore those people. I could tell they were afraid, and their fear made me want to chase them down." The admission that I'd wanted to hunt them had been a hard one to own up to.

My head dropped in shame. I didn't want to be a monster, and it seemed like maybe I didn't get a choice in the matter.

Gabriel reached out and put his hand on my shoulder, then rubbed it gently. Usually, I would have appreciated his efforts, but I was worried, so I didn't rise to the occasion.

"That's totally normal; the most important thing is that you didn't do anything."

"Have you ever felt like that?" I stepped closer, and he wrapped his arms around me in a hug.

"Um, no…not really. But to be fair, I don't have more practical experience with being a wolf than you do." He rubbed his hands along my arms, which were covered with goose bumps. "What happened exactly?"

I could hear the change in the tone of his voice from scared to curious. I hoped that it was a good sign.

"I don't know. I saw them backing away, and it made me want to chase them. Some part of me knew I shouldn't, and before I could think about anything else, I started running back toward your house." I pulled back a little and looked him in the eyes. "Then we got back here, and I realized I didn't know how to change back, and I freaked out."

He smiled. "Changing is easy, you just relax and think about being a human and it happens."

He was so confident that I felt stupid for having problems with it at all. So much for me being some Super Alpha.

"The worst part was thinking that my fear would make my change permanent," I said, rubbing the back of my neck.

We walked back inside the house at this point and sat back down on the couch in the living room. Gabriel looked confused, and I could see him trying to work through what I had said in his mind.

"I guess I don't understand what your fear has to do with changing?" He had turned to face me and his brows were scrunched together.

I watched him closely to see if he was playing a joke on me, but he seemed genuinely confused.

"Well, you know how to change into a wolf you have to think about something that makes you angry?" I began, "it was along those same lines, but I assumed that fear would make me do something else."

Gabriel's mouth spread in a smile, "Are you messing with me?" His question caught me off guard, and the look I gave him must have made that clear because he didn't push the issue. "I don't focus on anger to change, I just get the image of my wolf in my mind, and I change. It's that simple. My emotions have nothing to do with it."

Now I was the one who was confused, and my mouth started moving, as my brain struggled unsuccessfully to grasp the words I wanted to use. "How did you know that would work?"

"That's how my mom taught me to turn. I thought that was how everyone changed. I've never heard of anyone using emotion to change. Why do you do it that way? Have you asked your mom about what it means? What did she say about it?"

His stream of questions made me feel sorry for not running things by Lorelai, but I was so excited when I shifted on my own, that I hadn't thought to question it. I explained how I had accidentally used anger in the past to shift, and how I had been able to trigger the change by using the same memories. He listened carefully, and surprisingly, never interrupted.

"I have no idea how you got that to work for you. If it was triggered by emotion, it seems like everyone would be changing any time they got emotional."

Hearing that I was apparently the only one who used emotion to change made me feel even more like an outsider, and I made up an excuse to get out his house as quickly as possible.

Before leaving, Gabriel pulled me close and whispered, "I'm glad you aren't like everyone else. You're unique, and there is nothing wrong with being different."

He looked me in the eyes when he said the last part and then touched his lips to mine. It was chaste at first, but then something changed, and it felt as if a floodgate had opened. Warmth spread through my body, and I could feel everything Gabriel felt. He was nervous that he'd offended me and worried that I was angry with him. His insecurities were laid out before me as our kiss deepened. I was able to see that he was as new to this whole thing as I was; he just had other people's experiences learn from.

I put my hand on his bare arm and thought about my feelings for him, and then forced that feeling down my arm and into his body. He gasped when they hit him, and his eyes went wide with a huge smile spread across his face.

"That was some kiss," he said, breathlessly.

"Thank you for being so understanding."

I leaned in and kissed him quickly again, and pulled back slightly, smiling at him. I was about to turn away when I felt his arms encircle my body, as he pulled me closer. His lips pressed against mine again, but this time when they touched, the heat was immediate. There was no push of emotion from Gabriel to cause the feeling; it was pure chemistry and attraction that caused my cheeks to flush and heart to speed up. After about a minute, the kiss lightened, and he released me from his embrace. Without his arms around me, I felt somewhat incomplete, but I tried not to let it show.

"I'd uh…" I couldn't get my brain to work correctly and had to concentrate to get the entire thought out. "I'd better get going."

I blushed at my inability to speak then headed out the front door, toward the car, all thoughts of my unusual ability wholly forgotten. "I'll see you at the party." I smiled at him as I shut the door, and then pretended to adjust the mirrors and radio, so I could catch my breath and collect myself before driving away. As I did, I looked back and saw the hint of a smile on Gabriel's face as he disappeared into his house.

Chapter Seven

All I had to do today was be a host and convince a room full of Awakened that I was capable of being their leader. While I showered, I tried to run down a mental list of the things I wanted to say to everyone later. I made sure that when the time came I was as comfortable as possible with the changes we'd planned. I was glad that we'd only changed a few things at this point, which I hoped would make it easier for the pack to cope. It also gave me less to worry about. If things continued like they always had, there shouldn't be many issues. But true to form, my brain decided to play devil's advocate, and before I could control it, I had begun to argue with myself.

What if the other members of the pack are used to doing things differently than the members of Lorelai's pack?

"If that is the case, they'll be able to bring it up to the pack council, who should be able to figure things out."

"That isn't what I'm doing at all. They're there to listen to pack issues and bring them to Gabriel and me to decide on, not to decide on their own."

Frustrated, and standing under rapidly cooling water, I decided I'd been in the shower long enough and it was time to keep my mind occupied with other tasks. I quickly finished up and dried off before getting dressed and joining Lorelai in the kitchen for breakfast.

"Good morning, how'd you sleep last night?" She was more of a morning person than I was on a typical day, that fact was made even worse since my argument with myself had soured my mood.

"I slept okay, thanks. Is there any cereal left?" I plopped down on a chair at the table and leaned my head on my hands.

"Why don't you check the pantry?" Her voice was kind, but it was enough to send my already lousy mood spiraling.

"I don't understand why I have to do everything myself!" I scooted out from the table and made a big deal about checking on cereal.

"Since when is it such a horrible thing to get help from others?" I wasn't mad about the cereal, and after my rant I realized what it sounded like, but it was too late to take it back.

"Caleb." Her voice was calm but I could hear the strength behind it. "Would you like to explain why you are yelling at me for not serving you breakfast?"

"I'm sorry. It wasn't you. I'm just getting nervous about tonight and how everyone will react. I wish I were as confident as you are about this whole alpha thing, but I don't know what I'm doing. I'm afraid people won't respect me and Gabriel if we have people around helping."

I poured the cereal and some milk into a bowl and went back to my chair to eat it.

"I feel like it's already weird that it's the two of us leading which seems like a lot, and then we're asking other people to help. I'm scared that no one will feel like we're ready to lead if we can't do it alone."

She walked over and sat down next to me, rubbing her hand along my back. It helped to calm me down enough that her words could sink in effectively.

"No one expects you to lead perfectly at the beginning. You are the alpha because you are powerful, not because you are perfect or the most knowledgeable. Alphas always have people they rely on for support and assistance. Your father and I did, the old alpha from Gabriel's pack did, so why would everyone suddenly expect you and Gabriel to be able to lead without help?"

I hadn't thought about that before. Before he'd gone a bit power hungry, Carlos had been the support for my parents, and before Carlos killed the other alpha, Dominic had been one of her close advisors.Remembering Dominic made me break out in goose bumps, and I shivered at the memory of our fight in the alley.

"It makes sense when you put it like that." I looked over at her, and she was smiling at me reassuringly.

"Don't be so hard on yourself if you can help it and remember that no one will ever be harder on you than you are on yourself. If you keep that in mind, you will already be more in control of whatever situations you encounter as alpha."

"Thanks for the advice." I finally felt as though I might be able to pull off tonight, but even if I slipped up, I knew there would be people there to help. With that in mind, I finished eating my breakfast as quickly as I could. Lorelai and I made small talk about the evening's events, and I ran down my plan for the announcement part of the evening to get her opinion. My brain thankfully stayed quiet, and I didn't break into another argument with myself. Once I'd finished my breakfast, I put the bowl into the dishwasher and went back to my room to call Gabriel to find out when he was coming over.

When I picked up my cell phone to give him a call, I noticed that I had a missed call from Megan. I realized how long it had been since I'd seen her, or even tried to talk to her. Fortunately, Adam had been keeping her busy lately, so I was able to focus on other things. As a result, she was less likely to notice my conspicuous absence from her life. I hit the redial button and sat down on my bed, waiting for her to pick up.

"Hello?" I smiled at the sound of her voice, happy to reconnect with her again.

"Hey, it's Caleb."

"Who?" There was a hint of sarcasm in her tone, which let me know that maybe she *had* noticed my absence lately.

"Oh, I'm sorry, I must have the wrong number. I thought I was calling my amazing best friend Megan, one of the most beautiful women I know, who happens to be very popular with the gentlemen. My mistake, I'll just let you go." I waited for a few seconds to see if she would take the bait.

"Oh, Caleb! Of course, how could I forget my best friend?" I laughed, glad that all it took to get myself back on her good side was a little flattery.

"Sorry, I know I've been a bad friend lately, I just had a lot on my plate and didn't want to drag you into the drama."

I knew this line would only last for so long, and I remembered that I would need to talk to Lorelai about letting Megan in on our little secret. I didn't know how the rest of the Awakened could maintain close relationships with humans and not share their secret with at least a small number of them.

"You know I love the drama, why would you deny me the thing I love most in the world?" She was laying it on thick, but I was used to it from her.

"I'm not denying you anything. I practically hand-delivered your boyfriend to you."

She started laughing at me then, and I knew everything was back to normal between us.

"And what a hot boyfriend he is too, you have no idea!" I briefly pictured Adam when he was barely clothed and staying at my apartment, I had a better idea than she realized, which felt a little strange. I shook it off and pretended I hadn't been daydreaming.

"I mean I guess…if you like that sort of thing."

"Oh, I do." I laughed at her response because she liked men, especially men that wanted her. The fact that he was muscular and tan was just a bonus.

"Well, there you go then," I said. Then I tried to change the subject, "I was returning your phone call. What's up?"

"Nothing really, I hadn't talked to you in awhile, and thought I'd see how you were doing. Adam told me you lost your job a little while ago. I'm sorry to hear that, but your boss was clearly a dick! You were attacked, and he fired you for missing work?"

I was surprised that Adam had shared so much with her about what happened. I always assumed I had to keep things secret, but then Adam almost always told her as close to the truth as possible. I felt like an ass for not telling her more, but I didn't want to cross the line. Right when I thought it, I realized I could set it. Maybe this whole alpha thing did have some great perks after all.

"Yeah, he pretty much didn't like me from the beginning, which kind of sucks because I enjoyed that job for the most part. But, on to bigger and better things now, I guess. I have to figure out what that means for me."

Pack leadership and the ruling position on the International Council of Awakened. Does that pay?

"I'm sure you'll find something in no time. Now that you don't have to work nights, we can go on double dates! We've never been able to in the past, and I think it would be a lot of fun, especially since you already know Adam. And it would give me a chance to get to know Gabriel better."

"We've never gone on a double-date because you and I can't seem to be in relationships at the same time, and you always seem to be in a relationship."

I let the implication that her dating was forcing me to be single hang in the air. It had been a long running inside joke, but it was surprisingly accurate. We never seemed to be able to date at the same time, and rather than admit that it was maybe my fault that I was single, I preferred to make it a massive conspiracy against me.

"I got a few weeks to a month, tops, to find, date, and breakup with a guy before you were in another relationship!"

"Well, that's obviously not the case anymore since we both have guys, so how about it? You, me and our hot boyfriends…dinner and a movie?"

It seemed like something was up with Megan, she'd never tried so hard to get me to hang out with her boyfriends. I'd never even met half of them, and she'd been with them for months. I suspected it was because they were much older than us, and it would have been weird, but she never admitted it.

"What gives? Why are you pushing for this so hard?"

She was silent on the other end for a few seconds before finally giving in and telling me what had happened.

"I don't think Adam likes me anymore." That was the furthest from what I thought she was going to say.

"What do you mean? Why wouldn't he like you?"

"I know, right? I'm not sure what happened. A few weeks ago, everything was great, but now he's distant and doesn't spend as much time with me. He doesn't make time for me like he used to, and whenever the topic of you comes up, it's like…" she paused as though trying to decide what to say.

"Like what?" I was nervous that she was going to tell me she already knew my secret.

"It just seems like he's more concerned about you than he is about me. Which is weird, because you guys don't even hang out that much anymore, do you? I mean, I get it, he saved your life, which is obviously something you don't forget, but it's not like you guys have all that much in common."

I breathed a sigh of relief; she had no idea I wasn't telling her what I was, and she had no idea that Adam wasn't who she thought he was either.

"I don't know what to tell you Megs; I haven't talked to him recently."

I thought about the countless hours he spent with the pack. Having to train me, then looking for Carlos and Rosa, all while trying to keep everyone safe.

"Even if he does have some stuff going on, that doesn't mean he isn't interested in you."

I tried to make her feel better while still protecting our secret lives.

"I think the double-date sounds like a great idea, and I would love nothing more than to spend the night watching a movie and vegging out with my best friend and boyfriend. You bring the movie, and I will bring the popcorn."

I realized I'd have to ask Lorelai if I could go back to my apartment for the night, so we had some space from the pack, and some semblance of normalcy. But it was a conversation worth having since I still held out hope that I could move back in full time. It wasn't the best apartment ever, but it was the first place I lived in on my own, and somehow it made me feel more like an adult.

"Talk to Adam and I will talk to Gabriel, and then you and I can figure out the best time for us all to get together."

She agreed and sounded a little less worried as we hung up the phone. I, on the other hand, still had seventy plus shifters to face, and now a double date to help plan. My to-do list just kept growing.

Chapter Eight

I spent the rest of the afternoon doing what I could to prepare the house and myself for the party. Even though I'd cleaned the night before, I went around straightening things that were perfectly straight, and dusting already dusted surfaces. If I'd been this concerned about keeping my own apartment clean, I wouldn't have ever had time to do anything else.

I was concerned that my nerves would somehow cause a change to happen in my body that I wouldn't be able to fix in time. Who knew what I would have become from too much nervous energy.

Thinking about my "strange" approach to shifting reminded me that I really needed to sit down with Lorelai soon and talk through some things. about some of the things on my mind. Was I allowed to share my actual identity with non-Awakened? What caused me to shift into a wolf based on my emotions? When would I need to meet the Awakened Council? All these issues were running around in my mind, and I had been so consumed by the party that I hadn't addressed any of them yet. I knew if I didn't start asking questions soon, I might do something I shouldn't or couldn't, and I definitely didn't want to screw up this early. I made a mental note to talk to Lorelai tomorrow so I could clear up as much of the confusion as possible, and also find out whether I'd be allowed back into my old apartment. I really hoped she'd say yes.

By the time my shower was over, my shirt had become a little less wrinkled, and I figured as I wore it, whatever wrinkles were still there would be worked out. I got ready as quickly as I could and then sent Gabriel a text to make sure he was on his way.

His response was almost immediate, which helped to calm me even further.

Ya, I'm on my way over now. Is everything ok?

Yep, no problems, just wanted to make sure. See you soon!

C U Soon

I didn't want to keep him texting if he was in the car. I assumed his mom was probably coming with him and didn't want to say more if she was the one responding.

I was glad it only took a little while to get from his house to Lorelai's because I had run out of things to do before people arrived and I was still wound up. When he pulled up, I could hear him whispering to someone else before the car doors opened and I realized they weren't speaking softly, they were just muffled by distance. I was surprised that I could clearly make out what was being said and smiled to myself when I realized I had been right, and his mother had come along with him. Fortunately, it sounded like she had been the one driving. I walked out to greet them and noticed that when she saw me, his mother still lowered her head and exposed her neck to me. I hoped that one day she would feel comfortable enough with me that she didn't feel compelled to do that. But I also took it as a good sign that she was willing to show submission without question.

"Welcome to our home!" I smiled as I walked to Gabriel's mother whose name I had found out was Celia. I wrapped my arms around her and was happy to feel that she returned the embrace without much hesitation.

"Thank you for having us, I look forward to the big announcement you two have tonight." She returned my smile, but at her reminder of the announcement I could feel mine falter slightly. While we'd hugged, Gabriel had walked around from the passenger's side and just as Celia released, he wrapped me in a hug of his own. I tried not to resist, but hugging each other in front of his mother felt like flaunting our relationship, which I didn't really want to do. I looked cautiously over at her, but if she had any issue with the hug, she didn't let it show on her face. Gabriel finally released me and took my hand in his own. Where our hands met, warmth began to spread up through my arm and helped me to relax.

Lorelai peeked out the door then, and when she saw all of us, opened it wide and essentially did a repeat of what I'd just finished.

"Welcome to our home, thank you so much for being here. I'm Lorelai." She walked out toward Celia and gave her a quick hug. "It's nice to see you again under better circumstances."

She smiled, but I could see that she was keeping a sharp eye on Celia and Gabriel, gauging their reaction. She had killed one of the top ranked people in their pack after all.

"Lorelai, it's our pleasure to be here and thank you for hosting the gathering. I'm Celia." She reached out for Gabriel, who took her hand with the one that wasn't holding mine. "And you already know my son Gabriel of course."

Lorelai leaned in and gave Gabriel a quick hug as well, which was a little awkward because both of his hands were being held, so he had to let go of my hand to hug her back.

"Well, let's all go inside and get more comfortable." Lorelai turned and gestured toward the front door, linking her arm through Celia's. "Caleb, can you help Gabriel with anything in the car before coming inside?"

She had just given me the perfect excuse to stay outside for a few extra seconds and talk to Gabriel.

Thank you Lorelai!

The door closed behind our mothers as they walked inside, but before shutting it, I was pretty sure I saw Lorelai wink at me.

"That seemed to go well for the first real meeting of the parents." Gabriel smiled at me and took my hand in his again.

"Yeah, I'm a little surprised. I could tell Lorelai was a little worried your mom might not be a big fan."

"Not at all, my mom hated the old alpha and most of her advisors. They were unnecessarily cruel, which is why she didn't fight the order to move away from everyone despite her high rank in the pack. She's glad to be back with them now that the alpha is gone."

I hadn't really thought about what life in their pack had been like, but I couldn't imagine wanting to be in the same room as anyone who'd killed members of my pack.

"We'd better grab the stuff from the car and get inside before they wonder what happened to us."

I walked to the trunk of the car and waited for Gabriel to pop it open. We grabbed the bags and then took everything into the kitchen to start setting up. Lorelai and Celia continued chatting in the front room, which allowed Lorelai to be close to the door to greet new people as they came in. It also gave everyone a familiar face no matter which pack they'd come from. Before long, the table was overflowing with foods of all types. There were finger foods, dips, plates of meat, platters of fruits and veggies, and perhaps the most enticing thing I'd seen all night; shrimp wrapped with bacon. Another table had all the desserts, which looked like they could send all of us into a sugar coma a few times over.

Gabriel and I walked around the party, mingling with people and introducing each other to people we knew. I had already had a hard time remembering everyone from my own pack, and now there were almost double the number of people whose names I had to remember. Fortunately, Gabriel knew everyone in his pack well, so that went smoothly. He'd always be able to help me remember names if I forgot, and he even seemed to be picking up the names of the new people he met, which I took as a good sign. Most people were smiling and seemed to have a good time, but I also met a few people from Gabriel's pack that looked a little nervous or upset about being at the party.

I pointed them out to Gabriel, concerned that they might prove to be an issue at some point, but while we were talking about them, I saw their eyes flick over to us. When they met my eyes, they lowered their heads and showed me their necks. It was enough of a sign that they were just as uncomfortable as I was at this party. Thinking about it, I realized that if I were in their shoes, I would probably have looked the same. I smiled, trying to look as friendly as possible in hopes that they would begin to relax and enjoy themselves.

Once everyone had arrived, Gabriel, Lorelai, and I made our way to the backyard, asking everyone else to join us. We had set up a small raised area that would allow us to address everyone and make sure they could see us while we did so. Lorelai climbed up first to welcome everyone.

"I just want to start by thanking you all for being here tonight and bringing your delicious dishes with you. I'm pretty sure I gained five pounds just looking at everything, so I don't want to think about what eating the food did to me!"

She laughed at herself, and the pack laughed along with her. She had a fantastic ability to calm the group. I realized that she was charismatic, but at least some of that had to do with her ability to send out emotions that made people like her. I tried to think positive thoughts and concentrated on sending out whatever indicated that I wanted the best for everyone at the party.

"Before I welcome Caleb and Gabriel up to address you all, I just want to say that I am excited to see us all together tonight. I cannot wait for our alphas to usher in a new sense of peace among our members. With that, please allow me to welcome Caleb and Gabriel, our alphas."

The crowd clapped as Gabriel and I stepped onto the platform, but once I met their eyes, I froze. Sensing my discomfort, Gabriel reached out and took my hand, which allowed me to find my voice.

"Thank you all. Gabriel and I have worked hard to come up with ideas that will help to bring us all together as the pack we have become. And with that in mind, we have a few changes that we are hoping to enact to make things more comfortable for everyone. Gabriel will explain the first change we are making, which is to create a pack council."

I stepped out of the way and gave Gabriel space to explain the purpose of the pack council. Unlike my thoughts on the subject earlier, Gabriel did not leave any visible holes in his explanation, which could have caused confusion. It was apparent that the role of the council was to provide additional ears for pack members to have their concerns or issues heard. The power of the final decision however, still rested with us. He also announced that Kevin, Lorelai, Lucas and Olivia would be the members of the pack council. As he named them, they stood and made themselves known to the pack. So far things seemed to be going well, which made me feel stupid for being so nervous about this whole thing.

Once Gabriel finished, it was my turn to explain the changes that were happening to training for the children.

"The other change we are implementing at this time deals with training for the newly awakened, and those who are nearly old enough to awaken. It is the responsibility of the alphas to make sure this training is completed well before the awakening takes place. Since we will not always be here to do it ourselves, we have named trainers to make sure the children always get the attention and training they deserve. I want Adam, Brent, and Tanya to join us at the front please."

I waited for the three to work their way to the platform before continuing. Once they took their places beside Gabriel, I looked back out to the crowd again.

"As most of you no doubt know already, I was not a typical case when it comes to awakening. Adam and Brent were among those who made sure my training was sufficient to help me get through my first challenge." There was a murmur that started on one side of the group, and it worked its way across quickly.

I continued, hoping to regain the attention I'd lost.

"For that reason, I have asked them both to assist with training. And Tanya was one of the former alpha's closest advisors, and from what I've heard, is an incredibly fierce fighter. We have asked that she also participate in the training process as well. Effective immediately, these three will take on the task of official training for the pack."

I looked at the three of them, Adam and Brent were smiling from ear to ear, but Tanya seemed like she felt uncomfortable being in front of the crowd. Everyone was silent, and just stared at us, so I started to clap quickly and told the three trainers that they could step down. I'd somehow lost the crowd during my announcement. No matter how much I concentrated on sending out positive thoughts to the group, they didn't seem like they cared.

Gabriel stepped in close and raised his voice. "Thank you for your attention, those are the only announcements we have at this time. Everything else will remain much the same as it has always been. Please enjoy the rest of the party and eat up!"

The crowd laughed at his final remark before breaking up into smaller clusters and redistributing themselves around the backyard and house.

"God, I totally suck at public speaking!" I stepped down from the platform and saw Adam and Brent waiting for me. Adam held a plate of assorted desserts, so I grabbed a fruit tart from it and shoved it into my mouth quickly.

"They hate me," I said around the tart, small pieces of the crust flying out as I did.

"They didn't hate you, you just kept dousing us with really uncomfortable feelings." Brent snagged a cookie from Adam's plate when Adam wasn't looking.

"Once you told everyone that we'd helped to train you, and they started talking, you sent out a massive dose of emotion that showed how uncomfortable you were. It was like watching a person who can't sing forced into doing karaoke and struggle through it. It's hard to watch, but you can't look away because that seems worse."

Brent's explanation made me feel even more self-conscious than I already did, but at least he was honest with me. I was about to say something else when someone yelling in the front of the house cut me off. I turned and ran toward the gate and Adam, Brent and Gabriel followed close behind.

Chapter Nine

When we made it to the front of the house, I saw Tanya yelling at a man and woman that I didn't recognize. I assumed that meant that they were from Gabriel's side of the pack. It was impossible to tell who had started the argument, but it was clear that if we didn't step in, they were going to start throwing punches.

"Hey!" I yelled before I could think better of it. "What the hell are you fighting about?"

Tanya kept her attention on the man, but stepped back and bowed her head in my direction. He followed suit, which meant they acknowledged that I'd spoken to them.

"I'm sorry, but Sean and Jacque don't seem to think that I'm a suitable trainer for their son."

"That's not what I said, and I told you that I meant no disrespect to you, Tanya. It's them that I don't want around my son." He pointed behind me to Adam and Brent, who stepped forward when I glanced back at them.

"What's wrong with them?" Gabriel addressed the pair, who didn't meet his eyes.

"We don't trust them, Alpha; they are not part of *our* pack."

His emphasis rubbed me the wrong way, and had I been in wolf form, I was sure my fur would have bristled at that statement. As it was, a slight growl escaped my lips, and it took Adam touching the small of my back for me to stop making the noise.

"And how did you get involved in this Tanya?" Gabriel turned his attention to her, and she bowed her head, and then met his eyes, a sign of strength, but not a challenge.

"They came to me complaining about the change for the training, and to tell me they were not going to let the pack train their son. I let him know that I was perfectly capable of teaching anyone that needed it, and that he was going to send his son to pack training whether he liked it or not. There were a few more exchanges between us that I don't care to repeat, and then you walked up."

Gabriel turned and looked at me, his face clearly asking what I wanted to do about the situation. I stepped up then, my back feeling cold as I moved away from Adam's touch and stood by Gabriel.

"I understand your concern for your child, but these three are more than capable of training your son, and you should trust that your alphas have selected those we think best suited to the task."

Sean refused to look at me and turned to speak to Gabriel instead. "Please don't make me send my son to these…" he seemed to struggle to find a word he wanted to use that wouldn't get him into more trouble. "These men."

"What about Tanya? If your son was only trained by Tanya, would that be acceptable?" Gabriel was trying to find a way to make the situation better, but Sean refused to budge.

"No Alpha, I do not want to send my son to train with the pack at all if they are involved." His eyes darted over to Adam and Brent as he said it, and that caused my anger to spike again. I must have made a noise or moved because I could feel everyone's eyes on me. I didn't know what to do, Gabriel and I had just officially taken on our role as alphas, and we were already being questioned. I wanted to be fair, but I also knew that I had to be strict. I worried that if I let this slide, it would set a precedent that we didn't follow through with what we said. I refused to be walked over this early in my time as alpha, and it was with that in mind that I finally responded.

"Sean, you will send your son to be trained by the pack trainers, or you will leave this pack." He started to respond, but I cut him off before he could do so. "Your alpha has spoken, but the choice is yours. Choose now. The protection of the pack or you go and lose everything."

I could see Gabriel's eyes from the corner of mine; he looked torn but stayed quiet.

Sean looked back and forth from his wife to us, and then finally his decision washed over him, and his body went slack.

"We will leave." He spoke his decision so quietly that if I hadn't already turned, I might not have heard it. But the reaction of the group seemed to suggest that he'd shouted it in my face. They were all shocked, including his wife, who held their son in her arms.

"I'm very sorry to hear that, and I know I speak for us all when I say that we will miss you and your family. I think it is best that you leave now and not contact the pack again."

I turned and walked back toward the house. Adam and Brent followed, but Gabriel and Tanya stayed behind with the family. I felt horrible for what I'd just done, and I could feel the decision sitting in my stomach like a rock. I'd just kicked someone out of their extended family for not following my rules. I was no better than the people that kicked their children out of the house for being gay, but deep inside somewhere I knew that this decision was different. I did not hate them for their decision; I respected their choice, which is why I allowed him to choose.

I never expected he would choose to leave the pack, and I didn't think he thought he would either until right before the words left his mouth. After the door closed behind me once I entered the house, the laughter from Adam and Brent stole my attention. I turned to yell at them for their lack of sensitivity, but their smiles were aimed at me.

"Wow, who knew you had that much power in you!" Brent's eyes were a little wide as he spoke to me, which only deepened my confusion.

"When you finally let your alpha out I had to back up." Adam looked impressed, but there was a glint of something else in his eyes that I couldn't place.

"What the hell are you two talking about?" I felt terrible, and their good mood was making my bad mood even worse. "I just kicked a family out of the pack, that isn't something impressive, that was a horrible situation!"

"Of course, it was, but that's not what we're talking about." Brent held his hands up in surrender, which placated me a little bit. "We're talking about the power you sent out to the group when he said he wasn't sending his son to train with the pack. You sent out a wave of power and anger that was incredible. I've never felt something like that before."

I turned to Adam, looking for him to explain what happened a little further.

"Remember when I told you that you would be able to let others know you were an alpha without having to tell them?"

I nodded, so he continued, "Well, you did that but multiplied it by about ten."

I realized that was why everyone turned and looked at me when I got angry. I must have made it clear that I wasn't happy about the way Sean was talking without realizing it.

"I'm surprised no one from the party came rushing out when you did it. There's no way they didn't feel what you did, they must have just been glad it wasn't focused on them." Adam smiled at me again, staying by my side.

"Well, I just didn't want to look weak on my first day as an official alpha of the pack. I think you two will make great trainers, and I don't want the pack to speak negatively about anyone else."

As I finished my thought, Gabriel and Tanya walked through the door and joined us in the front room. Tanya bowed her head at me, and then smiled at me, which was a first.

"Thank you for what you did, Alpha. Not that I needed any help," she said, glancing around the room at Adam and

Brent. "I appreciate your support; my old alpha would never have taken my side of the argument. She liked to have me around, but I think that was just to make her seem even more powerful when she contradicted me."

There was a pain in Tanya's voice that I could hear because it so closely resembled the pain I felt when kids harassed me at school.

"Of course Tanya, Gabriel and I both value you and what you will do for the pack in the years to come." She smiled at me again, and I realized that it was very different from the first time I'd seen her smile when she came to my hotel. Then it had been a baring of her teeth; now it was happiness that caused her eyes to crinkle at the corners despite her young age. As I watched her talk to the other people in the room about what had just happened, I realized that she often used her long blonde hair as a shield to hide her face. She looked about twenty years old. Even though she was only 5'8", her heels allowed her to look eye-to-eye with Gabriel and I. I also saw that whenever Brent spoke, her cheeks flushed a little, but he didn't seem to notice her attention, or if he did, he wasn't interested.

At a lull in the conversation, I spoke up quickly, "Gabriel, can I talk to you?"

He nodded and we excused ourselves from the group and walked down the hall to my bedroom. I closed the door and took a deep breath before turning around to look at him.

"I'm so sorry for what I did out there. I didn't want them to leave the pack. Do you think we can persuade them to come back?"

He shook his head and smiled sadly at me. "It isn't your fault Caleb. Sean and Jacque have always been that way. They push and push, trying to get everything to go in their way, and when it doesn't, they complain until something else comes up that bothers them. This wasn't going to go away; they would have refused and gotten worse until they either gave in or left on their own. All you did was speed up the process."

His words made me feel a little bit better about the situation, but not about how I'd reacted to the challenge he posed to our leadership.

"I just don't want to be one of those people that cannot deal with being challenged. I am happy to compromise with pack members, but he just didn't want to budge."

I walked over and sat on my bed, then put my head in my hands.

"You can't blame yourself for what happened. He chose to leave the pack; you didn't force them out. I gave him the option of dealing only with Tanya, and he refused. There was nothing else to do at that point. The pack handles training and he knew that."

As he spoke, Gabriel sat next to me on the bed and rubbed his hand along my back, helping me to relax.

"Thank you," I said.

"For what?"

"For being better at this than I am, and for knowing what to say to me to help calm me down. I just got so worked up out there that I spoke without really thinking about it, and felt horrible for what I did."

He reached his hand through my arms and cupped my face before he softly pulled it toward his own. When my eyes met his he spoke again.

"You did what you thought was best, and that is all you can do. But I am not better at this than you are. I didn't react at all; I just asked what had happened. I'm not sure I'm cut out to be an alpha. I think I'd be better suited to stand by you and help you lead rather than leading anything myself. If you weren't here, there's no way I would be able to do any of this on my own."

"I guess it's good that we have each other then."

With that, I leaned forward and kissed him. His lips parted as mine pressed against them, and the kiss deepened and pulled us into each other's arms. He reached over and lifted my shirt up and over my head, and I quickly did the same. He dragged me further onto the bed so we could both lie down, and I followed him eagerly. I could see the hunger and curiosity in his eyes as we took things further than we ever had before. My heart raced as he traced his finger along the side of my chest and down my arm. I grabbed his neck and gently pulled him toward me again, which also brought him on top of me. As our lips met, I felt the total weight of him push down on me, and then I felt him jump up at the sound of a loud knock on my door. I looked up at the door and let out a frustrated breath then dropped my head to rest on the pillows. Sometimes I really missed living in my own place.

Chapter Ten

"What is it?" I tried but failed to keep the anger and frustration out of my voice.

"Caleb, we need to talk." It was Adam, which caused even more frustration to fill me. Now he wasn't just playing around with me; he had actively stopped me from taking my relationship with Gabriel further.

"Can it wait?" I held Gabriel near me, and tried to keep him from putting his shirt back on.

"Not really. Someone's died."

At those words, my anger subsided, and tons of thoughts started to race through my mind. Had I done something wrong? Was our pack under attack already? I ran down a mental checklist of faces from the party, trying to remember if anyone had decided not to come. I was sure that everyone had made it and probably still mingled with the rest of the pack somewhere in the house. I grabbed my shirt and pulled it back over my head as I walked to unlock the door for Adam.

"Thank you," he said, as he moved past me and into my bedroom. I noticed his nostrils twitch, and I tried to see if I could smell what he had, and then blushed when I realized it was probably a mixture of charged pheromones and sweat.

"Who was it?" Gabriel asked, sitting on the bed.

"Huh?" Adam turned to look at him, and I noticed he never greeted him with any deference for Gabriel's position as alpha. "Oh, one of the Council members. She got attacked and killed this morning. Word of the attack just reached us."

My heart started to race before I realized the timeline made it impossible that it was someone from our pack council, which meant it was someone from Europe.

"Who attacked them?"

"We don't know, and they aren't freely sharing information. We only found out about it because of connections to other packs on the Council. She was one of the leaders of the Council, however, which puts you in an awkward position. You'll need to travel to Croatia, where the Council has convened and take over as the new leaders."

When he said it, Adam only spoke to me, even though he indicated that both Gabriel and I would need to go.

"When do we have to leave?" Gabriel asked as he came to stand with me.

"Tomorrow morning if possible. We'll arrange for your transportation, but you two will need to get yourselves ready to go tonight so we can leave at dawn. We'll need to drive up to L.A. so you can fly out of LAX." This time Adam did address Gabriel, but I could feel him wanting to look at me instead.

"We knew this would happen eventually; I just thought I'd have more time to figure things out here before we had to face the rest of the Awakened."

I sat on the bed and rested my head in my hands then tried to soothe the ache that suddenly appeared at my temples.

"Megan is going to be pissed at me," I blurted it out without thinking about it and realized I'd forgotten to tell Gabriel that we were supposed to go on a double date with her and Adam. From Adam's look, he didn't know about the date either, so I had to explain.

"We were all supposed to get together. I promised her we would do something soon since I'd avoided her for so long."

"Let me worry about that, you have bigger things to deal with." Adam reached out to touch my arm but stopped before actually doing it. His arm hovered in mid-air for a few seconds, and then he dropped it back to his side.

"Screw this." I picked up my phone and scrolled through my recent calls to her name, then hit the call button. She picked up after a couple of rings, and when I invited her out to Lorelai's house, she agreed without questioning it. I was in for a lot of questions when she got here.

"Okay, we've got about an hour to get packed and ready. Gabriel, why don't you go home and pack then come back and spend the night? We can leave from here in the morning, and that will give you some time with your mom to let her know what's going on."

"That's fine; I'll go find her and head out now. I'll be back as soon as I can." He leaned over and kissed me again before leaving Adam and me alone in my bedroom. Where his lips touched mine, I could still feel the warmth of his skin, which radiated through the rest of my body. Afterwards, I felt happy and safe; a feeling that disappeared after a few minutes of being with Adam. It wasn't that I didn't feel safe around him, the opposite in fact. He made me feel like nothing would ever hurt me, but he also made me feel like my stomach was twisting itself into knots, and like I might hurl as a result.

"I need to talk to Lorelai. Would you mind finding her and bringing her here while I figure out what I should pack?" I turned and walked toward the closet, taking care to avoid getting too close to Adam as I passed him.

"Sure. We'll be right back." He quietly left the room, and I could breathe again.

I took the time I had to sort through my clothing, which was a little tricky because San Diego winters, even out this far east, were mild in comparison to European winters. Or at least they could be, depending on where we went. Adam hadn't said where we were going, so I decided I should pack for all occasions, just in case. I pulled down all of my long sleeve shirts and folded them neatly in a pile before moving to pants. I figured it wouldn't be warm enough anywhere in Europe to require that I have shorts with me, so I skipped those entirely. I sorted through jackets, which were primarily light weight and only meant to keep out the wind, not protect against snow, when Lorelai and Adam walked into the room.

"Caleb?" Lorelai called quietly into my bedroom before entering completely.

"Back here, I'm in the closet," I called out.

"Oh honey, I thought you were finished with all of that." Her voice was so severe that it took me a few seconds of confused silence before I realized she'd just made a coming out joke at my expense.

I laughed so hard I fell to the ground.

"That…was…amazing," I said in-between gasping for breath. She just smiled at me, and Adam did his best to hide his smirk behind her.

"So, what did you need to talk to me about? Adam and I have already discussed that you need to go to Croatia. I'm happy to stay here to keep things as normal as possible while you're gone."

I hadn't even thought about what would happen here in California while we were away, which is why we'd implemented the pack council in the first place. They were here to help when we were unavailable. I knew she would take over, which was a comfort to me, and made me feel better about what I had to do.

"I appreciate that, but it isn't what I wanted to discuss with you. I wanted to talk to you about coming out actually."

It was her turn to look confused, and she tilted her head as she looked at me. "I'm pretty sure everyone knows about you and Gabriel."

"Yeah, I figured that as well. But I'm not talking about being gay; I'm talking about being Awakened. I want to come out as Awakened to Megan and my parents. It feels so wrong to hide this part of myself from them, especially when they were so often my support system when I was coming to terms with being gay."

She looked a little hurt by my reminder that she'd given me up for adoption and hadn't been there while I was growing up, but she kept a calm expression.

"I'm just not sure that's a good idea right now Caleb. They could get hurt if they said the wrong thing to the wrong person. It isn't just the other Awakened that we have to watch out for." Her revelation that there were other issues we had to worry about was news to me. "I just don't want to see them get hurt for something that isn't their secret to keep."

I wanted to ask about the other things we had to worry about, but I was afraid to get off the topic before I explained my reasons for telling my loved ones about who I was.

"I get where you're coming from, but I didn't know anything about our world, and it still came after me. Who's to say someone won't be able to track their connection to our world back to me? At least if they know what to look out for, and that this world exists, they will have all the information we can provide to keep them safe."

I could tell she wasn't convinced, but she didn't immediately say no, which I took as a good sign.

"He does have a point. There's no reason to assume they're safe just because they're ignorant of our world," Adam spoke in my defense, which surprised me a little.

I remembered back to the night he rescued me from being attacked and how he'd appeared to be a little afraid of Lorelai's power. Now he seemed able to overlook her history as alpha since she no longer possessed the title.

Lorelai was quiet for a few minutes, her face gave away only brief moments of expression, which made trying to figure out what she was thinking nearly impossible.

"I'll leave it up to you, Caleb. If you want to share this part of yourself with them, it is your decision. You are an alpha of this pack and leader of the Council. I am no longer above you and cannot tell you what to do anymore. And I certainly would not want inadvertently to cause harm to your parents or best friend by asking you to keep this secret. I would strongly encourage you to be as discreet as possible, and tell them only part of the story. I can only imagine how your mother would feel finding out you're traveling to Europe to hunt down killers."

She made an excellent point; if I thought my mother could use emotions as weapons, worry was like a bomb. It destroyed everything around her, and the effects of her anxiety could be felt for years.

"Maybe I'll just start with Megan and see how that goes." Lorelai smiled at me and kissed me on the forehead.

"I'd better get back to the party, so people don't wonder where we've all gone." She left the room and closed the door behind her.

"How do you think you're going to do it?" Adam grabbed a jacket of mine off of the hanger and folded it for me while I searched for matching socks to roll into pairs.

"Tell Megan?" I asked. "I figured I'd just tell her I had something I needed to explain, which was why I'd been so distant lately. And I hoped you might be willing to do a little shifting like you and…"

Carlos's stuck in my throat and refused to come out. I could tell from his flinch that Adam knew what I was about to say. "Uh…like you did when you first brought me to the house."

"It's okay, you can say his name. I do." He picked up a pair of socks I pulled out and rolled them up for me, his face an emotionless mask. "Carlos was my friend and my mentor, but in the end, he was too interested in power, and that took over the best parts of his personality."

He added the now rolled socks to my pile and refused to look at me.

"I'm sorry, I didn't mean to bring him up, I wasn't thinking." I reached out and touched his shoulder gently. He leaned into my hand as if seeking comfort from it. I rubbed his upper back, trying to make him feel better, but unsure if it helped at all. After a few seconds of silence, he cleared his throat and reached for another pair of socks.

"You don't think she'll freak out if I shift in front of her?"

"Nah…Megan has dated a lot of freaky guys…do you think one that can change into a wolf is anything different?" He laughed at that, and then lightly punched my shoulder.

"Gee, thanks for making me feel special."

I laughed. "I doubt that you need me to make you feel special!"

He looked up at me then and I could feel my insides knot up again.

"I mean, look at you…close to the former and current alphas of the pack, a leader among the other members of them pack. Plus, you have a great girlfriend…"

My words cut off as his expression changed. I didn't realize what the look was at the time, but I was suddenly rendered mute. I dropped my gaze and refolded some already perfect shirts.

"Caleb, I should tell you something…"

"I'd better go find some luggage to put all of this in…I'll be back in a minute."

I walked out of the room and into the hallway where it was somehow cooler, and my stomach didn't hurt as much. Letting myself into Lorelai's room, I went to the closet to find something large enough to hold all the clothes I was bringing with me. I didn't know how long I'd be gone, but I figured it would probably be more than just a weekend trip. I took my time so I could avoid as much alone time with Adam as possible, hoping that Megan and Gabriel would make it to the house soon.

I rolled the suitcase into my bedroom and found Adam lying on his back on the bed. His eyes followed me into the closet where I'd left my pile of clothing. I could hear the springs groaning under his shifting weight as he got off the bed and joined me in the closet.

"Is everything okay?" He reached out and picked up the pants I'd folded and placed them neatly in the large compartment.

I looked up at him; my mouth opened and closed, but nothing came out. Was all of this tension in my head? Was I making things more awkward than they needed to be? He had already told me he thought I had the wrong idea once. It was possible that I was reading further into things than I should have been.

"Yeah, everything's fine, I'm just nervous about the trip." I was nervous—that was true-- and there was no reason to tell him I'd thought he was coming on to me. "I've never been that far away from my family and friends before. I just don't want anything to happen while I'm gone I guess."

I let the thought sink in and realized I really was worried about my parents and Megan. I did my best to block it out because there was nothing I could do to keep them safe, and I had to leave, there wasn't any way around that.

"I understand how you must feel, but you're going so you can protect other people. Your family and friends are important, but you have additional responsibilities now, and you have to worry about more than just your close circle."

He made me feel ridiculous for worrying, but it was hard for me to worry about people I'd never met. I found it even more difficult for me to put them before my parents and best friend. Regardless of my fears, I understood that by accepting my position with the pack, I had responsibilities I couldn't abandon. The fact that I'd awakened early also meant I had the ability to do something to keep the Council safe. It made me miss the days when all I had to worry about was checking people into their rooms for the night.

Chapter Eleven

The crunch of tires against gravel let me know that people were beginning to leave the party, as their cars started up in the driveway and goodbyes were trickling down the hallway to my ears. I figured I'd better be there to see as many people off as I could, so I jumped up and reached out for Adam's hand. He grasped mine firmly and pulled himself up, but held onto my hand as he pulled me from my room and toward the foyer. I tried to slip my hand free of his, but he held on tightly. When we finally got to the door, he dropped my hand, and I could feel the sweat that had built up in my palms in the short walk. I wiped my hands on my pants and shook hands with as many people as I could as they slowly made their way out of the house. I thanked them for coming and did my best to maintain a confident but friendly smile as they bowed their heads.

As the last few stragglers made their way to the front door, Gabriel walked back through it holding a large blue duffel bag, and he smiled brightly at me. Seeing him made me feel much better, and I relaxed knowing that even if I were leaving some of the most important people in my life here in California, I would at least have him with me. My smile matched his, and I nodded my head toward my bedroom.

"Go ahead and drop your bag in my room."

He disappeared down the hallway and returned a few seconds later and stood by me as we said goodbye to the last of the pack members left in the house. We followed them out to the front porch, where Brent, Tanya, and Olivia were all standing in a small group talking quietly. When they saw us walk out of the house, their conversation stopped, and they smiled genuinely at us.

Lorelai, Adam, Gabriel and I walked over to the threesome, and I realized that these were the people I trusted the most in my life right now. Kevin and Lucas, the other pack council members, were part of the group as well, but since I'd only met them tonight, they hadn't yet earned my complete trust. If Tanya had reacted differently after the confrontation earlier, I might not have included her in the group either, but I felt like there was a level of mutual respect between us now.

"So what's the plan?" Gabriel was the first to speak.

Brent, Olivia, and Tanya looked a little confused, so Lorelai filled them in on what had happened and how we were going to deal with it.

"Olivia and I will be here with Lucas and Kevin to keep the pack stable while you two are gone."

Brent spoke up next: "And we will get started on training the young, so they are all ready for the awakening when it happens."

He gestured to himself and the other two in the circle. I smiled at everyone again; glad they were taking on their responsibilities so willingly. I still had some trouble adjusting to the idea that I would be leaving the following day, but having a solid support system in place in our absence made the trip easier to handle. I reached over and took Gabriel's hand in my own.

"Thank you all for your help. I know that we both appreciate your support." I squeezed Gabriel's hand, and he smiled at the group as well, nodding in agreement.

I could hear Megan's car pull up in the driveway and laughed quietly at her singing along with the radio.

"Now, I think we will leave you all for the night." They all said their goodbyes and I walked with Gabriel toward Megan's car, so we were there when she got out.

I could see her face through the front windshield as she took in Lorelai's house. It was undoubtedly grander than the apartments we lived in back in Twentynine Palms, but not as large as some of the other homes in the area. She pushed her door open and climbed out of the car.

"Where the hell are we?"

Her bluntness never ceased to catch me a little off guard, and I laughed loudly at her question.

"Seriously Caleb, why are we hanging out all the way in the boonies?" She looked over at Gabriel then and seemed to realize that maybe we were at his house.

"Oops, sorry. Hi Gabriel, I love your house." She smiled at him, which caused him to start laughing as well. Just then, Adam came up from behind her and swept her up into his arms. She let out a little scream, but when she saw him, she laughed along with us.

"This isn't Gabriel's house; it's my birth mother's."

Megan stared at me, confused.

"My birth mother lives here. And now, so do I. At least for now."

I added the last part in because I was determined to get back to my apartment when Gabriel and I returned from our trip. I wanted the option of being closer to the rest of San Diego if I needed to be. I could see that Megan was confused, but she was trying to hide it behind a perfect mask of makeup.

"C'mon, I'll introduce you. Then I have something else I need to tell you…"

"There's more!?" It sounded like she was going to freak at any moment, but I knew she was more upset at being kept out of the loop than she was truly surprised.

"Unfortunately." I smiled at her, and then led the group into the house. Lorelai was in the kitchen putting leftover food away in the refrigerator, but she turned and smiled at us when we walked into the room. "Lorelai, this is my best friend from home."

"Megan, it's great to meet you." She walked out of the kitchen and gave her a hug.

"Uh…yeah, it's nice meeting you too." I held in the laughter caused by Megan's discomfort.

"Do you need any help with cleaning up?" I took a step toward the kitchen to help, and Lorelai put up a hand to stop me.

"I'm fine, you kids have fun."

That was all I needed to hear. I grabbed Gabriel's hand again and started to walk back to my bedroom. "Okay, I think we're gonna go watch a movie then. If you hear any screams, it's just Megan."

Lorelai gave me a knowing look, which seemed a little sad before nodding. "I'll keep that in mind. See you in the morning."

I mouthed a "thank you" as we all walked toward the hallway. When we were finally in my room, I closed the door behind us so the noise from the movie wouldn't disturb Lorelai if she decided to try to get some sleep before we had to leave for Los Angeles.

"Okay, before we start the movie, there is something I need to tell you, Megs."

She looked at me strangely, but we'd been through a lot in our friendship, and I knew this would be just another bump in the road.

"There's something you should know about the three of us." I motioned toward Adam, Gabriel and myself.

Her face paled, and she looked like she was about to throw up. "Oh my God Caleb, if you tell me that the three of you…"

I knew where she was going before she got there, so I cut her off. "I would never do that to you, you should know better!"

She took a deep breath and relaxed a little.

"But we do all have a secret we've kept from you, and I wanted to make sure you knew what it was since you're my best friend. I've always told you everything, and I don't want this to stop me from sharing parts of my life with you."

"Caleb, you're freaking me out a little bit."

"Sorry, it's just that this is a big deal, and I don't want to blurt it out, but I guess maybe that's the best way. Megan, we're not human."

Now it was her turn to laugh at me, which she did without an attempt to hold it in.

"You ass! I thought you were going to tell me something real. You had me worried!"

I could tell from her response that she didn't believe me, so I looked at Adam and nodded my head. He walked out of her line of sight and shifted into his wolf form while I kept her attention.

"I wish I were kidding, it'd make things a lot easier. But I'm serious. There's a reason I've been so distant lately, and even though Adam did pull me from my car after I crashed, that isn't the whole story."

I looked over at him now, and his wolf form sat perfectly still, waiting for Megan to turn and look at him as well. When she did, she let out a scream that rivaled the one from earlier.

"There's a fucking wolf in your room!"

"It's not just a wolf; it's Adam." I nodded at him again, and as we all watched, he shifted back into his human form. "Like I said, we aren't exactly human."

"So you're trying to tell me what? That you're a werewolf?" She laughed nervously. "There's no such thing!"

How she was able to simply disregard the evidence that was right in front of her was beyond me, but I continued carefully.

"Technically, you're right, there is no such thing as a werewolf, but we do become wolves."

At her silence, I continued. "When we turn 18, we gain the ability to shift into a new shape."

I looked over at Gabriel then, and he smiled reassuringly at me.

Her expression was a mixture of confusion and hurt feelings. "You turned 18 months ago, and you're just telling me this now!"

"That's another thing, apparently I was born a bit later than I thought, and I'm still only 17."

She looked confused, but I was on a roll, so I kept explaining.

"Gabriel and I oversee the group here in California and will be leaving in the morning for the Mediterranean, where we will take control of all the Awakened in the world."

She gave me a blank look as Adam joined us on the bed again. "So you're telling me that you, my best friend, are somehow the leader of some weird race of whatever you called them?"

Her choice of words was a little offensive, but I remembered my reaction when I'd first heard the news, and she seemed to be taking it about as well as I had.

"Basically, yes."

Her smile spread across her face so quickly that I wasn't sure what was happening.

"That's awesome! Does this mean I get some fringe benefits?"

I laughed at her question. Of course, she would see the positive in this situation. That was just who she was, always looking on the bright side, or for whatever was better than what she had. A best friend was good, one who was gay was great, but a gay best friend with power was better.

"I don't know what sort of benefits you're looking for, but sure, you could get some fringe benefits. I'm glad you didn't freak out because we might have had to eat you if you did."

I looked at her with a serious expression and watched her squirm for a second before she smiled at me again.

"That's kinky!"

Leave it to her to find the sexual side of anything. We all laughed at her joke, and I could feel the tension in the room drop dramatically. Since she was clearly not going to freak out, we popped in a movie and the four of us crawled on the bed and got comfortable. Gabriel was on the outside, and I was next to him, followed by Megan and finally Adam, who was on the other side of the bed. When the movie ended, Megan and I hugged goodbye, and I told her I'd call her when I could. Adam walked her out to her car and after a few minutes I heard her engine turnover and listened as she backed out of the driveway and headed home.

Adam came back into the house and locked the front door before rejoining Gabriel and me in the bedroom. Gabriel had fallen asleep during the movie and was still snoring quietly on the bed. Adam helped me carry the luggage out to the car and get everything loaded for our trip to L.A., including an extra bag I didn't recognize. When I gave him a funny look, he took both of my arms in his hands, to hold me in place.

"I'd like to go with you to make sure you two are okay."

Admittedly I hadn't thought about having anyone there to help us out, which was a little scary, so the idea of bringing Adam with us was comforting.

"That's fine with me, but how will you get there? Were you able to get three tickets on the same flight?"

"Sort of…" He smiled at me. "It's a private plane, so there's enough room for me to join you."

My level of excitement amped up quite a bit at the prospect of a private plane. I'd never been in one, nor had I ever thought that I might have the opportunity to get in one. Maybe Megan's hope of fringe benefits wasn't too far off.

"Then I'd say it's a good thing you packed a bag."

We smiled at each other, and he pulled me into a hug. I pushed back softly after a little while.

"I'd better get at least a little sleep before we leave, or I'll be useless." When he released me from his arms, I turned without looking at him and walked back to my room. I felt his eyes follow me the whole way there, but I made sure not to turn around. I pulled off my shirt and pants, then climbed into bed next to Gabriel and fell asleep.

The darkness of my dream surrounded me and I began to look around for some indication that it was just part of my subconscious mind taking me on a nightly journey through my hidden fears. When the mirror popped up in the distance again however, I knew I was in for more confusion. I slowly wandered toward it and tried to shape the dream to my will along the way.

"It sure would be great if I were on a tropical island instead…"

I waited to see if anything would happen, but the mirror only seemed to grow larger as if it were trying to get my attention. I sighed and walked over to it where my annoyed reflection stared back at me.

"Don't give me that look, I didn't do anything!"

I spoke to my reflection as though it were another person in my dream, but he didn't change his expression, so I just stared back defiantly.

Then he opened his mouth to say something and when he did, his facial features changed slightly and my birth father now spoke to me through the mirror. This time however, I could understand what he was telling me, and so I watched his mouth closely to make sure I didn't miss anything he said.

"Caleb, I'm sorry that I cannot be there for you when you may need me most. Now that you have awakened, the challenges facing you will only increase. There is so much that I wish I could have told you before I died but your mother will have to share it all now. Never forget that I love you son, and I always have, even when you were far away from us."

He reached out and it looked like he was trying to touch the mirror, but his hands disappeared into the frame. I realized then that he had gone beyond what I could see in the mirror and now appeared to be talking to someone who was just outside my field of vision.

"If I could take on your challenges, I would do it in a heartbeat, but I know you will be strong enough to handle things yourself. You are incredibly special son, more than you can imagine. Time will prove that you are only limited by your own mind. Once you eliminate your perceived limits, you will be unstoppable."

He looked up at me again and smiled, and then his features disappeared and were replaced by mine. I could feel tears stream down my face, but I let them fall as the mirror faded away and I was swallowed by darkness once again.

Chapter Twelve

The next morning came much faster than I'd hoped, and I was still groggy when Lorelai knocked on the bedroom door to wake Gabriel and I up for our drive. I grumbled then rolled over and looked at Gabriel, who was still fast asleep. He had a little line of drool trickling down from the corner of his mouth, which made me laugh. It was adorable, and I felt even more excited about our trip because we would have a lot more uninterrupted time together, where we could hopefully get closer. I reached over and nudged his shoulder gently until he woke up and absently wiped at his mouth, before opening his eyes and smiling at me.

"Good morning handsome," he said, his voice deep and gravelly from still being tired. He lifted his head up off his pillow and his multicolored hair stuck almost straight up. I just smiled back at him, and then leaned in for a quick kiss before realizing I had morning breath. Since he didn't cringe away from me, I figured he wasn't too concerned about it, so I sat up and stretched before getting out of bed. I kept one eye open as I slowly made my way to the bathroom, and left the light off to avoid making myself temporarily blind. I moved around the room as quickly as I could manage, getting ready for our trip and a long flight ahead of us. After about ten minutes, Gabriel walked in and flipped on the switch, causing me to cry out in pain from the sudden increase of light in the room.

He smiled and turned off the light, apologizing to me. I wrapped my arms around him and squeezed lightly, which made him cry out a little. I forgot he hadn't used the restroom yet. I laughed and set him down and allowed him to pass by me while I walked into the closet and looked for something to wear. I grabbed a comfortable pair of jeans and pulled those on, and as I was searching for a shirt, I heard Lorelai knock on the door again.

"Come on in, we're almost ready," I called out, and waited for her to open the door. I heard her turn the latch and walk toward the closet, but I jumped when I heard a deep voice behind me.

"Good morning."

I spun around and saw Adam standing in the doorway to the closet. Without thinking, I reached out and pulled the first shirt I touched off the hanger and held it up in front of my body. I could hear the vibration of his deep laughter that he somehow kept inside. I looked down at the shirt I was holding and noticed that it was a little small since my body had begun to take on some bulk. I decided to try to put it on anyway, to avoid looking like an idiot.

"Good morning. How'd you sleep?"

I was mentally scolding myself at my awkward behavior, and then last night's conversation came racing back into the front of my mind and I remembered that Adam wanted to go with us. Suddenly, my alone time with Gabriel didn't seem like it was going to be so easy to come by as I'd initially thought, and my disappointment was immediate.

"I slept pretty well actually, how about you?" He stepped a little closer, his eyes locked on my face.

I knew my eyes were bloodshot, and my hair was a mess, so I just shrugged noncommittally.

"Eh, I slept okay. Are you and Lorelai ready to go?"

As I said it, I heard the toilet flush and the sink turn on from behind Adam. His face took on a new expression, which he quickly hid.

"Whenever you guys are dressed, we're ready to go."

Just then, Gabriel stepped out of the bathroom in his t-shirt and boxers. He smiled at Adam and said hello, then padded back out to the bedroom where he pulled on the clothes he wore to the house last night.

"Ready to go!" He yelled from the other room, which caused me to look down at my shirt that was way too tight to be comfortable.

"I'll just be a minute. You two go on ahead."

Adam nodded and walked out of the room. I pulled the shirt off and grabbed a new one that fit, slipped on some shoes, and then joined the rest of the group by the garage door.

"Let's go!" I tried to smile, but there was an uncomfortable weight in the air, that no one else seemed to notice.

"Can we stop on the way, though? I'm going to need something to eat." My stomach rumbled as proof of my hunger and caused Gabriel and Lorelai to laugh.

***

Getting through security was pretty simple, there weren't that many passengers heading to the private and commuter planes, which made the process a lot faster than it was usually. And thirty minutes after Lorelai dropped us all off, we were on the plane and getting ready for our flight. Gabriel and I chose seats next to each other, and Adam sat a couple of rows behind us. Each row had two oversized seats, which reclined back to an almost horizontal position and had a foot rest that made them feel more like tiny beds than airplane seats. There were only seats on one side, and the other side was open, with a small refrigerator, sink and lower cabinets I assumed had pillows and blankets.

The only other person on the plane was the pilot, and though she greeted us as we boarded the plane, she quickly excused herself to finish her last minute checks before the flight departed. After we were airborne for a while, I could hear Adam walking around behind us. He was looking through the cabinets, which had plates, glasses, napkins, cutlery and snacks. Even though we'd stopped and gotten something on the way, I could feel my stomach growl, and I got up to grab something small to munch on in my seat.

When I approached Adam, he nodded but didn't say anything to me. He grabbed a couple more things then quickly went back to his seat, which left me to hunt through the cabinets on my own. I found some granola bars, individually packaged cookies and some fruit bars, so I grabbed a few of each and a small bottle of orange juice and returned to my seat.

"What'd you find?" Gabriel looked over interested in my stash as soon as I sat down, and when he saw the cookies, he snatched one up quickly before I could even respond.

"Please, have a cookie." I laughed at him.

"Thank you, I will."

He joined my laughter, and I realized that even though things between Adam and I were a little strange this morning, Gabriel was still laid back and as happy as ever. It made me glad to know that we were in this together. Even if he wasn't sure he wanted to be an alpha, he was still here supporting me, and I couldn't have asked for anything more.

We slept off and on for the next few hours, and then watched a movie on the small screen we found built into the ceiling of the plane. Even though he kept his distance, I could hear Adam laughing from behind us at the funny parts of the movie. I decided maybe all the weirdness was coming from me, and I should do something to try to show I wasn't going to let it bother me. After the movie ended, I got up to use the lavatory, and as I reached for the handle, it opened and the door swung out, nearly smacking me in the face.

"Caleb! I'm sorry, are you okay?" Adam reached out and lightly held onto my arm. He checked to make sure he hadn't hit me and let go when he was satisfied.

"I'm fine. Don't worry about it." I smiled and stepped back a little to let him pass by me. After a few seconds he got the hint and walked back to his seat.

So much for it just being in my mind. I closed the door to the lavatory and looked at myself in the mirror. My eyes still looked red from lack of sleep, and my hair was even more disheveled than it was early this morning. I ran some cold water and splashed it on my face. It didn't really help, but it made me feel a little better. Soon enough, I was able to rejoin the others.

By the time I walked back out, Adam and Gabriel were sitting at a small table with some playing cards lying face down between them. They each had a small handful and eyed each other carefully.

"What are you guys playing?"

"Strip poker," Gabriel replied without looking up.

My mouth dropped open, and Adam's head whipped around, his cheeks flushing red.

"We're just playing regular poker, no one is stripping!"

Gabriel burst out laughing at Adam's discomfort, and my complete shock turned into loud laughter.

"You wish we were playing strip poker…" Adam said under his breath as his cheeks returned to their normal color.

"Deal me in." I sat down with them, determined to keep my thoughts to myself, and to let this tension ease in its own time.

Adam gave me a small stack of cards and the game began in earnest. It turned out that Gabriel had a pretty big tell when he had a good hand, and Adam's dimple became visible when he was lying. Having no real idea how to play poker, I was the best of all, because I never knew if I was doing well or not. I either won big or lost half my pile. Gabriel found potato chips, which we used instead of money. They were certainly a delicious prize, but we had to quit playing after a few hands because we'd eaten all our winnings.

Having eaten just about everything on the plane, and watched the only movie any of us had with us, we were now out of things to do and still had about three hours of flying ahead of us. Now was the best time to talk about what the plan would be once we landed. I wanted to make sure that I was ready for whatever we were going to encounter, and that there were no surprises if I could help it.

"What happens when we land?"

My question threw both Adam and Gabriel off for a second, but Adam responded.

"We'll find a taxi and go meet Ouriel, who will fill you in on what has been happening with the Council since the murder. And then tonight, you will meet with the rest of them for the first time as their leader."

The thought of meeting the other alphas of the Council made me uncomfortable, but Gabriel slipped his hand into mine and squeezed lightly, sending warmth and comfort through my body. He reminded me that I wasn't alone in this effort, and I couldn't have been more appreciative than I was at that moment.

"Who's Ouriel?"

"He's the other elder on the council. He's been on the council for the longest, now that Deanna has been murdered. Then there is the rest of the Council. Kenai, Jae, Stephen, Maeve and The Greek." I was impressed by Adam's knowledge of the Council but realized it was probably only my ignorance that made it seem so incredible.

"What is the Greek person's name?"

"That is his name, The Greek. It's more title than anything I guess, but that's what he goes by. No one knows if he has a real name. And don't say anything about it, he's apparently short-tempered."

Great, we were walking into an uncomfortable position with a group of Awakened that probably thought we were stupid kids, and at least one of them already has an attitude problem. What could go wrong there?

"The Greek it is."

We continued to talk about protocol for meeting the other alphas and what we would be expected to do once we were all together. When the captain came over the intercom and asked us to prepare for landing, my stomach began to cramp as the nerves set in. A few minutes later, we were on the ground and moved toward a small hangar off to the side of the main airport. I could see a sleek white car waiting next to the hangar and a man dressed in a suit standing in front of it. As we rolled to a stop next to the vehicle, the captain came out of the cockpit and opened the door, while the man in the suit moved a staircase up to the opening.

"Who is that?" I asked Adam quietly as we gather our belongings.

He shrugged, barely noticing. "The driver I guess, based on the car."

"Ass," I said under my breath.

Adam just laughed as he walked away.

Gabriel squeezed my arm before giving me a kiss on the cheek.

"Try to relax, we are here to help."

He made a good point, and yet I couldn't shake the feeling that nothing good would come from this meeting. Even if we thought we were here to help, there was no certainty that they wanted our help in the first place. I tried to force myself to look at the bright side and made my way off the plane. The man in the suit took my luggage and placed it in the trunk before he helped me into the backseat. Gabriel was already waiting for me, and Adam had taken his place next to the driver in the front. Without a word, the driver maneuvered the car out of the airport and onto the main road toward the city.

Chapter Thirteen

Gabriel and I were making small talk in the back when the car suddenly made a sharp left turn, and then a right almost immediately. I slammed into the door and then felt like I was being choked by the seat belt. The driver didn't bother to slow down and the tires had begun to lose traction with the speed and angle of the turns. We slid around tight corners in the road and ran over medians as he changed lanes and cut across oncoming traffic without any notice.

"What the hell?" I looked at the driver as I said it, but Adam was the one to respond after he looked back at me.

"Caleb, get down!" He didn't yell, but there was a forceful strength to his tone, and I knew better than to question him. Gabriel and I ducked down as low as we could get.

"What's going on out there?" I asked as the driver accelerated again, and then narrowly avoided running off the road as it curved in front of us.

"Being followed." His gruff voice and broken English made me feel like I was in one of those movies where the American gets abducted while on vacation.

I remembered back to the photos Adam had shown us of some of the other Council members, and I wondered if they were already trying to get rid of me. It wouldn't be the first time I had gotten in someone's way, and it probably wasn't going to be the last either.

"We just got here, how does anyone even know we've arrived?"

The answer seemed obvious to me, but I couldn't exactly point fingers at the Council without having met them first.

"I don't know, but whoever it is, they clearly don't want us to make it to our destination."

Adam's voice was low. He spoke quietly to the driver who nodded and grunted an agreement.

The car swerved back and forth as we continued to speed through the city. I could see buildings and the tops of the trees that hung over the road fly by as we darted through tight alleys and careened around an almost unending series of switchback turns. After a couple minutes of this, I began to feel sick, but that at least took my mind off of my panic, which had started to subside a little. Gabriel was less worried than I was, and he peeked out of the window every couple of minutes.

"What are you doing?! Get down!" I pulled on his arm as his head popped up.

He dropped back down and looked at me with a frustrated scowl on his face. "I'm just trying to see what's happening. Relax."

He lifted himself up again to get a better look before dropping back down almost immediately. As his head cleared the window, it shattered, and a bullet hole just to the right of where his face had been sent a very clear message of the intentions of whoever was following us.

"I told you not to do that!" I hit his arm, angry with him for being so stupid. He looked back at me, his eyes wide with shock, but didn't respond. When it seemed like things couldn't get any worse, our car began to slow down and drift to the right.

"What's happening now?" I asked, hopeful that the attack on the car was over.

"Oh shit!" Adam's voice from the front seat made it clear that we were nowhere near safe yet. I tried to get myself into a position where I could see him without being visible from the window.

"What happened? Did we lose them?" Ever the optimist, I hoped I had just been over reacting to his outburst.

"No, they shot the driver." His tone was flat, and there was a complete lack of emotion, which made it seem like he'd said something about the sky being blue, rather than someone getting injured.

"Oh shit!" I agreed. "Can he heal himself?"

"Not exactly…"

"What do you mean?" I got up again to try to look at the driver and see what was wrong. As I did, the back window exploded inward, and small pieces of glass cut my neck, face and arms. I ducked back down, and could hear some grunting and cursing coming from Adam in the front seat. Followed immediately by the driver's door opening, then closing as the car ran over something big.

"What was that?" Gabriel suddenly spoke up.

"It was the driver; I had to push him out so I could take over." Adam's voice was now coming from the other side of the car, and we picked up speed again.

"You threw him out of the car? Why?" I could feel my body try to shift as fear began to take over my body, but I concentrated and held it off. I figured that a wolf in the car wouldn't make the drive any easier for Adam.

"Is that what we ran over?" Gabriel and I spoke at the same time, but he asked the most important question, so I had to make an assumption.

"He was already dead and more importantly, he was slowing us down. There was nothing I could do to help him, so I pushed him out."

Adam's voice was strained, which I assumed was due to his extreme concentration as he attempted to navigate the streets of an unfamiliar city.

"Call the Council and find out what we can do!" He barked the order at us and thrust a cell phone in my face.

"What's the number?" I opened the contacts on the phone and scrolled through. There was one that was simply listed as "Council" so I gave it a shot. "Never mind, I think I got it."

I pressed the call button and waited. It took a few seconds, and the ringing noise sounded different for some reason, but after a few rings someone picked up.

"Halo?"

It was close enough to English that it took me a second before I remembered I wasn't in America, and English was not the primary language here.

"Hello? Ouriel?" I hoped the person spoke English, or I was in trouble.

"Pričekajte minut…" I could tell that he had put the phone down and was walking away.

"Wait! No please wait, come back!" I yelled into the cell phone, hoping he would hear me and pick up the receiver again.

"What's happening?" Gabriel leaned closer as we sped around another curve in the road, and Adam cursed from the front seat.

"Someone answered, but they put the phone down. I don't know what to do!"

As I tried to decide whether I should hang up and try again or just stay on the line, another voice came through the phone.

"Halo?" The voice sounded older than the first and was speaking English this time.

"Hi! This is Caleb and Gabriel; we're being chased and shot at. Our driver is dead, and we don't know where to go."

I was yelling into the phone to be heard over the string of expletives coming from the front seat as Adam slammed on the brakes, swerved and sped up again.

"Caleb, this is Ouriel, I'll do what I can to help you, but can you tell me where you are right now?" He spoke to someone else in what I assumed was Croatian, and whoever it was seemed to be getting an ear full.

"Ouriel wants to know where we are, Adam, any idea?"

"We're on Route 105, heading toward Krka."

I was surprised that he gave that much information, but then I saw a sign fly by the car with the word 'Krka' on it, which made more sense.

I shared the information with Ouriel, who in turn relayed the news to his counterpart and then returned to the phone.

"Keep heading in the direction of Krka, and Jusuf will intercept you along the way. Caleb, when you see him, make sure you get out of the way as fast as possible. Jusuf will take care of the rest."

With that, he disconnected from our phone call, and I was left wondering what he meant.

"He said to keep heading in that direction, and someone will meet us, and he said to get out of the way when we see him."

"What are we supposed to get out of the way of?" Adam asked, apparently as confused as I was.

"He didn't say, he just told me to get out of the way and then he hung up."

I dropped the cell phone back over the seat so Adam would have it if he needed it. My legs had begun to cramp from being curled up tightly against my body. I tried to stretch them out in front of me, but there was no space to accommodate my extremities. I tried to take my mind off of my discomfort, by reaching for Gabriel. I placed my hand on the side of his face, and he winced from the minor cuts the window caused. He looked up at a high-pitched noise that came from behind me and his eyes widened as he did.

"Caleb, watch out!" He tried to pull me out of the way, but Adam reacted and swerved rapidly, hitting something on the driver side as the glass above me shattered and rained down on Gabriel and me. I heard what sounded like metal nails scratching across a chalkboard, and shivered involuntarily.

"What the hell was that!?" I brushed glass carefully out of my hair and checked Gabriel for fresh cuts. I could feel something warm trickle down the back of my neck, and I knew I was bleeding, but my fear and confusion proved to be a pretty good anesthetic.

"A guy was pointing a gun at you; he shot out the window as Adam swerved into him."

Adam spoke up from the front, "Are you two okay? Sorry about that, he came up out from behind the car that has been following us. I thought he was just trying to pass us until he pulled out a gun." Adam's voice still sounded strained, which concerned me a little bit.

"We're fine, thanks to your quick reflexes. Are you okay?" I ventured a quick peek out the back window, and it looked reasonably safe, as the next closest car was a little bit behind us currently.

"I think the bullet ricocheted off something in the car and hit me, but I should be fine. Just get back down, we're coming up to a roundabout, and I'm going to have to slow down, or make it a 'straight through'."

His ability to joke with me while he was clearly in pain helped me worry a little less. The car slowed slightly, but Gabriel and I were still forced from one side of the back to the other. Adam let out some choice words again, which suggested that the pain had started to get to him. I took hold of Gabriel's hand, and we reached out and touched the back of Adam's neck.

I could feel the warmth of our healing ability flow through my hands and into Adam, who was quiet and held as still as possible. The skin under my hand flushed and warmed while the little hairs on his neck stood on end for some reason. I had no idea how our healing ability worked, and I couldn't see his wound, so I wasn't sure if he was still healing or wondering why we were still touching him. Finally, I looked over at Gabriel and noticed the small cuts on his forehead and cheeks had closed. I figured if he had healed, Adam was probably fine, so I carefully moved my hand away and felt Adam lean into it again.

He seemed to notice what he'd done, and he let out a soft apology. "Sorry about that. You can stop now; I think I'm fine. Thank you."

The sincerity in his voice caught me a little off-guard, and I smiled despite the severity of our situation.

A couple of minutes later, Adam shifted in his seat and seemed to lean forward.

"Get back in your seats, now!" His instructions were confusing, and my legs were asleep, so I didn't make any effort to move quickly.

He insisted more forcefully, "Get your asses in those seats and put on your seat belts, or I swear you will wish you'd been thrown out of this car with the driver!"

That was enough for me. Gabriel and I untangled our limbs from each other and slid back into the seats, careful to avoid the glass shards wherever possible. When both of us clicked our seat belts into place, Adam swerved again, but this time I could see that we were not going to stay on the road. I looked beyond the front of the car to see where we were going to end up, and saw someone with an enormous gun, and he appeared to be aiming it right at us. I turned around and saw the car behind us drive off the road as well and saw the front windshield of that car implode as the man with the gun, Jusuf I assumed, opened fire.

"So that's what Ouriel meant by 'get out of the way'? He could have just said he was sending a guy with a giant gun," Gabriel said next to me.

"Too true," I agreed.

Chapter Fourteen

We climbed out of the car, and I was happy to have survived my second crash in a matter of months and all those years of previously uneventful trips in cars seemed somehow impossible since I had the worst luck with things now. I tried not to worry about it and walked over to where Adam and Jusuf stood. I noticed that Jusuf was typing something into his smartphone and then handing it over to Adam, who would type back and return it. When I got closer, I realized they were using a translation app, which never seemed to work quite right when you needed them to. Hopefully, they were able to understand the critical pieces, and we'd get out of here soon.

Finally, Jusuf walked back toward his car, which was partially hidden behind some bushes along the street, and Adam popped the trunk of our car, grabbed his bags and followed Jusuf. I figured we were changing cars here, so Gabriel and I followed suit. Once we'd loaded our luggage into the new vehicle, Jusuf handed Adam the keys and took the keys to the car we'd been driving.

"Okay kids, time for another car ride, hop in!" Adam's fake cheery voice was a little condescending, but I refused to react. I calmly opened the door for Gabriel, and then walked around to the other side and got in—no need to start something when there was nothing to start.

"What'd he say?" I asked.

"What do you mean?" Adam glanced at me in the rearview mirror while maneuvering his way back onto the road.

"You two were texting, what'd he say?"

"We talked about his family and where he was from, his childhood hopes and dreams; what do you think he said? 'Give me your keys, you take my car and follow me back.'"

I reached over and gently took Gabriel's hand in my own. I thought about the night we'd first shifted, and everyone around us had reacted to our power. I tried to channel that feeling and focused it all on Adam's snarky expression. After a few seconds, though, nothing had happened. Adam was stronger than I thought, or I had no idea what I was doing. I was willing to bet it was the latter.

"Where are we going?" I finally asked since there was no tidal wave of power ripping through the car.

"I'm not sure, but I'll bet Ouriel will be there, and that is all that matters to me right now. It will also give me a chance to call Lorelai while you two are meeting the rest of the Council. I need to let her know what happened today."

I didn't like the idea of him sharing with Lorelai that we were chased through the city by some crazy with a gun, but it felt like she ought to know.

"Will you just make sure to let her know we are all okay?"

"Of course."

Without all the gunfire and sharp turns, the drive was uneventful. I looked out the window and watched the country go by, surprised by how much the road reminded me of the freeway in California from San Diego into Riverside. There were houses and shops along the way, but it was mostly expanses of open space, small mountains and tree filled valleys. As we got closer to our destination, the trees became more plentiful, and the buildings thinned out significantly. Jusuf, who was still in front of us, took an exit off the roadway and began to head deeper into what appeared to be a tree lined compound. We arrived at a large, solid looking gate, complete with a guard stand and guard, who waved us through once Jusuf showed up.

Once the gate opened and the house came into view, I was at a loss for words. Even the word house didn't seem to capture its scale accurately, but castle felt too old world for the modern building that stood before us. It was all white, and straight lines with large windows that made the facade look like a Mondrian painting. There was a large wooden door that seemed to pivot rather than swing open on hinges, which was wide open and waiting for our arrival. On the other side of the house was a balcony that probably had a fantastic view of the garden that spread out beneath it, and the trees beyond that.

Jusuf had already begun unloading our bags by the time I had gotten out of the car. I rushed to grab what I could, so they didn't think I was rude or expecting a certain level of treatment while I was here. Gabriel did the same and smiled nervously at me, then moved to my side as we walked toward the open front door and a smiling man who stood there.

"Caleb, Gabriel, I am Ouriel. It is so lovely to meet you finally!" He looked at both of us as he spoke, and I realized he probably didn't know which one of us was which.

I stepped forward and held my hand out to him. "Caleb," I said. "Nice to meet you."

His smile got even bigger, now that he was able to put a face with my name, and I could feel something from his handshake, but it was unlike anything I'd felt before. When Adam forced ideas in my head, it was as though he was pushing something into me, but this felt almost like something was being taken away. I wasn't sure what to do, so I focused on the one thing I was sure he'd expect from me, hunger, and pushed that into his hand until he released me.

He stepped up to Gabriel then and grabbed his hand and shook it.

"Which means you must be Gabriel! It's so nice to have you both here in my home. Please, won't you come inside? I don't know about you two, but I am hungry all of a sudden."

I tried to cover my laugh by coughing, and if he noticed, he didn't say anything. He simply led us into his home and swiveled the door closed behind us. The inside of the house was even better than the outside, but instead of a cold modern functionality, the furnishings were warm, inviting and looked like they were over-stuffed for comfort.

"Your home is gorgeous, thank you for having us." I spoke to the rooms while my head swung from side to side, taking in everything I could.

"Thank you, Caleb, I do hope you will all enjoy your time here. I only wish your arrival had not been so exciting."

The way he said 'exciting' sounded almost like an apology, which I took as a good sign. Even Gabriel seemed to relax a little and drifted away from me a bit more. As he did, I could feel Adam take up his position on my other side, almost as a slight tickle along the edge of my body. I'd have to ask him about that later, as well as the strange feeling I got from Ouriel when we shook hands.

Ouriel led us into a small informal dining room, and I was surprised to see that there was already food waiting, and more was being carried in as we walked into the room.

"Please, everyone, have a seat. I thought you might be hungry after your travels and the events of the day. A small meal may help you feel more relaxed and will hopefully help with the time change you have experienced. After we eat, Jusuf will show you to your rooms, and you can get settled. The Council will convene tomorrow to meet our two new leaders, and we will have much to discuss at that time. But for now, please eat and try to relax, we have plenty of time to talk now that you are here."

With that, he grabbed a bowl next to him, which appeared to have some small pasta mixed with fruit; I picked up a plate of cured ham and took a few pieces. Gabriel took what appeared to be rolled up lasagna, standing on its end, and Adam took a few pieces of meat that looked like little sausages, which also had some onions and a reddish-orange sauce. We passed the dishes around until we all had a little bit of everything and then began eating. The food was delicious, and we all took a bit more of everything, which left the large plates nearly empty and our stomachs incredibly full.

Once we finished eating, Ouriel called for Jusuf, who had changed since our arrival, and looked a lot less imposing than he had previously. After a few words in Croatian, Jusuf motioned for us to follow him, and led the three of us out of the dining room and back toward the front entrance of the home. Before we got there however, we turned down a small hallway and took stairs up to the second story. Jusuf gestured toward three rooms that were on either side of the hall, which I assumed was his way of saying, "Here are your rooms."

I looked into one of the rooms and saw that Gabriel's bags had been placed on the bed inside. Adam found his stuff at the end of the hall in another room and was already inside unpacking. My things were in the room in the middle, so I walked in and was happy to see that I had an expansive view of the grounds from my window. The balcony I'd seen before jutted out from an opening between my room and Adam's.

I unpacked my clothes and then realized that I hadn't seen a bathroom yet, so I set out in search of that. It ended up being next to Gabriel's room and had a large, claw foot tub that fit with the large and comfortable nature of the rest of the furnishings in the home.

"Hey…"

I jumped at the quiet voice behind me and spun around to see Gabriel covering his mouth to avoid laughing at me.

"Holy crap, you scared me!"

He smiled at me and moved out of the doorway as I followed him into his room.

"Sorry about that. I saw you walk past my room so I figured I'd see what you were up to."

"I was just exploring a little, seeing what there was to see up here. How's your room?" I looked around and noticed that the furniture in the room was pretty similar to my own. His window and view were from a different side of the house, though, so he could see some of the mountains we'd passed on our way here.

"It's beautiful, look at it all." He sat down on the bed and practically disappeared into the comforter. "This is the softest bed I think I've ever sat on in my life!" He laid back, and it almost looked like he was buried in snow and not laying on top of the bed. I plopped down on the bed next to him and reached for his hand as he reached for mine. We were so in sync sometimes it was as though we'd known each other for years and not a few weeks.

"I should send a picture to Megan, she would be so jealous of all this. I wonder if there is a Wi-Fi signal here?"

To my delight, when I took my phone out and searched for a signal, I was able to log on to a nearby network. I sent her a couple of quick messages with pictures of Gabriel and me in bed. I made him pretend he was making a snow angel and sent that as well. A few minutes later she replied with a couple pictures herself, but then the text came through that explained why I had received them.

Please show those pictures to Adam so he can see what he's missing out on. I could practically hear her laughing all the way from California.

Only a little from what I can tell. I texted back.

She responded with a series of emoticons that I assumed meant she knew I was kidding and then a very clear, *Bitch!*

I laughed. *I love you too!* I had to keep it short because I had no idea what my cell phone bill would look like when I got home. I hoped that the Wi-Fi connection meant these conversations were free, but I wasn't going to chance it until I figured it out.

I sent one final text before turning my phone off for the rest of the day. *I've got to go, but I miss you! Tell my parents I said hello and I will be in touch soon.*

I had to remind myself that I was here for the good of my other family, and I just hoped my parents would understand. I set my phone on the bedside table, curled up with Gabriel in my arms and drifted into the darkness of my dreams.

Beginnings

Excerpt from
<u>The Awakened History:</u>

Gilles Garnier
October, 1572:

Gilles felt his hunger overwhelm him and threaten to rend him in half. It had been too many days since he and his family had eaten a proper meal, and his wife was becoming ill from a lack of food. He felt helpless; he had already done everything he could to provide for his family. His tired and broken body was not as quick as it had once been, and catching game in the forest was almost impossible.

"Papa, I'm so hungry, do you think we will eat tonight?" His daughter looked up at him from where she sat on the bed, her cheeks, long sunken, had lost the fullness of youth making her look much older than her five years.

"Yes, my darling, we will eat tonight, I will make sure of it. Look after your Mama, and I'll go get us our meal." Gilles removed his clothing, not wanting to ruin what little he had, and he walked outside. The pain in his stomach disappeared for a merciful second as he became completely encased in darkness, but returned with a fury as his increased senses bombarded his brain with the scents of meats and bread in the distance. Drawn in by his animal instincts and burning hunger, his feet began to carry him toward the small town of Dole. As he got closer to the cooking food, the intoxicating smells distracted him, and he didn't realize a small child of nine or ten, playing at the edge of a vineyard, had spotted him.

She stared at him, unblinking, the fear apparent on her face. Forgetting his form, he took one step toward the girl, hoping to comfort her. He watched as the girl ran screaming back to her town to warn her neighbors. Knowing her screams would jeopardize his search for food, he pursued her.

Lyse knew the wolf was behind her. She'd heard of the creatures in the forest but didn't think she would ever see anything so terrifying this close to her home. She ran as fast as her legs could carry her, but when she turned, her foot caught in a crevice in the ground. She stumbled, hitting her temple against the sharp edge of one of the rocks along the road.

Gilles watched as the child struck her head. He could hear her shallow breathing, but she made no move to get up. After ten long seconds, Gilles began to fear that he would be discovered on the road with the girl and killed for attacking her. To make sure she was not injured further, he grabbed the girl by the hem of her dress and began to drag her into the protection of the rows of grapes in the nearby vineyard. He nudged her until he was finally able to flip her onto her back and began to lick the wound to try to clean it. Gilles hoped to get a better look at how much damage had been done to try to assess the situation. As he licked, however, new blood rushed to fill in the space as though her body was fighting the inspection from the outsider.

Gilles waited with the girl for hours, hoping she would open her eyes. Finally, as the sun began to dip below the horizon, her shallow breathing stopped, and he could tell she had no life left in her body. Her delicate features relaxed, and she reminded him of his daughter, whom he had left that morning in search of food. How could he return to her and tell her he had failed? She would soon follow this girl into an endless sleep if he didn't do something to get her food soon. His desire for food had begun to rise in his stomach again, and before he could stop himself, he had bitten into the exposed muscle of her calf and removed a small piece. Instinct took over as he continued to eat small portions of muscle and fat until the pain of his hunger had stopped. He removed a few larger pieces and brought them home to his family, ashamed of what he had done, but unwilling to allow them to follow the young girl into death.

Over the following weeks, Gilles continued to try to find a regular food source for his family through hunting in the traditional sense. By November, the winter had driven large animals away from the area, and many of the smaller prey had disappeared as well, leaving Gilles without any hope of providing food to the others. Since the first girl, he'd attacked two others and provided more meat for his starving wife and daughter. The townspeople were now even more wary of the forest than they had been, and he had to venture closer to their homes than he wanted to. Now he was more exposed and vulnerable to being caught, which didn't stop him, but made him more cautious. If he were discovered and killed, his family would be unable to care for themselves and would surely perish soon thereafter.

To avoid raising suspicion, he walked to the town as a man, so he was able to get close enough to be able to find a small child or perhaps a stray dog or cat, which would be easy to carry off into the vineyard. As he neared the town, he tried to keep out of the public areas rather than walking along the main thoroughfare. He used alleys and small spaces between buildings to move through the village instead. Finally, he saw a little boy playing outside his home. He got as close as possible without calling any attention to himself and then watched and waited. No one else in the area moved about, which meant it was now or never.

Gilles sprang forward, grabbed the boy and clamped a hand firmly over his nose and mouth to keep him from making any loud noise. Gilles ran as quickly as he could along the path he'd taken to the town to get back out again, and sprinted for the vineyards once they were in sight. When he reached the cover of the vines, he looked down at the young boy, who was now dead, as a result, of Gilles' hand blocking his airways.

"I'm so sorry, I wish there was another way, but my little girl has to eat to live, and you are already dead."

It was the same thing he'd said to the other small children he'd killed and eaten, trying desperately to justify his actions. He laid the boy's body down gently and had begun to shift into his wolf form when he heard them. Men from the town were coming closer, and from the sounds of their voices, there were quite a few of them. He stopped the change and began changing back into his human form so he could escape and hopefully carry the child further into the woods. After he'd shifted back, he reached down and picked up the child, cradling him close to his body.

"You there, what are you doing?" A gruff voice called out to Gilles from the road. He tried to walk calmly away from the men, but they didn't allow him to get far. "I asked you what you were doing, answer me now!"

Gilles could hear them getting closer, the fallen leaves crunched under their feet. "I'm just resting a while on the road. I've been traveling for so long." He continued walking away, careful to keep the boy's body hidden from view.

"What are you carrying?" Another man, who was walking to the side of Gilles and had a better view than the rest eyed him closely.

"Just some clothing and other goods for my family. As I said, I've been traveling for quite some time." Gilles attempted to remain calm, but his body was struggling to hold the boy, and the effort was apparent in his voice, which made him nervous.

A large hand squeezed Gilles' shoulder and spun him around roughly. His grip on the boy faltered, and the body slipped, falling a short distance to the ground. Horrified,

Gilles looked into the eyes of the men who pursued him and saw that they knew his real intentions.

"The Devil made me do it!" Gilles screamed out suddenly, afraid that the men would realize who he was and follow his tracks to his waiting family. The men grabbed Gilles and dragged him back to the town, where he eventually confessed to the murders of the children and was sentenced to death. His wife was also found and put to death for her knowledge of the murders.

Their daughter, who was still quite young, was taken in by the community and lived with an older couple that did not have children of their own. One night, when she was 15, she disappeared and was never seen again. But shortly thereafter, the sightings of a wolf near town increased.

***

Part Two

Chapter Fifteen

I woke up with Gabriel still in my arms and realized that we'd slept much longer than I initially anticipated. I checked the clock by the bed; it was nearly 3:30 in the morning. The room was dark except for the glow from the crack under the door. Carefully, I slid out of bed, making sure that I didn't disturb Gabriel as he slept and crept to the door. Once I was in the hallway, I walked back toward my room, but stopped when I saw the door leading to the balcony open slightly. I saw Adam standing outside, pacing back and forth slowly.

I opened the door, which caused him to stop in his path and look up at me.

"Caleb, what are you doing awake?"

"I slept about as much as I could, what time is it back home?" I continued out onto the balcony; the cold air wrapped around me, helping to wake me up even more.

"It's about 6:30 pm." He watched me closely as I moved toward him.

"Have you spoken to Lorelai yet? Told her what happened?" I sat on the railing of the balcony, and looked out over the yard below.

"Yes, I told her about the attack and that we made it to the house safely. She said that she wanted to hear from you when you can call her, but she is working to make sure everything at home continues to run smoothly. I'm sure she's worried about you but was trying to hide it because of your position in the pack now. You should call to calm her soon."

When he sat next to me, his knee brushed up against my own. I could feel the warmth of his body seep into my own, and it felt like I'd wrapped myself in a blanket fresh from the dryer. The heat soothed me while the cool air kept me from overheating.

"I will call her and let her know we're fine, but first, I was hoping we could talk about what was going to happen today. I want to make sure I am ready to meet with the rest of the Council. Ouriel seems nice enough, but the last time someone like us sat on the Council, she became a puppet for the other alphas. I want to send a very clear message that Gabriel and I are united and not going to give in to pressure from the other members."

With the mention of Gabriel, Adam shifted his body slightly, but it was enough that his knee was no longer against mine. The space between us was small, but all of the warmth disappeared, and I began to feel uncomfortable in the cold morning air.

"Have you slept yet?"

He turned his face away slightly as he answered, "No."

"Why not?" I leaned forward and touched his knee with the tips of my fingers then tried to get him to look at me again.

When he turned around, there was a look on his face that I'd never seen. Pain, confusion, hope, and fear all seemed to play across his features. He opened his mouth to speak as his hand moved toward my hand on his knee.

"Caleb? Adam?" Gabriel's voice from the doorway pulled our attention away, and Adam quickly stood and moved to the other side of the balcony.

I was confused by Adam's change in behavior, but happy that Gabriel had joined us, it would be better that we all discuss the meeting together.

"Morning, sleepy." I smiled at him, as he walked toward us, still wrapped in a sheet from his bed.

"What did I miss?" He sat down next to me and snuggled in close. He smelled so good that I leaned closer than was absolutely necessary and he wrapped the sheet around my shoulders. It brought back the warmth that I had been missing. And I relaxed into him and breathed in his sweet scent some more.

"We were just about to discuss the meeting today, so you have perfect timing." I responded before kissing him gently on the lips. I could hear Adam sigh behind me, so I broke off the kiss and turned to face him.

"What do you think?"

"I've already shared about as much as I know about the Council members with both of you, all that's left is for you to figure out what you need to do in order to get them on your side."

Gabriel shifted next to me. "Why do we need to get them on our side? Aren't we already on the same side?" He asked as he looked between me and Adam.

"I was telling Adam that I don't want to be taken advantage of since we are still very young, so making sure they see us as allies and not pawns to move as they please would be a good thing for us to do."

"I don't want to be used either, but don't you think it sends the wrong message if we start our relationship with the Council by putting ourselves above them?" He sat up straighter, and looked me in the eyes.

"Gabriel does make a good point as well, Caleb. They have all been Alphas for a long time, trying to position yourselves as being separate from the Council or above their advice may not be the best decision." Adam continued to pace on his half of the balcony but stopped long enough to make his point heard. When he finished speaking, he began to walk again.

"I'm not saying that we should go in there with our figurative guns blazing. I just think we need to be ready to stand up for ourselves and prepare to defend our positions on the Council if they are questioned."

Gabriel appeared to consider my suggestion but Adam merely shrugged and kept walking.

"How do we do that?" Gabriel asked.

"I think one thing that we can do is show them that we are together, which gives us an advantage the others don't have. They may know each other, and be powerful among their own packs, but they are from different parts of the world. We're from the same pack which means we have support on the Council that they don't."

I noticed that Adam had stopped pacing, as he understood the power in the truth of my statement, a small smile played on his lips.

"I can do that," Gabriel said. "I want to be near you during the meeting anyway, and if that happens to demonstrate the power of our being together, so be it. I'm just hoping they don't challenge us so we can go home as soon as possible."

"It's settled then; you will go in together and make sure you let everyone know how strong your bond is. They don't have a chance to consider the possibility of trying to bend your wills to their own." Adam's smile had spread but still didn't cause the dimple in his left cheek to become visible. He was happy but it was controlled. "What do we do until then?"

An idea popped into my head, and I smiled in return, my body flushed with excitement. Both Gabriel and Adam turned to look at me without me saying a word, which apparently meant I was so excited I had shared that feeling with everyone.

"I know what we should do!" I stood and began to pull off my shoes and socks, and then I unbuttoned my pants and pulled my shirt over my head.

"Well, are you going to join me, or am I going to have to do this alone?" I looked at them both expectantly. They each just watched me, quietly. The expression on their faces was a mixture of embarrassment, excitement, and confusion.

"Um, Caleb…what are you doing?" Gabriel's head was cocked to one side, and he looked at me with a question clear on his face.

"I'm going for a run, obviously. What else would I be doing?" I looked down at the pile of my clothing, as I stood there in nothing but my boxer briefs and realized that maybe my body had only told them I was excited, but not why.

"Oh, you thought I…" I broke off the thought there. "No. No. NO!" I laughed at the misunderstanding. "I just wanted to explore the countryside a little bit before we have to deal with anything else here."

My explanation cleared up the confusion, and Adam and Gabriel began to remove their clothing in preparation for the change as well. Gabriel's six-foot frame glowed in the moonlight, and his belly, which made him so comfortable to cuddle with, began to sprout hair as he quickly changed from himself into the sleek black wolf that matched mine. Adam's massive chest, already covered with golden hairs, thickened until he was covered in the sandy fur of his wolf form. I stood there and watched in awe as they became something so different from what they'd been moments before. It took Gabriel nudging my hand to snap me out of my stupor.

I harnessed all of the pain and anger that I learned helped me shift and let it fill me until I could see the edges of my vision getting darker. Once I reached the tipping point I gave in to the change, and it came quickly. When my senses returned, I stretched my legs and spine, which caused my tail to stick straight out behind me. Once I'd finished, I looked up at the other two wolves, who waited for me and let my tongue roll out of my mouth, which caused Adam to shake his head and Gabriel to rub his body along mine. My fur slid along his and it was an amazing feeling, which felt incredibly intimate.

Adam jumped onto the railing, and looked for a way down from the balcony, then leaped. Gabriel and I rushed over to make sure he was okay and saw that he had landed in some yard clippings that were piled near the house under us. He got up and shook the leaves and grass out of his coat and then turned around and looked up expectantly. Gabriel climbed onto the ledge next and launched himself off the second story, then landed safely in the pile. Once again I was last to do anything, so I made sure I followed quickly to avoid being made fun of later.

In my haste, I didn't judge the distance very closely and landed half in and half out of the pile, which caused my right front paw to curl up under the rest of my body. I yelped in pain, and Adam and Gabriel came over to see what had happened. I stood carefully and made sure not to put too much pressure on the paw, but when I did, pain shot up my leg, and I had to lift it immediately to avoid further discomfort.

Gabriel touched it and then jumped back as the shock of electricity coursing through our bodies no doubt stung the tip of his sensitive nose. I put my paw back on the ground and put more weight on it slowly, to make sure that it was not going to hurt again. After a couple of seconds, I put my total weight on it, and when there was no pain, I let my tongue roll out of my mouth again to show that I was okay. Without waiting for the other two, I started toward the main gate that we'd entered when we had first arrived at the house. Once I'd reached it, I was surprised to find that it began to open on its own. I looked around and noticed there was a sensor that must have picked up my movement. That was handy.

When there was enough room to slip through, I took off into the darkness and ran full speed, enjoying the feel of the wind as it rushed past my furry face. The scents of the woods around the house found their way to my nose, and I drank them in as if they were water, and I had gone days without a drop. I could smell the musty fragrance of leaf litter, the fresh scent of saplings, and the sweet spice of flowers that bloomed in the moonlight. I could hear the sound of small animals burrowing, and birds that begun to wake and rustle in the branches above me. Gabriel and Adam were close behind me and the sound of their paws provided a bass rhythm that allowed us to keep a constant distance, without the need to see each other.

As we ran my mind began to wander and I thought about some of the amazing things that had happened in my life over the past few months. I had met Lorelai and Gabriel and finally felt like I was part of something larger than myself. Of course that sense of belonging hadn't come without a price and without meaning to, my mind drifted to thoughts of Karen and her death at the hands of Dominic. The memory of her home after the attack began to overwhelm the gentler fragrances of the woods until the only thing I smelled was the coppery warmth of her blood.

When I finally realized that Adam and Gabriel had quit running behind me, it was too late, and I stopped just before I stepped on the body of a young man that laid in pieces in front of me. The blood I smelled wasn't coming from my mind, but rather from him. I was so distracted by my memory that I had almost tripped over him. I backed up as quickly as possible, and stumbled when I ran into Adam, who had stepped forward to protect me in case whoever had done this was still in the area.

When we were certain no one else was in the area, Adam raised his head to the sky and let out a howl that communicated the fear and anger we were all feeling. Within minutes, Ouriel, Jusuf, and others had joined us, and the safety and joy I had felt up to this point was replaced by a sense of fear I could only describe as déjà vu.

Chapter Sixteen

The calming experience of our run turned into loud voices, bright lights, and anger. All of which made it very difficult for me to calm myself long enough to change back into my normal body. When no one was looking, I snuck back toward the house to be away from it all. I hoped that by leaving the chaos behind, I could relax enough to shift back naturally.

I was able to get back onto the property because the main gate was wide open now that everyone had rushed out to find us. Fortunately, the front door handle was easy to open with my paw, which was probably an intentional design choice. I padded my way up the stairs and onto the balcony, where my clothes were still sitting in a pile. Gabriel and Adam's clothes were still here as well, and I could smell the sweetness of Gabriel surrounding the items he'd left behind. I imagined being wrapped in his arms, which meant I imagined having arms, a good start. His touch had helped bring me back to myself in the past, and I hoped his scent would be able to do the same for me now. I closed my eyes, inhaled deeply, and let his scent fill my mind. A hint of chocolate, and something wild, which made his smell unique.

Then my mind went off track, and suddenly I was in the alley behind the hotel where I used to work. I followed Dominic, whom I thought had abducted Gabriel at the time. My heart raced as I relived that night in my mind, and I had to open my eyes to avoid full-fledged panic. After a couple of minutes, I had cleared my mind of the memory and tried it again. This time, the wind had shifted, and I couldn't smell the sweetness of Gabriel, but instead I smelled the spice that I realized was Adam. I tried to move myself to pick up Gabriel's scent again, but Adam's seemed to follow me wherever I moved. It was almost like him, hanging around me at every turn, refusing to leave me alone with Gabriel to enjoy myself. It was then that I realized I had begun to relax because my mind had completely forgotten about the carnage I'd just left. Unconsciously, I moved toward Adam's discarded clothing, breathed in his scent, and relaxed.

"What are you doing?"

The unknown voice snapped me out of the moment, and I looked up at the man standing in the doorway to the balcony. He wasn't very tall; I would guess maybe 5'8" or so, but he was very broad, and his large chest and shoulders filled the frame of the door. The light behind him made it impossible to see his face clearly, so he was just a muscular silhouette.

"What?" Hearing my voice was even more confusing, and I looked down and saw my hands, which were gripping Adam's shirt like it was a lifeline, and I was adrift in the ocean.

He repeated himself more slowly this time, being careful with his accent. "What are you doing?"

His voice was deep, and he sounded angry, which, of course, made no sense to me since it wasn't his shirt I was holding.

"Nothing." I stood before realizing I wasn't wearing anything. "I just came back to put on some clothes to help."

I moved quickly to my pile of clothing, careful to keep as much as possible from his view.

"What are you doing here? I thought everyone was already down examining the body?" I had been sure the house was empty when I'd come back, and a stranger showing up after a murder never ended well in the movies.

"I left something behind," he said, his hand moving to his hip, where a rather large gun sat in its holster. "Then I saw you smelling the clothings."

"Clothing." I corrected without thinking about it.

"What?" He yelled at me.

I cowered a little and then realized that if he was meant to be here, he apparently didn't know who he was speaking to, and I was not about to back down.

"You said 'clothings' just now, but that's not right, it's clothing." I spoke loudly, but without any anger. I could still be a kind leader, no reason to yell at people.

He started muttering in a language I couldn't understand, and his hand twitched on the gun handle, which freaked me out. It was probably a bad idea to antagonize the random guy who had just found me sniffing someone's shirt. He took a few steps closer to me, and I could finally make out his face.

"Tell you what, when you start speaking perfect Greek, you can give me advice on my English. Until then, shut up." He turned and left me alone on the balcony as he headed downstairs and out the front door. It wasn't until after he mentioned speaking Greek that I knew who I had been talking with. Less than 24 hours in Croatia and I'd been in a car chase and shootout, found a dead body, and pissed off The Greek. Things could only get better from here. Right?

I finished getting dressed, grabbed Adam and Gabriel's clothing, and then ran back to the group, hoping no one had noticed my disappearance. When I got there, The Greek was standing next to Ouriel, speaking quietly to him. When he saw me, his eyes changed and began to glow in the lights that had been set up around the perimeter. The effect on me was immediate. My heart began to race again and sweat started to pour down my back. I needed to stop pissing off the people who were supposed to be on my side.

"Caleb, where have you been?" Adam walked up behind me and pulled my attention away from the death stare I was getting.

So much for my little absence going unnoticed. "I went back to the house to get changed."

I spun around without realizing that if Adam was speaking, he was human, and I was holding his clothes. I looked at him long enough to eventually realize he was naked and then quickly looked away, holding his stuff out in front of me.

"Here, I brought yours so you could change as well. It looks like you didn't wait."

I could hear the smile in his voice as he took his clothing from me. "I appreciate that, thanks."

"Caleb, can you join us, please?" Ouriel called from behind me. "Gabriel as well."

It was then that I realized I hadn't seen Gabriel in his human form, so he was probably still running around as a wolf for the moment.

"Gabriel," I called out into the darkness. "I brought your clothes so you can change back. I'll leave them over here for you." I set them down and walked over to Ouriel and The Greek.

"Caleb, this is The Greek, he is one of our council members. I had intended to introduce you to all of the other members at the same time tomorrow, but circumstances have changed." He gestured to the body on the ground in front of us as he said it, which seemed callous, but probably came from years of dealing with death.

"We've already met, back at the house. Didn't we Caleb?" The Greek's eyes still reflected the light back at me, making it uncomfortable for me to meet his eyes, a sign of weakness I was sure.

Never one to back down from a bully, I put a fake smile on my face and looked him in the eyes.

"We did indeed." I turned to Ouriel, smiled, and said, "I helped him with his English."

Ouriel smiled back at me and then looked between the two of us.

"Well then, now that introductions are out of the way, we need to discuss what happened here."

He either didn't know or didn't care that there was tension between us, and he pulled our focus back to the task at hand. "This is the second body to show up near the house in the last three months. The first body, it seemed at the time, was the result of an accident on a nearby road, when a motorcyclist hit a stray branch, and the rider was thrown against a tree."

The image of that accident played out in my mind in slow motion, and I had to shake myself to stay focused on what was happening at the moment.

"There is no doubt that this was no accident, however; this was murder. And it is going to implicate us because of its proximity to the house. We have to search the area for any signs of who may have done it, and then I will call in the authorities, so we have plausible deniability. For the time being, I think it would be best for anyone who does not need to be at the house to leave so we can avoid as much suspicion as possible."

As he finished his directions, Gabriel stepped up next to me, dressed in the clothes I brought for him. He took hold of my hand and smiled sadly at me. We both turned back to Ouriel and The Greek, as Ouriel introduced Gabriel. The Greek had bent to examine the body closer, and when he stood his face went pale and his eyes, now back to their normal appearance, were filled with confusion.

"Nikolas?" The Greek took a step toward Gabriel, his hand outstretched.

Gabriel paused for a second and then shook The Greek's. . "No, my name is Gabriel. Nice to meet you Mr. The Greek."

The Greek's eyes remained on Gabriel's face, but his expression was now a blank mask, impossible to read. Just then, a voice called out from the woods that she'd found something, and the moment ended.

We all rushed to the woman who had yelled to the group and found broken branches, with small tufts of hair at the end, and large paw prints in the mud. At first, I needed clarification about what was important about this discovery. I imagined that these were not the only large prints in the area, and fur was bound to stick to some of the branches we brushed by. Then I noticed that everyone except Gabriel and Adam was looking at me, and they didn't look friendly.

"What happened? What does this mean?" Gabriel asked of the group, now that he'd noticed they were all looking at me.

"I didn't say anything earlier because I didn't think it was possible, but there were bite wounds on the body, which suggest it was a wolf attack." Ouriel looked at Gabriel, Adam and me as though we were the murderers, and not the ones who had found the body.

"Surely you don't think we did this," Adam said, addressing Ouriel and The Greek. "Why would we leave the body so close and alert you to it if we'd done it? Why not just hide the body somewhere else?"

Adam's point seemed valid to me, but then again, I knew we hadn't killed anyone, so I was more easily convinced.

162

Ouriel's eyes flicked to the woman who had called out to the group, and she bent over and smelled the hair, which clung to the broken branches. She shook her head slightly, which caused Ouriel's eyes to change and his teeth to lengthen, making what he said next harder to understand.

"Jae is our best tracker, and this fur doesn't belong to any of us, which means it belongs to one of the three of you, or there is an unidentified wolf in the area. And if that's the case, they are trying to get us killed."

"What if we could prove that we had nothing to do it?" Gabriel asked.

"What do you propose?" The Greek spoke quickly, with something like hope in his voice.

"We ran through these woods less than an hour ago; our scent must be all over the place, along with our fur. Find ours and you'll know this wasn't from one of us."

I was impressed with Gabriel's quick thinking, especially in a situation like this. I hadn't had time to think through another idea, so I hoped his worked.

"How would we know it was yours if we found it?" This came from one of the men who were already searching the woods. Gabriel looked to me for help, but I wasn't sure how to answer his question because I didn't know how to track anything, I just assumed someone else would know.

"That isn't necessary," Adam said. He was bent over, examining the fur that had created the whole situation in the first place, and was being very careful not to get close enough to get anything from his body on it. "This fur is gray, none of the three of us has gray fur. Caleb and Gabriel are black, and I am light brown. It obviously didn't come from us."

I let out a huge sigh of relief.

"It may not have come from you or Gabriel, we all saw you, but Caleb wasn't here during the search. How do we know what color he is?" It was the same man who had questioned me earlier.

"He is right I'm afraid," Ouriel said. "I saw both Gabriel and Adam with my own eyes, I can attest to their coloring, but I did not see you, Caleb."

Panic began to set in as I realized that by leaving the area to avoid the gore, I had made myself a suspect in the murder. I began to worry that I might not be able to shift back to my wolf form to prove my innocence, and how could I possibly lead if I couldn't change on command.

"Are you sure you want to do this?" Adam spoke so quietly that I thought he was speaking to me, but when I turned to respond, I noticed he was looking at the man who asked the question and the rest of the group. "Caleb and Gabriel are the first Awakened to shift before they were eighteen in nearly five centuries. They are the born rulers of our race, and they do not need to prove anything to anyone, let alone someone below an alpha. Are you sure this is the impression you want to leave on your leaders on their first night in your territory?"

Ouriel laughed in an attempt to reduce the tension that was palpable. "Adam, you make a good point, but the fact remains, none of us is above scrutiny when it comes to the good of the whole group. Caleb can just shift to show us all that he is not the person who committed this crime, and we can go back to searching for the real killer."

It sounded so easy, shift and prove it, but the fact was, I had never shifted quickly in my life except for my first shift when I was facing Carlos. That had been because I didn't know what I was doing and didn't have to worry about gathering my emotions; they were just there on the surface. I realized then that the emotions were always there, and I just needed to keep them close enough to allow me to turn quickly. Gathering my anger, I ripped off my clothing and… nothing happened. I tried again, and nothing. I opened my eyes, and they were all staring at me, waiting for something to happen, but I just stood there. Embarrassment flooded through my body, which washed away the anger and left me feeling hollow. Gabriel reached out and put his hand on my shoulder, and our now familiar spark stung me. Suddenly the world around me went dark, and when I emerged from the darkness, I was a sleek black twin to Gabriel's wolf.

Ouriel smiled broadly and spoke to the group, who dispersed and went back to look for evidence, then he and The Greek turned and left Gabriel, Adam and me alone. At that moment, I didn't care what it took, or how long I had to try, I was going to figure out how to shift quickly, even if it killed me. I just hoped it didn't come to that.

Chapter Seventeen

We spent the rest of the night in the woods to help search for more evidence. Around seven in the morning, Ouriel called the authorities, which now swarmed the area and looked for evidence. Ouriel spoke with the person in charge of the search, who was wearing reflective lenses, making it impossible to see her eyes. She nodded slightly every few minutes but was otherwise motionless. Her stoic features made it easy to tell she was in charge at first glance. . I tried to remember the way she held her arms and head so I could put it to use later when I needed to seem like I was in charge when I had no idea what was happening.

Gabriel and I ended up spending the rest of the morning in his room. There was so much noise and activity going on around the house, and we didn't have a great excuse for being in the area, so we stayed out of sight. I could already tell that today was going to be a long one.

There was a soft but noticeable knock on the bedroom door before it opened, and Adam walked into the room. Gabriel and I were lying in bed and hadn't invited him to enter, but the way he continued into the space made it seem like we'd rolled out the red carpet for him.

"What the hell? You can't just barge into the room like that! What if we'd been…" I stopped, I realized a little too late that what I was going to say was something Gabriel, and I had never even talked about doing.

"Relax, I listened through the door for a few minutes before I knocked. If I had been interrupting anything, it wouldn't have been worth continuing anyway." His wry smile grated on my nerves, but I admitted internally that we hadn't even been close to doing anything worth hiding, so I couldn't be too upset about it.

"Whatever. What do you want?" I asked, cranky from the lack of freedom and the intrusion. Gabriel moved closer and put his hand on my upper thigh under the covers, which took my focus off Adam long enough for me to calm down. Adam's eyes immediately went to the spot where Gabriel's hand was resting on my leg as if he could see it through the covers.

"I just came in to make sure you two were ready. We need to get out of here soon to avoid having to explain why we're here. The police will want to talk to everyone in the house, and we have no obvious connection to anyone. Our presence is more suspicious than anyone else's. I don't want to have to try to explain to a foreign government why I have no idea how someone died the night we arrived in the area. Do you?"

He looked at Gabriel; his face was serious and a little angry looking, as if Gabriel had been the one to ask why he had come in the room.

Gabriel shook his head and looked at me with a grin. "We can go check out the town and actually do some sightseeing!"

His excitement was what I needed, and I did my best to absorb his positive attitude. I'd need all the help I could get to make it through the day without biting someone's head off.

Adam started to say something, but I ignored him and replied to Gabriel, "That sounds like fun. I was reading about the waterfalls in Krka, the water there is apparently some of the cleanest in the world, and you can go swimming!" Any chance to see Gabriel with his shirt off was worth it to me.

I turned to Adam, "You in?"

"Probably too cold for swimming, don't you think?" Gabriel said, causing the little bit of excitement in me to fade away. "But we could walk around and check it out." His positivity made it impossible to stay disappointed for long.

I looked at Adam to see what he thought, but he just grumbled something unintelligible and walked out of the room. Fortunately, he closed the door behind him as he went, so I rolled on top of Gabriel and kissed him as loudly as I possibly could. He responded with kisses and appreciative noises of his own, which rivaled mine in volume. A few seconds later, we heard Adam's door slam closed, and we both started to laugh. It served him right for listening to things he shouldn't. We continued kissing for a while. As things began to heat up, Gabriel laughed and rolled away toward the edge of the bed.

"We'd better get up and get ready, or we may get left behind to fend for ourselves with the police."

I couldn't argue with that logic, even if my brain wasn't fully focused on what that meant.

"Okay, do you want to use the bathroom first, or should I?"

I was hoping he would volunteer to go first so I could avoid standing right then, but he just shrugged.

"I'm easy, what do you want to do?"

I didn't want to seem like I was bossing him around, so I made some adjustments and rolled out of bed, trying to walk in a way that looked natural.

"Are you okay?" Gabriel was sitting up in bed, a look of concern plain on his face.

So much for looking natural. "Yep, I just got a cramp, I should be okay after a shower."

Feeling my cheeks flush red, I hurried from the room and walked quickly to the bathroom. I hoped I'd be able to avoid anyone else in the house, but as I pushed open the door I ran into Adam, who was standing in front of the mirror, doing his hair. He wore a towel and shook little droplets of water from his hair which then splashed all over me. It took me a couple of seconds to realize what I'd done and to react accordingly.

"What the hell Caleb? You can't just barge into a room like that!" Adam's voice was full of anger, and I looked up to apologize, but I saw that his face was on the verge of cracking into a wide smile. Then I realized his words sounded oddly familiar.

The redness in my face deepened, but I did my best to pretend that I wasn't bothered by it in the slightest.

"I listened at the doorway, and you weren't making any noise, so I figured it was okay just to walk on in." I tried to use his words against him, but it only made him laugh, which caused his dimple to come out. I smiled at his smile because it was so rare, and I couldn't help it. Then realized I was staring at him, smiling, as he stood there in his towel.

"S-sorry about that."

"It's okay; I was done. The bathroom is all yours." Adam walked out of the small room, squeezing past me, careful not to touch me again, and closed the door behind him, which trapped me in the room with the steam and my embarrassment.

I quickly showered and got ready, and then let Gabriel in so he could get ready as well. Thirty minutes later, we had snuck off the property, and avoided the police; on our way to what I hoped was a day of exploration and relaxation. Adam seemed to be in a better mood, and Gabriel smiled at me whenever our eyes met, which helped me relax. Ouriel had Jusuf leave a car a short distance from the house, which helped us get back to the main part of the city. We stopped in a small restaurant and ordered breakfast, which was a mixture of fresh fruit, tomatoes and small balls of mozzarella, a sampling of thinly sliced meats and a basket of sweet bread. It was light but filling, and I felt better with the food in my stomach, it gave me energy.

After we finished our breakfast, we picked up a map with directions to get to the waterfalls in Krka National Park, some international sim cards so we could call home, and set out. The road included numerous switchbacks, which gave us a great view of the lush vegetation and views of the river that wound through the park. Once we got to the parking lot, we noticed that we were one of the only cars in the area. The pathway to the main waterfall was similarly empty, so I took the opportunity to be as touristy as I could and took a bunch of pictures along the way. We eventually came across an open clearing that was a little off the trail and seemed like a good place to practice shifting.

"Can we hold up here for a minute? I hoped you two could help me with something."

Adam and Gabriel both turned to look at me. Gabriel's face was open and waiting for my question while Adam looked like I was somehow annoying him.

"I'm not exactly sure how to get my body to change on command, and I thought we could practice. I know I've asked you both about how you change in the past, but I still don't have control of it. I don't want to face whoever it is that attacked the council without being able to shift when I want."

Adam's expression changed slightly, and he seemed more interested in helping now that it related to something he was supposed to help me with anyway.

Gabriel just smiled at me. "Of course we'll help, let's get it on!" His word choice made me laugh, and when he realized what he'd said, he started to laugh as well.

"Okay, let's keep it in our pants for now." Adam said, but he was trying to hold back his laughter.

"We kind of have to get out of our pants for this though, don't we?" Gabriel asked smiling at me.

Adam just shook his head and looked at the ground like there was something interesting happening below his feet.

"First things first, why don't you try to change now and then we can see what you could maybe improve to make it happen faster." Gabriel moved up next to me and rubbed my shoulders, which helped me to relax a little.

"Okay, I'll see what I can do." I pulled my shirt up and over my head, took my shoes and socks off, and stepped out of the pants I wore. I started to shiver in my boxer briefs almost instantly, but I tried to focus on something other than the cold to get the lesson started. I thought back to the memories that I had used in the past to help with the emotion I needed to harness in order to change and tried to pull them into the front of my mind. I started to focus on it, but the wind would suddenly pick up, or there would be a noise that broke my concentration, and I would lose it just as quickly.

"Nothing is happening, that's the point I'm trying to make. I don't know what I'm doing and trying to get mad when I'm cold isn't easy."

I complained aloud hoping one of them would give me something better than 'just try it on your own.'"

"Why do you use an emotional trigger to change?" Adam stood next to me; his broad shoulders blocked most of the breeze and helped me to feel slightly warmer for the moment.

"That's how I did it on my own the first time. I was in the shower at my apartment; you had just…" I stopped, looked up at him, and then at Gabriel before continuing. "You made me mad."

I refused to say he'd reacted poorly to my offer to let him sleep in my bed. "When I got in the shower, my hand turned into a paw. I used anger later, at Lorelai's house to change completely, and it seemed to work, so that is what I have done when I had to shift on my own."

"What about the night of the fight between the packs at the ranch? You and Gabriel shifted together for the first time, as soon as you touched." Adam's voice didn't seem to hold any emotion other than curiosity.

"He grabbed my hand, and everything went dark. I didn't even think about it, I just shifted." I looked at Gabriel and smiled, which he returned with a confused look.

"I think I may have an idea," Gabriel said before he touched me on the shoulder and everything around me went dark. Once I could see again, I looked up at both of them and I could feel four legs beneath me. I looked down and saw my shiny black coat and my ripped boxer briefs lying on the ground. Guess I was going commando later. Gabriel reached out and touched me again. This time when the darkness cleared, I was back to myself again.

"How'd you do that?" I asked, making sure to keep everything carefully covered by my hands.

"That night, when I took your hand at the ranch, I imagined us shifting. Last night, when I touched you, you shifted, and I think it was because I wanted you to shift. I didn't think anything of it until you said you hadn't done anything because I just assumed it was a coincidence."

"What does that mean?" I looked at Adam, hoping he would be able to shed some light on the situation, but he looked just as confused as I felt.

"I'm not sure, I've never heard of anyone doing anything like that before. I think we may need to talk to someone else about this, but first, I wonder what happens if someone else touches you." Adam reached out and gently rested his hand on my arm, but nothing happened. I looked up into his eyes and then he said, "Shift."

The world around me blacked out again, and when it came back into focus, I was on all fours again. When I looked up at Gabriel and Adam, they both looked scared and a little shocked. I looked behind me to see if someone had wandered into the clearing, and it was when I turned back around that I noticed the color of my tail. I wasn't the same solid black that had been the twin of Gabriel's wolf. It was sandy and so was the rest of the fur I could see. If I didn't think it was impossible, I'd have said I was now a perfect twin to Adam.

Chapter Eighteen

I could see the panic and concern in their eyes so I did what I could to relax and change back into my normal body with a mouth that could form human speech.

"What the hell just happened?"

Adam and Gabriel looked back and forth at each other, and then looked at me and shrugged at almost the same time. If it hadn't been so annoying, I might have said it was cute. But given my current emotional state, I didn't find anything adorable.

Adam was the first to speak, "You looked like me when you shifted."

"Yes, I got that much, thank you. What I'd like to know now is, what the hell does that mean?" I tried to control my anger, fear, and frustration so I could avoid changing back into a wolf, but it got more difficult to hold myself together.

"I honestly have absolutely no idea; I've never seen that happen before." Adam looked at me seriously; his eyes scanned my body as though he was looking for something he'd missed. "When I helped you shift, you took on characteristics of my wolf, and when Gabriel helped you shift, you looked like his wolf. Maybe it has something to do with us forcing the change on you."

"But Caleb has changed on his own, and he still ends up with black fur, so maybe this was just a fluke, and he really does have black fur." Gabriel's voice held a note of optimism, which helped to calm some of the anxiety I felt. Even in the most strange and scariest situations, Gabriel seemed cool and collected. It was one of the things about him that I found attractive. He helped balance out my hair trigger emotions with a sense of calm that eventually worked its magic on me.

"That's a good point. The first time I changed on my own I was still all black." I looked at Gabriel and smiled, hopeful that this was easily explained away.

"Can you try to shift on your own? Don't worry about your whole body, just shift your arm to see what happens." Adam moved back a little to give me some room, and it was the first time I noticed just how close he had been.

I concentrated on my arm and saw it shifting into a wolf paw, it was covered in ink black fur and the claws were sharp. I could feel my fingers begin to shorten, and the tiniest smile played on the edges of my mouth as satisfaction rolled through me. When I opened my eyes, I was not surprised to see the dark black hair covering my new limb, which looked exactly like the fur I was used to having.

"Okay," Adam said. "I'd like you to try to change your other arm, this time I am going to try something." He reached out his fingers to touch the skin of my shoulder. "Now, shift."

He hadn't given my body a command. This time the change didn't rip through me unexpectedly. It was a request, and I was able to take my time.

I concentrated again on shifting my other arm, saw the same black fur and felt the same physical change in my body. Before I could open my eyes to see what happened, Gabriel's gasp let me know that something wasn't quite right. I opened my eyes and saw that my arm had changed into another paw, but this one was a little larger than the other one, and of course there was the other thing. The hair that covered it was the same sandy color that I had been before, and was without question, a match to Adam's.

"What does that mean?" Gabriel asked, looking at Adam expectantly.

"I have no idea, I just thought about Caleb having the same fur as me, and it happened to work out. I don't know why it happened, and I have never seen a wolf with different colored limbs before." I looked down and saw the stark contrast between the two, so I shook the change off and was pleased to have normal looking arms again.

"We need to talk to your mother about this," Adam said, as he walked back toward where we had parked the car. "She might know something about it that I don't, and she may be able to clear all of this up."

"And if she can't?" I let the question hang in the air, and looked at Gabriel and Adam, hoping one of them would have another option to throw out there.

"Let's worry about that when and if we must. For now, let's get back to the house, you two have a meeting to attend."

With all the commotion about the dead body the night before, and my confusion about shifting, I had completely forgotten about the Council meeting. Chills ran down my back as I thought of the icy reception I had received from The Greek, and I hoped the other members would be warmer. We climbed back in the car and drove to the spot where we'd found it on the side of the road, which is where we left it to be picked up later by Jusuf. By the time we'd made it back to the house, the police were gone but there were still signs of their presence. Yellow tape was strung between branches of trees, and their footprints were all over the place. If they hadn't already found something, there was little chance of them finding anything now.

"You two go ahead, I am going to call Lorelai and see if she knows anything about what your change means. We can meet up again after the Council meeting." With that, Adam left us outside the house, and walked deeper into the trees, no doubt trying to avoid being overheard. The idea of sharing with the Council that one of their new leaders couldn't change on command, but when he did, he had yet to pick just one wolf didn't seem like the best idea.

"We'd better get inside; we don't want to keep the Council waiting." Gabriel grabbed my hand and we walked toward the back doors we had come through earlier that morning. The doors led us into the kitchen, where Jusuf waited for us.

"Follow me." Jusuf's accent was incredibly thick, but I appreciated that he'd switched to English for our benefit. He led us through a series of hallways, and down a few different flights of stairs until we reached what appeared to be an immaculate conference room. There were multiple flat panel televisions hanging on the walls, outlets for power and Internet built into the large circular table, as well as some strange object in the middle of the table that looked like an asterisk. I assumed it was a phone that must have been used for conference calls.

Already seated were Ouriel, who was laughing with a woman with dark red hair, his belly shook slightly as he did, and he reminded me of a mall Santa. Seated next to them was The Greek, who immediately stood when he saw Gabriel and I walk in. I got the impression that it was not out of respect based on the glare he gave me.

A few seats over from The Greek sat a man in his early thirties, with a dark beard that was trimmed close to his face. It gave him a ruggedly handsome look. Beside him was the woman who had found the fur in the woods. She had straight black hair that was cut at a severe angle, accentuating her already angular features Finally, seated closest to us was another bearded man, whose golden skin made me jealous, if only for an instant. His flawless skin paired with is dark hair and eyes made him look as though he'd stepped out of the pages of a men's fashion magazine. Ouriel looked over at us finally and excitement spread across his face.

"Gabriel, Caleb, I'm so glad you are both here! Now we can get started and figure out what it is we need to do to stop the killing."

I gave the room a slight smile, followed Gabriel's lead to approach Ouriel before taking a seat.

"First, I want to introduce you to everyone. This lovely woman next to me is Maeve; she is one of the alphas for Western Europe."

Maeve gave us a smile that was all teeth, but in the friendliest way possible. "Nice ta meetcha both." Her accent and red hair made it clear that she probably hailed from Ireland, but who was I to assume?

Ouriel continued, "Next to her is The Greek, whom you've met already."

He had finally taken a seat, but his glare had not wavered, and I began to feel little beads of sweat roll down my back.

"Next is Kenai; he's the alpha for Southern Africa but is here on behalf of all of the African alphas." Kenai smiled briefly and gave a slight nod in our direction.

"Continuing on is Jae, whom you met briefly last night. She is here from Seoul, representing most of the packs from Asia." She nodded her head, her expression still unchanged..

"Lastly," he gestured to the man closest to us. "Stephen is here representing the alphas from the packs of the Middle East."

He reached over and shook our hands. "Hello, so nice to finally meet you both." His deep voice was friendly but impartial.

I smiled back and responded, "Thank you so much, we are glad to be here, I just wish it were under better circumstances."

That sentiment drew a collective muttering from the group, which was silenced by Ouriel, who was very clearly the real leader in the room of alphas.

"Caleb and Gabriel are here, representing the packs of the Americas, and both have a unique story to share, which I have left out of the information I have already provided to you all." Ouriel turned and smiled at Gabriel and I.

"Would you like to share information with the Council about why it is you two who are sitting here before us and not another alpha?"

Gabriel looked at me and smiled encouragingly. "We're here because we changed together and beat the challenger for the alpha to my pack, who had recently become the alpha of Gabriel's pack. Our packs are now united with us as alphas because neither of us has turned 18 yet."

With the last few words, an uncomfortable silence filled the room as the alphas looked at one another then back to Gabriel and me.

"You see," Ouriel began. "We have hope to stop the attacks against our kind because new alphas have awakened before their time. As a result, they have brought with them the power to heal."

I looked at Gabriel, who looked as confused as I felt, and let that emotion show plainly on his face.

"How did you know that?" Gabriel asked.

"It would be a stupid alpha indeed who did not know what powers the new leaders of an entire species brought with them to his home. But do not worry; your gifts will be a closely guarded secret by the others in this room. We cannot let our enemy know we have a secret weapon to stop their attacks against us."

He smiled confidently and looked around the room at the commotion his announcement had created. It had begun to feel like our being here had started out as some stunt for Ouriel's benefit. But before we left, I had a hunch we would no longer be just an exciting addition to the collection of alphas on the Council.

"You're telling us that these two are the True Alphas?" Stephen looked past us and stared at Ouriel with tightness in his body that spread to his face. If I were old enough to gamble, I'd bet money on him not being happy with the news.

Ouriel opened his mouth to speak but was interrupted by Jusuf, who had just entered the room. Now that we were all in the same space together, I realized that he smelled differently than everyone else in the room, and it suddenly hit me that he was human. He silently walked toward Ouriel, whispered something in his ear, and then stood along the wall behind him. Ouriel gave Jusuf a meaningful look but didn't respond. If Ouriel trusted a human with the Council's secrets, I saw no reason for me to have to keep anything from my parents. I decided that I would tell them as soon as I had a chance.

Satisfied with Ouriel's non-response, Jusuf walked back out of the room and shut the door behind him. Ouriel turned his attention back to the Council, and his smiled returned.

"They are indeed. Not since Céline Garnier has the Council had a True Alpha. Rest assured, when I said we had hope for defeating our enemy, it was not just because we had new alphas joining our ranks. But rather, because we have the leaders, we have been waiting for."

Ouriel smiled at the gathered alphas and seemed pleased with the reactions he saw from around the room.

My left leg started to bounce uncontrollably under the table but fortunately Gabriel reached over and quietly placed his hand on my thigh. It helped to calm me, and as I watched the others, there was a wave of relaxation that seemed to go through them as well.

I must have been giving off an uncomfortable vibe again without realizing it. Thank GOD for Gabriel.

I looked into his eyes and mouthed a "Thank you" before turning back to the rest of the Council, who all seemed to be watching us, waiting for something to happen. I figured now was as good a time as any, so I decided to share the other mystery they would find out about sooner or later.

"In addition to being able to heal other Awakened, I also haven't quite figured out how to shift in a way that always produces the same wolf." I inhaled loudly at the end of my announcement and let it out as a sigh. Then the room erupted into a cacophony of voices all shouting to be heard over the others. I turned back to Gabriel, who smiled and shrugged.

"That went about as well as I expected."

Chapter Nineteen

Once the meeting ended, Gabriel and I ran back upstairs to find Adam. He was in his room, lying on his bed listening to music on his phone. He sat up as soon as we burst in and closed the door.

He looked from Gabriel to me and back to Gabriel again. "Well? How'd it go?"

"Well, they already knew about our ability to heal. Or Ouriel did and told the rest of the alphas. Then we told them that we awakened earlier than we were supposed to, and Ouriel called us 'True Alphas.'"

Gabriel had walked over to sit on a chair in the corner of the room, which left me standing awkwardly by the door since there was nowhere else to sit. "And then Caleb told them that he hadn't figured out his wolf yet."

"What!?" Adam's yelling was really nothing when compared to the Council, but it still surprised me, and I flinched a little bit.

"In my defense, Ouriel said he already knew about us before he invited us to come. I assumed he probably knew that as well; how was I supposed to know it wasn't part of the dirt he'd already collected?"

Adam seemed to do his best to stay calm. "Probably because we only figured it out right before the meeting." He sounded angry, but he wasn't wrong, so I just accepted his anger without saying anything in return. "Tell me exactly what happened."

I sat down on the floor with my back against the wall and tried to get as comfortable as possible.

"I told everyone that I hadn't figured out the whole shifting thing, everyone went a little crazy, asking questions, yelling and trying to talk over everyone else. Finally, The Greek got everyone quiet and asked me to clarify. I told them that I was working on shifting on command, but that so far, I had become two different wolves. I didn't specifically mention that they were your wolves--" I gestured to Adam and Gabriel "--so they don't know about that. Jae asked what that meant, and no one seemed to have an answer to that question. Then Maeve asked what else I could do, and if Gabriel could change into multiple wolves, which he said he couldn't do. Ouriel called Jusuf back into the room and said something to him, but I couldn't understand what he said. Jusuf nodded and walked out and then Ouriel told everyone that he was going to see what he could find out about my shifting. Then we talked about the body we found in the woods, and how to keep the police from finding out anything else about the Council. After that, it was pretty much over."

Adam continued to stare at me for a moment before looking at Gabriel to see if either of us would add anything else.

"So they didn't say anything else about the murder that happened before we got here? That was the whole reason we had to rush to get here."

Gabriel shook his head and then spoke up, "Ouriel told the other alphas that we were the secret weapons to defeat their enemy but didn't specifically mention the alpha who was killed, or who exactly the enemies were."

Adam looked concerned. "That just doesn't make any sense. The whole reason the Council is here was because of that murder, and he completely avoided the topic." He looked down at his phone and started to type something quickly.

"What did you hear from Lorelai?" I asked.

Adam looked up from his phone. "Nothing. I left a message but couldn't get through to her. I was texting Brent to see if he had any news about things there, but he said everything is fine."

"Would he know anything about my shifting?" I figured it was worth asking.

"Who Brent? No, he's more of a protector than a scholar. If it didn't happen to him or in front of him, he doesn't know about it." Adam's description of his friend was a little mean, but based on what I knew about Brent, it also seemed true.

"What are we going to do now?" Gabriel asked, as he stood up from his chair and crossed the room to sit on the ground next to me. He grabbed hold of my hand and instinctively I looked up at Adam to gauge his reaction.

Adam's eyes had narrowed a little before he smoothed his reaction away, but I couldn't tell what the expression meant.

"Now, we are going to start asking our questions of Ouriel and the others. He must tell us what happened here with the other murder so we can figure out how to address it." Adam stood up from the bed and started to pace. "We'll see if we can get him alone at some point tomorrow and get as much from him then as possible. That will give me more time to connect with Lorelai about everything and see what she thinks about all this and find out if she knows anything more. Since you two took control of the pack right after this happened, the information would have been relayed to her, and may have continued to go to her until your arrival here in Croatia."

Adam glanced back at his phone again and smiled, before clicking out a few letters and slipping his phone into his pocket.

"What happened?" I asked.

"What do you mean?" He responded.

"You looked at your phone and smiled. What happened?" It was unusual to see him smile much at all and now seemed like a strange time for him to find something funny.

"Oh, that. I got a message from Megan. I was just responding." Hearing him talk about Megan made me realize I hadn't talked to her or my parents much since arriving and they would be angry if I went much longer without getting in touch.

"Well, tell her I said hello and that I'll call her later." I replied.

Adam just nodded but didn't pull out his phone again. I was about to say something when my stomach growled like it was being cornered by a village full of angry people with weapons. Not an experience I ever wanted to go through personally. Gabriel and Adam both laughed at me.

"We'd better see if we can find something to eat around here, I feel as hungry as you sound." Adam walked over to me and reached both hands down to help me stand up from the floor before ushering Gabriel and me out of his room and into the hallway. On our way toward the kitchen, we passed Jae and Maeve, who were deep in conversation, but stopped as soon as we got close enough. As we passed, they both bowed their heads slightly, exposing their necks to us. I saw Gabriel nod back in recognition out of the corner of my eye, so I tried to do the same.

"Why do people keep doing that?" I whispered.

"It's a sign of respect and deference to your power. You two are alphas that even other alphas have to bow down to. They're showing you that they acknowledge and respect your position above them," Adam replied.

"And we just what? Nod at them to acknowledge the gesture?" I wasn't sure I understood how showing me their necks was a sign of submission, but what did I know?

"We're supposed to bare our teeth at them and look them in the eye to show them our dominance," Gabriel said, taking my hand into his own.

"So we just smile and look at them? That sounds pretty easy." I was happy to hear that my response was simple.

"It's not a smile, it looks kind of like one, but it's all teeth. Maeve did it in the Council meeting earlier when Ouriel introduced her." Gabriel said.

Adam spoke up then, "A lot of alphas do it out of habit but based on the limited information she had, she also probably thought she was above you in terms of the Council hierarchy. She was next in line to lead the Council after Ouriel until you two came along."

I suddenly felt like I had a bullseye on my back, and it wasn't a pleasant feeling. Fortunately for me, after a few more stairs and a couple of hallways, we made it to the kitchen where The Greek and Ouriel were sitting at the table eating. They both looked up when we entered the room, and Adam ducked his head in their direction. They flashed their teeth at him but did not show submission to Gabriel or I. I flashed my teeth and hoped I didn't look like a complete idiot. I was rewarded for my effort with a growl from the throat of The Greek, who stood almost immediately and stared at me. I held his gaze for a few seconds before Ouriel stood up and blocked my view.

Ouriel nodded to each of us in turn as he greeted us. "Hello Caleb, Gabriel, and Adam. What would you like to eat? I can have something prepared for you, anything you want."

He smiled, all teeth, at us and gestured to a woman who was standing off to the side quietly.

We all looked at each other and then at the woman and said in almost perfect unison, "Cheeseburger."

With a shared laugh--even Ouriel joined in the levity--while The Greek stood quietly and glared at me. We sat down at the table with Ouriel and The Greek, who only sat down after the rest of us had been seated.

"How do you like Croatia so far?" Ouriel asked no one in particular.

"I love what I've seen of it," Gabriel replied. "The park this morning was beautiful, and the architecture has been so impressive. I didn't really know what to expect since I'd never thought about coming here before, but it has been much more amazing than I imagined."

Ouriel smiled at him then turned to Adam and me then asked, "How about you two?"

"It's been great so far," Adam replied, talkative as usual. Then he looked at me, waiting for my response.

"I'm with Gabriel, I've enjoyed everything we've seen so far, thank you so much for your hospitality." I smiled, but it was forced, and I could tell that he knew it. I was hoping to have more conversations with the Council about what the hell was going on here. With the murders and the dead body I almost ran over during our run, I felt like we were being purposefully kept in the dark. "Whenever you have some time, I'd love for us all to have a conversation to give us a better grasp of the gravity of the situation here."

Ouriel looked from me to The Greek but didn't say anything. Adam and Gabriel were similarly silent. The only sound in the kitchen now was the sizzle of the burger patties being cooked.

I continued, now that I apparently had everyone's attention. "You said Gabriel and I were going to be the key to stopping everything. I think it's only fair for us to know what it is you expect from us before we agree to help with anything."

When I'd finished speaking, The Greek stood again, growling at me from across the table.

"Who do you think you are to come in here and demand this kind of information? You are nothing but children and this fight is not yours to dictate." He didn't yell it exactly, but the anger was evident in his expression.

"You're right," Adam cut in. "Caleb and Gabriel are young, but they are also True Alphas, and whatever they say is law. Caleb and Gabriel weren't the ones who came here and tried to insert themselves into this situation. Our previous alpha was summoned here as a result of the murder of Deanna, and they came to help if possible. Please don't presume to tell them what is or is not their business. Everything that happens with the Awakened is their business now, and under their control."

Adam's interruption caused The Greek to start to shift, which made his facial features longer and more deadly.

"That's enough!" Ouriel yelled, and the power that came from his words felt like a physical slap in the face. The Greek sat back down, and his face returned to normal, but he was grinding his teeth so hard that I imagined he could probably feel his molars getting smoothed out.

"Caleb, in response to your request, I am happy to talk to you and Gabriel about everything to make sure you are both aware of the situation. As the True Alphas, you will, of course, have access to any information you need to make informed decisions."

The Greek was practically turning purple in his seat from anger but was surprisingly holding his tongue.

"Furthermore, any member of the Council who seems to be blocking your access will answer to me and will be dealt with swiftly and severely."

He turned and glared at The Greek, and then back to the rest of us.

"But for now, I am going to retire for the night, so we will have to discuss everything in the morning if that is suitable for you two."

It wasn't a question, and we both nodded in response.

Ouriel stood, smiled his toothy smile at us all and exited silently. As soon as he was gone, The Greek sucked in a large breath, and began breathing rapidly, which made me think that maybe his silence and purple color hadn't been anger induced after all. He glared at the three of us and stalked out of the room after Ouriel without a word.

The woman who had been making us dinner set our large burgers down in front of us. She added a few plates with smoked meat, cheeses, and fresh fruit down as well before leaving us alone to eat in peace. Once we were alone and had taken a few bites of our burgers, we all seemed to relax.

"Well, that wasn't how I thought things would happen," Gabriel spoke up first.

I laughed. "I know, sorry about that. I just figured there wasn't any reason to beat around the bush, so I just told him what I wanted to know. It seems like it worked out well enough; we didn't want to have the discussion until we talk to my mother, so hopefully she'll get back to us tonight. That way, we will have talked to her so we can make sure to ask the right questions."

Adam nodded and added, "I think we should also spend some time tonight talking about what it is that you want to know and need to know to stay as safe as possible."

We finished eating dinner and then headed back up to my room to figure out a plan for the following day and our conversation with Ouriel. While we were discussing things, Lorelai called Adam back, so he stepped out of the room to fill her in on everything and find out what she knew. While he was gone, I pulled out my phone and sent a text to my parents.

Hey, guys! I miss you so much right now; it isn't even funny! How are things going there?

A couple of seconds later, my mom responded. *Caleb! How are you doing babe? We haven't heard from you in forever, are you okay?*

Leave it to my mom to be levelheaded and not overreact to things. I got those qualities from her.

I'm fine; everything is fine. I took a trip out of town now that I don't have to work, so I've just been busy with all the travel and stuff. I don't have a lot of time to chat right now, but I just wanted to say that I love you and miss you, and hope to see you and dad again soon!

Her response came in right away and was what I'd expected to see. *Enjoy the time off and the trip, but keep me posted along the way! We love you too babe, talk to you soon.*

Since Adam hadn't returned, I sent a quick text to Megan. *Hey girl hey!*

It took her a minute, but she responded. *Caleb, how's everything going there? Why haven't you texted me until now?*

I just barely got my head out of your BF's lap, so I haven't had the time. I knew she would love that.

Jealous! I haven't even gotten to do that yet…wait a minute! Keep your paws off my man! I could imagine her laughing as she responded.

He likes my paws. We found out today that we have a matching set. Long story, I'll have to tell you later. I just wanted to say that I miss you and that I got an international sim card so that we can talk soon!

It felt good to be able to share things with her now that she knew, especially because we could joke about it, which helped me feel a little less anxious about everything.

I miss you too babe, call me whenever you can, and give my man a deep, passionate kiss for me.

I laughed and then shook my head to clear that mental picture.

On second thought, don't you dare kiss him, he probably couldn't handle that. ;-)

Being able to connect, even briefly, with my mom and Megan had made my night a whole lot better. I looked over at Gabriel, who appeared to be texting on his phone as well and smiled. He glanced up at me and returned my smile.

"My mom says hello by the way."

"Tell her I said hello back."

"I will," he said as he returned to his cell phone.

I started scrolling through games on my phone but was interrupted by one of the loudest screams I had ever heard. Gabriel and I looked up at each other and then ran out into the hallway, where Adam was already running toward the stairs.

Chapter Twenty

"You two stay behind me just in case," Adam said, without waiting for us to agree. We continued to run toward the screaming until we found the source. Maeve had collapsed on the ground and was holding Ouriel's head in her lap. He was covered in blood and didn't appear to be moving except for his mouth, which opened and closed as though he was trying to speak.

"Shh, hold on, we'll get you help, just hold on." Maeve was slowly rocking back and forth as she held his head, wiping away as much blood as she could.

"Caleb, come on." Gabriel grabbed my hand and pulled me forward. I knew what he wanted us to do because I was thinking the same thing. We knelt beside Ouriel and put our hands on the bare skin of his arms. I thought about the skin under our interlaced fingers and the damage beyond, that I was unable to see, healing. The jolt of electricity I usually felt was noticeably absent, however, and nothing seemed to happen.

Maeve leaned in closer, crowding us slightly. "Is it working? Can you heal him?"

She was on the verge of an emotional breakdown, and Adam gently reached down and pulled her up to a standing position to give us more room. She clung tightly to him, her eyes never leaving Ouriel.

We continued to try to heal him; our hands worked together to mend his wounds, but there was no change and his mouth slowed until it finally stopped moving. Seconds later, I could feel that the soft beating of his heart was noticeably absent.

Gabriel looked up at me and shook his head before looking at Adam and Maeve.

"I'm sorry, but we were too late to save him. Ouriel is dead."

Minutes later, the house erupted into a blur of activity. Multiple members of Ouriel's pack were called to the property, as they tried to figure out what happened to him and how he could have been attacked without anyone seeing a thing. After thirty minutes of that, the front of the property was filled with bright lights and for the second time since we'd arrived in Croatia, the police had swarmed the house. This time, however, Gabriel, Adam and I were unable to avoid them. We truly had been one of the few to witness Ouriel's death, and Gabriel and my fingerprints were all over his body. Had we not been available for the questioning, we would likely have become suspects. I'd watched way too many shows about international prisons to have any desire to try and chance it.

The same detective from the previous incident returned to the house and separated Adam, Gabriel, Maeve and me into different parts of the house before asking us questions about what happened. I wasn't too nervous because I knew that I had no real idea what happened, and Gabriel and I could explain our fingerprints away by saying that we were trying to slow the bleeding. I was less sure what would happen after the police left and the actual investigation began. The rest of the Council would no doubt bring us in for their line of questioning, which I imagined would be even more uncomfortable than our first meeting.

I was mostly concerned about what happened to Ouriel and how something like this could have happened inside his home, seemingly protected by a host of guards and seclusion from the rest of the town. And what would happen now that Ouriel was gone? Gabriel and I had no allies on the Council, but it felt like now we would have nothing but enemies.

"What did you see?"

I was pulled out of my head by the detective, who had finally shown up to ask me the questions she'd likely already asked the others.

"I was in my room when I heard screaming from inside the house, Gabriel, Adam and I ran toward the screaming and found Maeve and Ouriel laying on the ground. Maeve was holding Ouriel's head, but then Gabriel and I tried to slow the bleeding while help was called. After a little while, he stopped responding, and we realized he had passed away."

She looked me straight in the eyes without showing any emotion and continued with her next question. "How did he die?"

I looked back at her confused. "I thought that was something you would tell us? But my guess is from blood loss. I'm not sure."

The corners of her mouth seemed to move up a little, almost making it look like she was about to smile, but then she realized what she'd done, and her lips became a straight line again. "What brings you to Croatia?"

I hadn't thought about what I should say if I were asked this, mostly because I had never been alone when anyone asked it, so I let someone else answer. Now I was left scrambling to decide what Adam and Gabriel would say, and what I could say without getting me into more trouble. I decided the best bet was to be as honest as I could be.

"We're here to try to figure out what is going on with our group."

At that, her eyes opened wide, and she looked surprised before restraining her facial expression again. "What do you mean, your group?"

I felt like I had already made a mistake by saying anything, but I couldn't backtrack now.

Why hadn't we talked about this beforehand? I won't last in prison!

"Did I say group? It's more like an extended family. Ouriel was our patriarch, and he asked us to come to help out." My heart sank as confusion and real fear set in.

"I have no idea what will happen now that he's gone."

She looked at me, seeming to chew on the next question before finally asking it. "Who will lead now?"

I was about to tell her I wasn't sure, when I realized that we'd gotten off the subject of Ouriel's death. "I'm sorry, what does that have to do with what happened here?"

"Whoever will take over now has a motive for killing him. Who is next?" Her eyes narrowed and she leaned forward, as if she were trying to listen to my thoughts.

"I'm not sure. I only just recently arrived, I don't know who would have been next in line to lead, but surely you don't think someone here did this?"

"What do you mean 'would have been'?"

"What?" I asked, confused.

"You said you didn't know who would have been next in line, which sounds like you know who is now." Her weight, which had previously been on her left side shifted to her right, and her head cocked to the side, as though she were listening to something I couldn't hear.

Flustered, I stammered about things being confusing, and not being sure what was happening. When it seemed like she wasn't buying it, I just started to cry. I decided that there was no way she could force me to talk if I were crying. Eventually she gave up, flipped her notebook closed and told me not to leave the area until she gave me permission because she would be back with more questions. With that, she left me alone in the room and returned to the rest of the police in the house. Meanwhile, I went straight upstairs to my bedroom but found Gabriel and Adam were already waiting for me at the top of the stairs.

"I think I messed up," I said as I got closer to them.

"What do you mean?" Adam asked as he ushered Gabriel and me into my room and then closed the door behind himself.

"She asked me why we were in Croatia, and I said we were trying to figure out what was happening with our group."

Adam's face turned red almost immediately, but he kept himself from yelling, aware that the police were still on the first floor and would likely hear him if he went ballistic. Rather than addressing me, he turned to Gabriel. "What did you say?"

Gabriel had a look of guilt on his face. "I said we were on vacation."

Adam seemed pleased, but Gabriel continued. "We hadn't talked about it really, but I assumed that would be the best option because we had technically been sightseeing."

He looked at me and mouthed, "Sorry."

"Which is what I told her when she asked me." Adam was looking at me again, his eyes accusing me of something terrible, I was sure.

"Well, I'm sorry that I don't know how to lie appropriately or think up stories that sound believable at the drop of a hat. I was going to say we were on vacation, but then I thought about what would happen if you said something else and I looked guilty because I was lying. It's not like being here as part of the Council is illegal!" I was whisper yelling at this point, trying to make my point while still staying as quiet as possible.

"Illegal, no. Dangerous if we confessed that fact to outsiders? Yes."

Adam sat down on the chair in the corner of the room and seemed to be thinking about all the ways this could go wrong. Different negative emotions kept streaming across his face like a stock exchange ticker tape in Time Square.

"I'm sorry, okay? I didn't mean to, I just panicked, and that's what came out." I fell back onto the bed and sunk into the mattress and comforter a bit. It felt like I was lying on a cloud and was being swallowed up by it. "But then she asked me who was going to be the next leader and said that they would have a pretty strong motive to get Ouriel out of the way."

Gabriel sat down next to me and took my hand in his, the electric current I'd been hoping for when we were trying to heal Ouriel buzzed through our fingers, and I took some comfort in knowing that at least our connection was still strong. "Who would have been next?"

Adam's head was buried in his hands, but he looked up and responded, "Maeve and The Greek."

"The Greek?" I yelled before I was able to contain myself.

Adam and Gabriel ducked, as though I'd thrown something sharp at them. I sat up slowly, and we all stared at the door, waiting to see if my yell had somehow alerted someone else in the house that we were in the room together. After about a minute of silence on both sides of the door, Adam finally spoke again.

"Yes, The Greek. But technically it would have gone to Maeve first, then The Greek. But it doesn't matter because you two are here, and you would have led even if Ouriel hadn't been attacked. Everyone on the Council knew that, so killing Ouriel didn't change the actual leadership of the Council."

"What if we're next?" I asked. "Carlos didn't come after me until the alpha of Gabriel's pack was already dead." As soon as his name was out of my mouth, I should have known it was a mistake, but hindsight is 20/20, and no one had ever accused me of knowing when to keep my mouth shut. Adam looked like I had slapped him in the face and said something rude about his mother.

"I'm sorry Adam, I shouldn't have brought that up. This is a totally different situation; that was stupid of me."

His face had softened a bit before he responded. "No, you're right Caleb. Carlos did kill the other alpha first, and I understand why you'd see the similarities between that situation and this one. That being said, I'm telling you that I don't think that's what's happening here. Like I said, Maeve would have taken over before The Greek, so why not start with a closer target?"

"Ouriel said he would make sure the rest of the Council shared all their information with us regarding the attack on Deanna. And at dinner, it seemed like he did something to The Greek to stop him from talking or breathing. Maybe it wasn't to get him out of the way, maybe it was to shut him up!"

I could feel that my eyes had gotten larger as I realized the possibility of the situation.

"You make a good point," Adam admitted. "But what information could the Council possibly possess that was worth killing Ouriel over?"

I shook my head slowly before finally responding, "I have no idea."

All I knew was that The Greek seemed to have it out for us, and now our only ally on the Council was dead. Things had just gone from bad to shitstorm in about 30 minutes, and I didn't want to stand around and wait for it to hit the fan and come raining down on me.

Chapter Twenty-One

The Council gathered the following morning, somber, confused, and lost given the recent events. Gabriel had asked Adam to join us in the meeting, and I was happy to have someone on our side in the room. He stood against the wall, just to the side of where we sat, and watched as we discussed what to do next. Though Gabriel and I were meant to take over the Council based on awakening early, it still felt like we had gotten the position from Ouriel's untimely death. Regardless, the circumstances made everything look shady.

"I just want to make sure that Gabriel and I are on the same page with the rest of you: Deanna was killed prior to our arrival, Ouriel's cause of death is still unknown."

At the mention of his name, people's faces dropped.

"There was a motorcyclist found by a tree near the property, plus the body we found just outside the walls. Furthermore, you're all certain that the person found by the wall wasn't anyone known to the local pack or connected to the Council? Is that correct?"

I was surprised at my ability to remember and recite this number of events, and even more shocked that I was able to do so without sounding overly emotional.

"Yes, that is everything we have so far." Maeve was the one to respond verbally, though there were heads nodding in agreement from around the room.

"And do we have any new ideas about what happened to Ouriel? Maeve, you were there when we arrived, did you see or hear anything?" I asked, hoping she would be able to take over the conversation for a little while.

"I found him almost exactly like you found him, he had collapsed where you found us. I saw him when I happened to walk past and screamed. It looked like he had been shot or stabbed from the amount of blood that covered his shirt."

Her eyes were glossy with unshed tears and unfocused while she relived the previous evening's events in her head.

"Gabriel and I tried to heal his wounds, but there was no reaction in his body. It was almost as though there was nothing to heal, but the amount of blood says otherwise. Could he have tried to heal himself, but only covered over the outer damage?"

The Greek spoke up now. "It is possible that he tried to heal himself and was only partially successful, but that isn't likely. We all know better than to seal an open wound that has not been mended internally. I don't think he would have risked trying something so reckless."

His aggressive tone sounded more threatening than usual.

I must have been radiating some powerful energy, because I heard Adam growling behind me, and the rest of the room was suddenly staring at me like I was on fire. Gabriel reached over then and placed his hand on my knee to help calm me. I could feel my stress level decrease immediately, and the rest of the room relaxed as well, and Adam stopped growling.

"If you're going to keep doing that, I would like to leave the room," Jae said from across the table. "I don't particularly feel like being in the middle of an alpha fight, especially one caused by a 'True Alpha.'" Before she said "True Alpha" I thought she'd been speaking to The Greek, but now I knew it was an admonishment aimed at me. I way she said it sounded like she didn't believe the title was warranted.

"My apologies Jae. I'd be happy to let someone else take over this role since Gabriel and I didn't ask to come here to help figure out what happened to Deanna. I never intended to be caught up in the middle of a power struggle for leadership of a group of people I didn't even know existed a few months ago. Please, be my guest."

I waited for her response, but she was silent. I looked around the room to see if anyone else would accept my offer, which was made with complete sincerity. No one, other than The Greek met my eyes, nor did they meet the eyes of any of the other alphas in the room.

"No? Not interested in switching places? Okay then, I guess it's down to Gabriel and me. Believe me when I tell you that we are doing everything we can to get up to speed and handle this as best we know how. As you can imagine, it can take some time to adjust before we know how to react."

"Now that that is over, can we get back to the business at hand?" Stephen asked. "I think we should fill in the new alphas about the Pressors, to give them a better idea of what is happening."

Gabriel looked at me and I returned his gaze before looking back at Stephen.

"What are the Pressors?"

"They are a *who* not a *what*; they are the hunters of Awakened. They have been tracking and killing us for as long as we have had a written history to record their attacks. They date back to Ancient Rome where they were hired to kill the wolves that came too close to the Roman towns and villages. Eventually, these hunters realized that some of the wolves they hunted were not regular wolves, and they began seeking them out specifically. We were almost eliminated from some parts of the world, but those who survived went into hiding."

"And politics," The Greek chimed in.

"Yes, and politics to try to stop the attacks on the Awakened. Over time, due to political pressures, the number of Pressors dwindled and the rewards for the profession became less desirable. Now knowledge of the Awakened has turned into lore and fairytale, and the truth was forgotten," Stephen concluded.

"So, there aren't any Pressors still around then?" Gabriel asked.

"They still exist and hunt us to this day. They are fewer in number than they used to be. They are usually family groups now, rather than professionals. They act like packs do, with leaders, and they seem to stay loosely connected with each other based on what we can tell," he responded.

Kenai continued, "I have heard about them following packs as they moved from one part of the world to another, continuing to track and murder the same pack and any rogues they come across along the way."

Gabriel looked at Kenai earnestly. "I'm confused, how is it possible that I've never heard of them if they are such a threat?"

I hadn't even considered what this news must have felt like to Gabriel. He'd been raised Awakened, and this revelation probably hit him hard, whereas I was so used to being in the dark. "No one in my pack had ever mentioned it before; are there not any Pressors in America?"

"They live everywhere," Kenai responded. "It's possible that your pack wasn't being targeted for some reason, but I couldn't say for sure."

"How do they know who the Awakened are?" I asked.

"It depends on what is happening in a given area. Some packs run freely and are easier to find, whereas others are much more secretive. Those that are more open with their changes are found more quickly because their openness makes them easy to track. My pack was hunted almost to extinction under a former alpha because he believed we were above humans and should not hide who we were. It wasn't until after his death that we started to be more careful about how we lived, trying to blend into society better."

Kenai's face had dropped slightly at the memory, but he looked resolved when his eyes came back up, meeting Gabriel's and mine.

"How do they target the packs that are integrated into the human world? I never once saw Ouriel shift or even leave the property. How would he have become a target of the Pressors? Or are you still not sure that's what happened?"

Gabriel seemed hungry for information, and he was practically vibrating with nervous energy.

"Ouriel and Deanna were the oldest members of the Council. They had probably been less careful in their younger days and were potentially already on the Pressor's list for a long time," Stephen spoke up again.

"In general, the more hidden packs are harder to find, and do often go overlooked for a while. There is always something that tips off the Pressors to the presence of a pack. Sometimes it's a rogue Awakened in an area that doesn't play by the pack rules, or one of the young who thinks rules are made to be broken. One way or another, the Pressors find the pack, and they are forced to move to a new area."

I looked at Gabriel then and watched as this news sunk in, and things started to click into place.

"My former pack did move from our territory suddenly. They sent my family on ahead to scout the area and Caleb's pack, which might be why I never heard about any threats."

He looked around at the other alphas gathered at the table. "Our old alpha never told us why she sent us and gave no warning about the rest of the pack showing up; they just all arrived one day without a word."

Kenai and Stephen nodded at Gabriel while the others silently listened.

"It's impossible to say for sure without knowing more, but that is what we do when we are discovered or compromised. The pack picks up and leaves the area, searching for a new home. Your family probably wasn't the only scouting family sent out to find a better place to live. Yours was likely the one with the best option for relocation," Stephen spoke like he'd experienced something similar. All the faces in the room suggested they'd had some experience with the Pressors in the past.

"What do we do now? Does the Council need to relocate somewhere else?" I wasn't sure I would like the answer, regardless of what it was. Staying seemed dangerous but leaving presented a larger issue of figuring out where. If Gabriel and I were meant to lead as the True Alphas, it likely meant the Council would come to us, and that was something I would not allow. I would not bring the Pressors' attention to my pack.

The Greek, who had been uncharacteristically quiet up to this point, stood and stared me down.

"Moving the Council to a new location is the only option, but it must stay in Europe, as it has always been."

He looked prepared to fight me on any objection, but he'd just given me the only answer I would have liked.

"I agree with The Greek. There's history and tradition in Europe for the Council. Moving it out of Europe doesn't seem like a good option."

He looked surprised that I had agreed with him, and his mouth opened then closed again.

"I think we should wait to make that decision until we know for sure what happened to Ouriel," Maeve spoke up again. "If it is the Pressors, we need to be strategic in our next steps. If it was something else," she paused and looked at The Greek. "I think staying here right now is the only option worth considering."

"We wait then and will decide once we know what happened to Ouriel."

I looked at the other alphas for their agreement, which they all provided with almost no hesitation.

"For now, everyone should stay close to the property. If you *must* leave, you need to be extremely cautious. We must assume the worst until we know more."

The group quickly broke off into smaller segments, each talking quietly amongst themselves. Maeve pulled me to the side to discuss Ouriel's funeral arrangements. While we spoke, I watched The Greek approach Gabriel and motion for him to exit the room. Gabriel glanced at me and smiled before he stepped into the hallway, followed closely by The Greek. My ears strained in that direction, but I could only hear them speaking, not what they were talking about. I took a step closer to the open door to give me the ability to see and hear what was happening without impacting my conversation with Maeve.

The Greek looked at Gabriel for a few moments before he spoke again, his voice low.

"Pressors killed my friend Nikolas." He looked at Gabriel when he said the name, as though he was trying to gauge his reaction to it.

Gabriel's face immediately softened. "I'm so sorry to hear that."

The Greek continued, as though Gabriel hadn't spoken. "It was back when I was young and stupid; they caught us one day out in the open. I was running too close to the city where we lived and didn't notice we were being followed. When I finally did, I tried to get away from them, which led Nikolas into the trap they'd set."

The emotion in his voice grew stronger, but his face never moved. It was as if he were wearing a mask that refused to allow emotion to escape.

"I should have known better, but I never thought something like that would happen to me. Nikolas was our alpha, I should have protected him, but he jumped in between that bullet and me. When I managed to break through their line, I ran until I collapsed from exhaustion. I was too afraid to go home, so I just hid for a week, waiting for someone to find and kill me. When they didn't come, I went home. The pack was so relieved to see me that when it was time for a new alpha to take over, mine was the only name they considered."

"Thank you for sharing this with me, I can't imagine what that must feel like," Gabriel said, his hand resting on The Greek's shoulder in a comforting manner.

He flinched slightly, and then relaxed into Gabriel's touch.

"I do what I must to protect my people, and soon, you will have to do the same."

Then Gabriel was alone in the hall. Once Maeve and I had finished our conversation, I walked out into the hallways to find Gabriel and saw him standing alone, waiting for Adam and me to join him.

"Everything okay?" I asked.

"Yes, everything is fine. I just think we have a lot to talk about."

I couldn't have agreed more.

Chapter Twenty-Two

After grabbing something to eat, the three of us walked outside to wander the property as we talked. It had the added benefit of being able to avoid the potential for prying ears. Gabriel walked on my right and held my hand. Adam walked on my left, close enough for us to touch, but he was careful not to brush up against me.

"What did The Greek say to you?" I asked Gabriel, as we rounded the side of the property and headed away from the front gate. I had heard most of their conversation, but I didn't want to seem like I had been listening in.

"He told me about his friend who was killed by the Pressors. That's how he became the Alpha in his pack." The empathy in Gabriel's voice tugged on my heartstrings.

"He sounded upset about everything; I don't think that he would have killed Ouriel to try to take over the Council. It seemed like he's leading out of guilt, not desire."

Adam's turn to interject, "He could also have said that to try to get you to lower your guard. I mean, why focus on you specifically? Why not tell both you and Caleb? The bottom line is that he benefitted from the death of a pack mate and stood to benefit from the death of the other alphas as well."

I looked at Adam, confused by his change of heart. "I thought you didn't think The Greek was behind the attack."

"I'm not sure that he is, but you brought up the fact that Ouriel had promised to share information with you before he was killed, so that makes anyone with secrets a threat. Even if it isn't The Greek, that doesn't mean I trust him. He doesn't like you, Caleb, there's no doubt about that… But his whole demeanor changes around Gabriel. He's never seemed violent or angry when his attention is directed at Gabriel, so I'm not sure what to think anymore."

I wasn't sure how to respond to that last part, so I ignored it and pushed forward.

"Adam has a point Gabriel," I said. "I know you want to see the good in The Greek, but the fact remains that he's been stand-offish since we arrived and has given us no reason to take him at face value."

Gabriel nodded in agreement but remained silent.

"For now, I say we treat everyone like a threat until we know exactly what happened to Ouriel. Once the truth comes out, we can go from there."

Adam and Gabriel nodded their agreement.

"Good, now we just have to figure out what happened to Ouriel before it happens to us."

"Hello!" A loud whisper cut off our conversation.

We looked around, confused, to locate the source of the noise.

"Hey! Over here!"

Adam pointed to the wall at the edge of the property, where there was a head sticking up above the rock.

"Stay behind me." Adam walked toward the wall and made sure to keep Gabriel and me behind him as he moved, to block us from a potential attack.

When we got closer, I recognized the woman as the lead police detective who had investigated the body we'd found and Ouriel's death.

"Can we help you?" I asked.

"I hope so, but I guess we'll have to wait and see." Her tone suggested that she didn't trust us, so at least the feeling was mutual.

"How can we help?" Gabriel asked as he stepped around Adam, who looked back and forth between the two of us and moved to stand in between us.

"I know what happened to the man here, and I'm willing to tell you if you promise to do something for me first."

Her eyes were sincere, but there was fear in them as well. My interest in the knowledge of what happened to Ouriel was intense, and she picked up on my desire for the information.

"Do we have a deal?"

"We need to talk about it first," I said, nodding to Gabriel and Adam.

"Figure it out soon, I'll be back tomorrow night. Meet me on this side of the wall as soon as the sun sets if we have an agreement. If not, I'll destroy the evidence about his death." With that, she dropped out of sight, and we could hear her running away.

"She never actually told us what she needed from us," Gabriel said. "There's no way we can agree to help without knowing what we're getting ourselves into."

"I agree with Gabriel, you can't show up without knowing what she wants from you first." Adam crossed his arms and faced me, as though he dared me to argue with him.

"I completely understand where you're coming from, but how can we not show up? She said she knew what happened to Ouriel. Without that information, we have no way to know what needs to happen with the Council. If it's Pressors, I don't want to walk into that situation blindly. And if it was one of the people on the Council, we need to know to protect ourselves and the rest of the Council from this happening again." I met Adam's eyes and didn't look away until he dropped his gaze.

"Caleb, how can we know for sure that she's telling the truth? It could be a trap."

I could tell Gabriel was uncomfortable with the situation as a whole, and while I couldn't blame him, I wasn't about to back down.

"We can't know anything for sure unless we hear her out. To do that, we have to show up. I don't like it any more than you two do, but this is our only lead so far."

"If this is what you think is best, I'll go along with you," Adam said.

Gabriel closed the distance between the three of us. "So will I."

I leaned in and kissed Gabriel, who pulled back slightly and didn't return my affection. When Adam cleared his throat, I pulled back as well.

"Sorry about that Adam."

He laughed. "It's okay, I just thought you should know that you have more company than just me." He jabbed a thumb in the direction of the house where Jusuf was standing there staring at us.

"Hi Jusuf!" I yelled.

"Phone," was his only reply to me before he turned and headed back to the house.

"I guess that's the end of that conversation."

We followed Jusuf back to the house, and I found a phone I could use in relative privacy.

"Hello?" I assumed it would be Lorelai, and when the voice on the other end came through, I was happy to know I was right.

"Caleb! How are you doing? Are you okay?" Her rapid-fire questions let me know that she was aware of everything happening here.

"We're fine, yes, everything is fine. How are things going there?" I was more curious about things at home since I hadn't had the chance to talk to her at all since leaving California. "How is the pack? Any problems we need to know about?"

"Everything here is going just fine. There have been some growing pains, but nothing the other's and I cannot manage." A newfound calm seemed to fill her voice now that she'd heard my own.

"Good to hear! How is training going with Brent and Tanya? Have they killed each other?" It was out of my mouth before I realized how it sounded in the context of what was happening here. "Well, not literally, but you know what I mean."

"Yes, I know what you mean. Things with training are… interesting. There are more kids being trained now than there were when things first started, but it is still slow going. Brent and Tanya weren't really on speaking terms at the beginning, but they seem to be working out the training schedules somehow, so that's good to see."

I wasn't surprised that they were having issues, my limited interactions with Tanya had not been the best, and she didn't seem like much of a talker. Whereas Brent was constantly gabbing and joking about things, they probably got on each other's nerves almost immediately.

"I'm glad to hear that things are picking up. Please let them both know how much Gabriel and I appreciate their help."

"I will," she said. "Now enough about things here, tell me what is going on there. Adam told me about Ouriel, what happened?"

"We're still not sure, but we may have a way to find out later this week." I purposely lied about the timeline in case anyone was listening.

"What do you mean you may have found a way?"

I laughed and then covered my mouth. "Straight to the point, I guess. The detective leading the investigation came back for a visit today and told us that she may have some information about his death. So we are going to go down to the station later to meet with her.' ”

I hoped that she couldn't hear my lie over the phone or feel the emotions I was sure I was sending out.

If she knew I was lying, she didn't let on. "Let me know what you find out. Hopefully, she'll be able to clear up some of this situation for you."

"I will, don't worry."

I hesitated before continuing with the only question I hoped she would answer for me.

"I was wondering if you could tell me more about…about the Pressors."

My question was met with a long silence that was so complete; I checked the phone a few times to see if it had disconnected somehow. Finally, she responded.

"How did you find out about them?" Her fear was palpable over the phone, which made me think that she probably knew I'd been lying before.

"They might be behind the attacks on Ouriel, but we aren't sure yet."

There was more that I wanted to ask, but I wasn't sure whether I wanted the answer. "Have you ever had any problems with them?"

"Only once." Her silence once again filled the space between us. "When I was much younger than you are now, my family and I lived in New Mexico. The pack had lived there for so many generations that there were some among us who felt like we were safe enough to open up to the humans around us. We shared our secret with those closest to us and lived together peacefully for a long time, but one day the Pressors arrived. One of the humans had shared our secret, and the word spread that we were living in the area. It was a matter of time before the news reached the hunters, and they came for us. My mother and all my aunts and uncles were killed in the attacks. My father and I had gone out to dinner on our own that night and when we returned home, there was nothing left of our community. The official police report said that a fire had started in one of the houses and spread too quickly for anyone to escape, but it was clear what had happened."

The emotion in her voice was so raw that I found it painful to listen to her story.

"We moved around every few months for the next seven years, hoping to keep the Pressors off our trail. It wasn't until I met your father that I finally settled down and stopped moving. When we took over as alphas of the pack we made sure that no one ever shared our secret with humans again."

I swallowed down my guilt that I had pushed so hard to break that rule only a few months into my time with the pack and planned to break it again when I told my parents. I knew they wouldn't tell anyone else; who would believe them? Still, I felt horrible for putting Lorelai back in a position that would remind her of that loss.

"I'm so sorry that happened; I wish there were something I could say to make things better, but--"

"Oh no, you are fine, it was a long time ago, and we have taken every precaution we can to make sure we do not draw attention to ourselves here." She seemed so sure of the pack's safety that it strengthened my confidence in my power to keep them safe.

"And I will do everything I can to make sure that doesn't change." We spoke for a few more minutes and then I told her I needed to go plan for the next evening's meeting. I knew there were a few things I needed to do before we met the detective, and I needed to make sure that I did everything right.

Once I ended my phone call, I wandered the house until I found Maeve and then I asked her for a favor that she was happy to agree to. Feeling better about things, I went to find Gabriel to see if we couldn't finish what I'd tried to start with our earlier kiss.

Chapter Twenty-Three

When the darkness surrounded me, I welcomed it. Emerging on the other side, I noticed that I still looked like myself, or at least the part of me that I could see did. The mirror appeared again. As I approached, my reflection looked back at me as it always had, but there was a look of terror on my face, and my reflection pointed behind me. I turned around, but there was nothing there. When I turned to look back at the mirror, a bullet whizzed past my head, and the mirror exploded into a shower of glass shards. I ducked and covered my head, but still felt the shards of glass as they landed on me.

I stood and looked at where the mirror had been, seeing Ouriel standing there instead, blood dripping from his mouth. It covered his chest and pooled on the ground around him. I reached out, freezing for a moment when he mirrored my movement. The surprise that I felt was showing on his face. Again, when I reached out, he mirrored the movement, but it wasn't until our hands touched and I felt the cool, smooth surface of the glass that I realized he was just a reflection, and the mirror was whole once more. He pulled his shirt away from his body and looked down at the blood that had stained it red. When I looked down at my own body, I was shocked to find my hand was holding my blood-stained shirt, but the hands I saw were not my own. I had become Ouriel and began to spit blood out of my mouth as quickly as I could to try and breathe around it. After a few minutes, I felt my consciousness fading and when the darkness surrounded me, I knew it was for the last time.

* * *

I woke up gasping for air, my body covered in sweat, my pillow damp with it. My heart raced as I pulled air into my body and tried to calm down. I flipped my pillow over to the dry side so I could avoid the dampness and rolled over. My arm was stopped by something warm and for a split second I thought it was Ouriel, then I remembered that Gabriel slept in my room. I took a deep breath, let it out, and released the grip my nightmare had on me. I was finally calmed my heart into a normal pace. I could smell the sweet chocolaty aroma of Gabriel, and it helped ground me in the present, which was much brighter and happier than my dream had been.

Moving so our bodies were pressed against each other, my mouth automatically widened into a smile. He started to rouse, and I held as still as possible to not wake him up completely. After a few seconds, his deep breathing continued. Replaying the events of the past few days in my mind I was trying to figure out what two teens from America could do to help. We had to meet with the detective next, but I didn't know whether we could trust her. The only thing I was sure of was that I would do whatever needed to be done to keep Gabriel safe. I just hoped he wouldn't hold it against me later.

"No more milk, he can't finish that," Gabriel mumbled quietly.

I did my best not to laugh, but I couldn't stop my shoulders from shaking. At least his dreams didn't seem to be weighed down by the deaths. Gabriel yawned and stretched, which drove his hips backward into mine.

"Good morning," he croaked.

"Good morning to you as well. Who were you protecting from more milk?" I asked, with a laugh.

"What're you talking about?" He asked, as he rolled over to look at me.

"You were sleep talking and said something about him not being able to finish his milk."

He looked confused and then understanding settled his features.

"I was with my little cousin, and she was giving her kitten a bowl of milk. She kept spilling, so I told her he didn't need more." He laughed, and I joined him.

"That's adorable." I leaned forward and kissed him on the mouth, careful to keep my lips closed to not offend him with my morning breath. "How'd you sleep otherwise?"

He stretched again, letting out a moan as he did. "I slept okay thanks. How about you?"

I smiled at him and took in the very appealing sight of his chest and arms as he stretched.

"I slept great, which is unusual for me. Normally I toss and turn during the night, but after last night, I think I passed out and just stayed in the same position all night."

He blushed and laughed at me. "That good huh?"

I laughed loudly. "I mean, I have no complaints, how about you?"

"None," he said, and leaned forward to kiss me, his teeth nipped at my bottom lip.

I shuddered and smiled.

"Good to hear," I replied with a smile.

"I should probably go back to my room to avoid any questions from everyone else in the house." He didn't have to specify for me to know who he meant.

"Yeah, I should take a shower and get ready for the day," I said, then lifted the covers off my body and rolled toward the edge of the bed. "Wait for me for breakfast?"

He smiled as he got out of the bed on the other side. "I'll wait, but you better take the fastest shower of your life, I'm hungry!"

To emphasize the point, his stomach rumbled loudly. We both laughed and headed for the door. When we opened it, we stopped short at the sight of The Greek, who stood right outside my door, looking angry.

"Oh, good morning," I said nervously, unsure what he may have heard through the door.

"Is it?" He growled, turning to stalk down the hall toward the stairs leading down to the main floor.

Gabriel and I looked at each other, and he shrugged, so we went our separate ways, and I tried to put the awkward encounter out of my mind. As I got to the bathroom, Adam's door opened, and he walked into the hall wearing an undershirt and boxers.

"Are you using the bathroom?"

"Yeah, I was going to take a quick shower before breakfast," I responded.

"Do you mind if I just jump in really quick and go to the bathroom?" He asked, walking toward the bathroom as though I'd already agreed.

"No problem," I said, as I stepped aside so he could get by me.

"Thank you," he slipped past me, thenlooked back at me like I was crazy. "Are you coming in or not?"

"I thought you were going to the bathroom?" I responded.

"I am, but it's not like you haven't ever been in a bathroom when someone else was going, right?" His question was so simple that it made my discomfort seem like I was crazy.

"I guess that's true," I said as I walked in and shut the door behind me.

"I wanted to talk to you about tonight anyway," he said as he lifted the lid and seat of the toilet. "Have you decided what we're going to do?"

I looked at imaginary things on my shirt to avoid looking at him.

"I'm going to talk to her to see what she wants, but I don't think we all need to be there."

He finished going to the bathroom and flushed the toilet before moving to the sink to wash his hands.

"I'm going to be there, that's not open for discussion." He gave me a serious look, as if he dared me to disagree with him.

"I assumed you would be. I just don't want Gabriel or anyone else out there with us. If things go wrong, I want to keep everyone else out of it."

He walked toward me, and I had to move out of the way so he could access the towel rack behind where I stood.

"I agree with you, keeping everyone else safe, just in case, is important. I can protect you on your own better than I can protect a group." He looked at me standing lamely as I waited for him to finish up and leave. "I thought you were going to take a shower?"

"I am," I said.

He looked at me expectantly. "Don't let me stop you. You don't have anything I haven't seen before."

"Right," I replied before I turned on the shower. I waited for the water to get warm before I took off my clothes and jumped in as quickly as possible.

Adam laughed behind me. "You really are concerned about nudity aren't you?"

"What do you mean?"

"Most Awakened don't care about or even notice nudity, we're so used to changing in front of our packs that the sight of skin doesn't bother us. Your heart is trying to break its way out of your chest right now, and it's all because you took off your clothes in front of someone else."

"Well excuse me for growing up thinking I was human. We tend to see nudity as a bigger deal I guess."

Ever since being caught with nothing to wear after my first change, I made sure I had something around to change into when I shifted back. I never noticed what the others did.

Adam continued to laugh, but didn't argue with me about my point. "Anyway, I think it would be best if you stay in your current form during the conversation tonight, and I'll shift to make sure she comes alone. If there is anyone else in the woods, I'll be able to tell a lot easier as a wolf."

He made a good point, so I agreed, and that pleased him enough to allow me some privacy while I finished my shower. I got ready as quickly as I was able to, and met Gabriel and Adam downstairs for breakfast. Maeve joined the three of us along with Jae, but they mostly talked amongst themselves. After a few minutes of silent eating, I decided I wanted to know what my dream might have meant, if anything.

"Can I ask a potentially strange question without being judged harshly for asking?"

I looked around the table, and all eyes were on me, and everyone nodded and encouraged me to ask. "Has anyone ever had the nightmare with a mirror in it?"

I was glad that I didn't need to explain what I meant by "the nightmare" since having to explain that would have made the real part of my question even harder to swallow.

They all looked at each other and waited to see if anyone would speak up but no one did. Finally, Jae asked a follow-up question.

"What happened to the mirror?"

I wasn't sure how far back I should go, but I figured without giving some history to this aspect of my dream it might not be as powerful.

"A few weeks ago, right after we awakened, I began to see a mirror hanging in the darkness. When I looked in the mirror, I saw myself and then my birth father would appear. He was always saying something, but no matter how hard I tried, I couldn't tell what until recently. He told me that he was sorry he wasn't around to help me out with things now, and a few other things…

"But then it seemed like he was talking to someone else that I couldn't see in the mirror, but he was still obviously addressing me."

I paused for a few seconds to let that information sink in, then continued with the details of my dream from the previous night. When I got to the part about looking down and seeing that I was Ouriel, Maeve and Jae gave each other a serious look and Maeve covered her mouth.

"What? What does that mean?" Adam asked what I wondered but was too afraid to ask.

"There are stories about the other abilities that Céline Garnier may have possessed. One was the ability to shift into forms other than her wolf. She was rumored to be able to disappear into a crowd of people by taking on the shape of someone else, get close to her enemies by becoming their loved ones, or harmless animals." Maeve spoke softly, as though she was afraid to be overheard by the others in the house. "There wasn't any proof of this ability, however, just stories and rumors, so we have always assumed it was just part of her lore."

"If Caleb is seeing himself as other people, it's possible that he may have the ability to become other people as well. And the fact that he can take on more than one wolf form already proves that he has more shifting capabilities than anyone else." Jae adopted the same hushed voice as Maeve.

"Gabriel, have you tried to shift into another wolf with any success yet?"

Gabriel looked shocked at the suggestion but shook his head no. "I never assumed I could become anything else, so I've never tried. Do you think I should?"

Maeve and Jae looked at each other and then back at Gabriel and me before they answered in unison. "Yes."

As if given the same prompt, we all stood at the same time and moved toward the door, which led to the back of the property.

"Caleb, how did you do it?" Maeve asked.

"I was holding onto them, or they were touching me when I shifted, and I took on the shape of their wolves," I replied, gesturing to Gabriel and Adam.

"Gabriel, why don't you try to take on the shape of Adam's wolf since you have seen him before, that way you have the ability to picture it in your mind before you try shifting?" Jae suggested.

"Okay, that makes sense I guess," Gabriel replied, before undressing and stepping closer to Adam.

"Ready?" He asked Adam.

"Whenever you are," he replied.

Gabriel's eyes went blank, and hair began sprouting all over his body, which was reshaping itself into a wolf. Unfortunately, it was the same sleek black wolf he'd always been. After the transformation was complete, he looked down at his paws and let out a noise that sounded like disappointment and then he began shifting back into his human form again.

"I guess I don't have the ability to do it," he said, his voice low.

"Try again, this time, just try to shift your arm rather than your whole body. And Adam, picture your paw on his body and see if you can help with the initial change," Maeve offered.

They tried again, but when the black hairs sprouted across Gabriel's arm, he looked frustrated and let go of Adam.

"This is pointless! It doesn't work with me, and it never will!" He sounded angry and embarrassed, which didn't make any sense to me.

"Don't get upset, we don't know how it is triggered the first time, we just have to figure out how it works."

Jae stepped closer and laid her hand on Gabriel's shoulder. Seconds later his other arm was covered in black fur, and we all looked on confused. "I thought if I forced the change on you, I might be able to get you to take on my shape."

"Does that work for me?" I asked, still trying to figure out if this was something I was able to do.

Jae approached me and laid her hand on my arm, and I could feel her will being forced into my limb, which stretched and reshaped into a slender gray paw.

"It seems like it does, yes. I wonder if I could…" her voice trailed off, but I could feel her will being forced into my newly formed paw, which reshaped into a perfect replica of Jae's arm, complete with longer nails.

"What the hell?" I backed away and shook my arm trying to get it back into its normal shape. I could feel my skin stretch and rip as my arm reemerged from the shape Jae put it in.

"It seems that taking on the shape of other people is within the realm of possibility, but why are you the only one able to do it?" Jae looked from me to Gabriel and back to me again.

"Don't look at me, I'm new to just about all of this." I rubbed the skin of my arm, which felt raw and sensitive after my most recent shift. I turned around to ask Gabriel something and was shocked to see that he had walked away and headed back toward the house without a word to the rest of us.

"Trouble in paradise," Adam said, as we all watched Gabriel storm into the house. I gave Adam a sharp look of disapproval. Inside however, I felt the first twinges of uncertainty bubble up to the surface.

Chapter Twenty-Four

I followed Gabriel into the house, which left Maeve, Jae and Adam outside to discuss the possible causes of my ability, or the future of the Council without Ouriel, or perhaps the weather. I didn't care enough to find out. I found Gabriel climbing the stairs toward our rooms.

"Hey, wait up!"

"Why? So you can embarrass me again?" The pain and anger were clear in his voice, but I was shocked that they were directed at me that I stopped and stared at him from the bottom of the staircase.

"What are you talking about? I didn't do anything to embarrass you. I didn't do anything at all. I had something done to me." I was trying to keep my discomfort in check to avoid any confrontation between the two of us.

"Ever since we awakened, everything has been about you, which was fine at first. I didn't even want to be an alpha, but now it's getting to the point where people are probably starting to wonder what I'm doing here."

I could tell based on the emotional waves coming off him that this wasn't new embarrassment that he was dealing with. That made it even more difficult for me to talk about because I didn't know the real reason for his anger.

"I don't think anyone is questioning why you're here, I think they're questioning whether the two of us can lead the whole population of Awakened. That likely has more to do with our age than any abilities we haveDon't forget that you have abilities; you have helped heal me and other people when they were injured."

His harsh expression softened a little at that, and he seemed to be thinking things over now.

"But you were also there, it's not like I did any of that on my own."

"I haven't done anything on my own either. It took you, Adam, and Jae to get me to shift into something else. I don't have any control over that stuff. I barely have control over shifting at all!"

I laughed to try to lighten the mood even further and was rewarded with a small smile from Gabriel. When it seemed like most of his anger had dissipated, I climbed the stairs and walked down the hall with him to his bedroom.

"I'm sorry. I know I'm being dramatic about all of this but being sent away with my mom for no apparent reason made me feel like the pack didn't want us. My mom was important back before we left It felt like I was being sent away, and she had to come because she was my mom. Then I awakened early, and I felt like I was finally going to be able to prove my worth to the rest of the pack. Now it feels like I'm in your shadow, which I know isn't something you're doing on purpose, but it still sucks."

He refused to meet my eyes, so I took his hand in mine and held it softly.

"I wish there were something I could say to make you feel better. I can't speak for the pack and I certainly can't speak for the Council, but I think you're important on your own and not because of what happened to us. I think you and your mom were trusted by your former alpha and sent out to find a new place for everyone to live. If they didn't value you, they wouldn't have shown up, right?"

"I guess that's true, but I had nothing to do with that, all I did was get a job at the hotel and watch you to make sure they knew everything you were doing. My mom was the one scouting the area to make sure it would be a good place to live."

It was still a little creepy that he'd been asked to watch me for the pack, but I tried not to focus on the negative.

"Well, if I'm as important as you say I am, and you were the one responsible for keeping track of me, doesn't that mean you are important to them as well?"

"So, you're saying I'm only important because of how important you are?" His anger flared up again, and he pulled his hand away from mine.

"What? No! That's not what I meant at all." I tried to backpedal; to take back any hint of reference to me.

"Because it sounds like that's what you're saying. *You're* so important that *I* must be important because I got to follow you around like a little lost puppy? Because there's nothing I could do in order to make me valuable on my own? Thanks a lot, Caleb, I feel *much* better now!"

He opened the door to his bedroom. "I'd like you to leave, I need some time alone to think."

"But I—"

"Caleb, just leave. Please." His eyes were beginning to tear, but his flared nostrils and scowl let me know they weren't tears of sadness.

I walked back down the hall toward my room and tried not to flinch when I heard the door slam behind me and the lock click into place. Adam was leaning against the wall, looking as casual as possible. He started to open his mouth, and I cut him off.

"Save it, we have other things that we need to discuss." I ushered him into my room and closed the door. "We need to figure out what we're going to do tonight. It seems like Gabriel is probably going to be on his own for a little while."

The one good thing about our fight was that I didn't have to make up an excuse to keep him away from the meeting now.

"I don't want anyone else to know what we're doing, but we need to make sure *someone* knows we are leaving to make sure no one follows us."

"I think we can leave that up to Maeve. She would be the next to take over the Council before you and Gabriel came into the picture, so the others will listen to her if she gives them directions," Adam offered.

"I agree, and I already spoke with her about distracting Gabriel, so she would be the best bet to keep the others distracted as well. Can you talk with her soon and make sure she knows what we need her to do? I want to call my parents before we go out just in case something happens. You may want to call Megan."

He simply nodded and stepped out of the room, leaving me alone with my thoughts and a cell phone that was potentially my last lifeline to my family back in California. I called my parents first. I figured they would be easier to talk to since they had no idea what was happening. As I waited for them to answer, I made a silent promise to myself to tell them everything if I made it back home after all this.

"Hello?" My dad answered the phone, sounding surprised that it had rung at all.

"Hi Dad," I said. "Sorry for calling so early, I just wanted to see how everything was going with you and Mom!" I tried to keep my voice as upbeat as possible.

"Caleb! It's so good to hear from you! Things are going well here. I'm just working on a few things around the house before it gets too late in the day. How are you doing? How's the vacation treating you?"

I had no idea what he was talking about for a second, and then I remembered I'd told my mom that I had gone out of town for a little while.

"I'm all right, thanks. The vacation is going well, just trying to figure some stuff out here, but I decided to take a break to give you a call."

I didn't want to lie, but I also knew he wouldn't understand what was happening with the limited amount I was able to share at this point.

"I'm glad you did. It's always great to hear your voice. What are you trying to figure out? Maybe I can help?"

I should have known he'd offer to help me; he'd always been the person I'd gone to with any problems in the past. He was a fixer, so he immediately went into resolution mode when he heard someone was having a problem.

"It's nothing really." I struggled to find the right way to explain the situation without making him even more curious. "I'm probably making a bigger deal out of everything it really is. I'm sure I can manage things on my own."

"Okay, well let me know if you need help, you know I am always here for you."

"I know Dad, thank you. I love you." The emotion of the situation started creeping into my voice.

"I love you too son. Do you want me to wake up your mom?"

Of course she was still asleep; it wasn't yet 9:00 am there.

"No, that's okay. Just let her know that I love her, and I'll call you later."

"Are you sure you're okay?" There was suspicion in his voice, and I knew I had to get off the phone fast, or I would spill everything.

I forced some extra happiness into my voice. "I'm sure Dad, thanks. Well, I'd better run. Good luck with the stuff around the house!"

"Thanks, talk to you later." He disconnected, and I sat on my bed with the phone still pressed to my face.

"Goodbye."

The next phone call I had to make was to Lorelai, and I was even less excited about this call. While she may have had a better understanding of the danger I was in, I didn't want to cause her to worry more than she already was. A couple of deep breaths, thumb hovering over the call symbol on her contact page before I finally pressed it. She answered after a couple of rings.

"Good morning, Caleb, how's everything going there?" Already, she sounded on edge, making it difficult for me to try to pretend I wasn't.

"Hey, things are going okay here, thanks. Gabriel and I got into a little fight, but Adam and I are going to check out the information from the detective in a few hours. I just wanted to call to check in with you and see how things are?"

I decided that honesty about the situation here, immediately followed by a question might distract her. If that didn't work, I was counting on the news about Gabriel and me fighting to be an excuse for any emotion she might hear in my voice.

"Things are going just fine here. There's nothing new to report since yesterday morning. What's on your mind Caleb, you sound stressed out?"

So much for my brilliant plan to try to distract her. "I'm just nervous about going to the police. We're making sure everyone here will be safe and taken care of while we are following up on things."

"Why are you nervous? It isn't like you've done anything wrong, right?" Her voice was more serious this time.

My resolve immediately crumbled when her tone firmed.

"I know, but we're meeting with someone who claims she knows what happened to Ouriel and is willing to give us information in exchange for something she wants."

"What does she want?"

"I don't know. I wasn't calling about this issue, I was just calling to let you know what was going on. If something happens to me, I wanted you to know that I appreciate everything you've done for methe past few months, and--"

She interrupted me. "Caleb, why does it sound like you're preparing to die?"

I refused to give in this time and kept talking as though I hadn't heard her.

"I am making Gabriel stay behind so if something happens to me the pack and the Council will still have someone to lead them. I will call you as soon as we make it back and let you know what we were able to find out. Thanks again for everything. I love you."

I disconnected without another word and sent a text to Adam warning him not to answer if she called. All that done, I turned off my phone so she couldn't get through.

Here goes nothing...

When the sun was about to set, I walked down the hall to Adam's room and opened his door as quietly as I could. He was sitting at the end of his bed and looked up at me as I entered. He was wearing basketball shorts and nothing else, which I realized would make changing a lot easier.

"Is it time?"

"Yeah, I wanted to get there early so you could scope everything out before she arrived."

"That's what I was thinking. I'm ready when you are." He grabbed his sandals then walked toward the door.

"Did you call Megan?" I asked.

"Yeah, I didn't say much, but she also seemed like she was busy, so it was a short call. Then I called Brent, and…" he looked away when I glanced up at him.

I thought about the things that could have been going wrong back at home that Lorelai might have kept from me.

"And what? What did he say?" I had gripped the door handle so hard that I felt my knuckles pop.

"Apparently he and Tanya are dating now."

Of all the things I could have imagined, that was the last thing I ever would have guessed. I felt the stress and worry that had flooded my body wash away as a wave of relief crashed over me. I didn't know if this was really the time or place for this discussion, but honestly, I didn't care.

"Really?" I asked in disbelief. "I mean, Lorelai did mention things were 'interesting' with those two, but I just assumed they'd divided and conquered training."

If those two could figure out a relationship, I hoped that things between me and Gabriel would work themselves out. This had been our first big fight, and I didn't know what to do.

Adam continued with his story. "Brent said that she's bossy, and one day they got into a huge physical fight that led to them wrestling. She apparently pinned him to the ground and then he kissed her. And from there…" He trailed off, wiggling his eyebrows and grinning to suggest things had gone a bit further.

I laughed, happy for the distraction from the nerves I was feeling, but realized we were wasting valuable time. "As much as I want to sit here and continue to avoid what comes next, we have somewhere to be."

"Right!" Adam walked out of the room and down the hallway. I hoped that whatever we discovered tonight was worth the risk we were taking, and I was about to find out. I followed Adam to the balcony, where he shifted and jumped down to the ground below. I looked over the edge, and he had landed safely. He looked up at me expectantly, and I dropped his shorts and sandals down to him before I crawled over the railing and dropped to the ground below. I landed better this time and rolled to absorb some of the impact. Having arms and legs made that surprisingly easier.

"You spoke to Maeve about everything, right?" I realized now that I should have asked him when he was still able to speak, but the look he gave me let me know that he had done everything I'd asked him to do. "Okay good, let's go."

Chapter Twenty-Five

We moved across the yard, which gave us a view into the windows of the house that were illuminated from the inside. While the air outside was cold, the interior of the house looked warm and welcoming. Gabriel's light was on, but the curtains were closed, which kept me from seeing into his room. I ran through the fight we'd had earlier in my mind again, and it only made me more certain that I was doing the right thing leaving him behind. He'd be upset if he found out, but he was the only person in the house I trusted other than Adam. Someone needed to live if things went badly for Adam and me.

Adam growled quietly behind me. When I turned to look at him, he motioned with his head for me to keep moving. We hadn't made it to the relative safety of the shadows cast by the wall, so anyone looking out the windows of the house would be able to see us sneaking away.

I followed him into the shadows and up and over the wall into the woods beyond the property.

Adam nipped my hand, letting me know I should stay against the wall as he explored the area. I waited patiently and worked on my tracking skills. Listening to the rustle of leaves under his paws, and inhaling the subtle fragrance of the forest that a cold breeze carried to me. Nothing seemed out of the ordinary, but then I heard Adam's deep growl off to my right, followed by the snarling of another wolf. Before I could react, I heard them thump against each other, and the growling got louder and more vicious.

I forgot about my safety and ran toward where I thought the sound came from. I hoped that Adam had somehow found a regular wolf roaming in the woods coincidentally, but I knew somewhere inside that I was lying to myself. An explosion of gunshots rang out followed by the loud yelp of what sounded an awful lot like Adam, and I knew this was much more than a clash between Adam and a random wolf.

Sprinting harder into the middle of the clearing where Adam was, I saw another Awakened and he were still circling each other. Off to one side, I could see the detective with her gun pointed at Adam. She yelled something in a language I didn't understand—her finger hovering over the trigger was enough for me to know she wouldn't hesitate to shoot if things got violent. I looked back at Adam, who was limping and dragging his right hind paw behind him. His eyes never left the other Awakened and now that I was in the area, he stopped circling to keep the other wolf from getting close to me. As I took in the scene, I noticed the wolf had the same gray fur that we'd found near the body, and my mind whirled through worst-case scenarios.

"What the hell is going on?" My anger and fear pulsed out in waves to the wolves as they stared each other down. The detective dropped her arms to her sides, but held onto the gun. My yelling caused Adam and the other Awakened to focus their attention on me. When I caught the eyes of the strange wolf, I forced my will into his mind with so much conviction that he whimpered and collapsed to the ground. I was so angry that I imagined my power strangling his brain and was shocked when it seemed to work.

"What did you do to him?" The detective asked me, moving closer to where I stood. My attention still on the unknown wolf, I didn't realize the detective's gun was pointed at me until Adam jumped between us. The sudden movement distracted me enough that I took my attention off the other Awakened.

"What did I do to who?" I asked carefully.

The detective realized her mistake and backed away; her gun was still pointed at my face. The other wolf had shifted back to his human form, and when he did, he ran to the detective and stood in front of her. He backed her slowly away from Adam and me. There was fear in his eyes, but I could tell that he wasn't afraid for himself.

I reached down to touch the top of Adam's head with my fingertips. Where we touched, I could feel a small shock followed by heat, and the bullets were being pushed out of his leg as his wounds knitted themselves back together. He shook his head and moved to stand in front of me once more now that he was back to full strength. It was the first time I had healed someone else on my own. I then realized that I'd healed him in front of someone who probably shouldn't have seen that.

The detective and the man that accompanied her watched what happened and their eyes widened as the bleeding slowed to a complete stop. They looked closer at his leg with extreme interest, then at each other before sharing the tiniest nod. Before they could act, Adam jumped up and grabbed the wrist of the detective, which caused her to drop the gun. Close behind Adam, I snatched it off the ground before she could react. I raised it and pointed it at her, ready to do whatever I needed to do to walk away from this night safely.

"Wait!" She cried, her hands out in front of her, with the palms facing me. She and the Awakened next to her kneeled on the ground and exposed their necks to me, their eyes cast down to the ground.

I was surprised by their submissive posture but didn't let it distract me.

"Who is he?" I motioned to the man as I spoke.

"He's my husband. Your friend attacked him as we were coming to meet you."

I looked down at Adam again, who gave what could only be described as the wolf version of a shrug.

"He was protecting me, you never said you would be bringing another Awakened with you; how were we supposed to know who he was?"

"You're right, but it was a risk I had to take. When I told you who we were, you may not have been willing to listen to me. We came together, so you knew we were honest with you." For a human, she seemed to know a lot about what Awakened could do, and that intrigued me.

"I'm listening." I took a few steps backward and allowed them to stand up to be more comfortable. Adam stayed between the three of us, which was just fine with me.

The detective and her husband helped each other up and then huddled close. Her husband spoke then for the first time.

"My name is Lorenzo. My wife Giuliana and I need your help, or our lives will end, just like you and the rest of your pack."

My skin prickled at his mention of my pack, but he motioned toward the house, making me realize he meant the others here in Croatia.

"That's an interesting way to ask for our help: threatening me and my pack. Why should we help you?"

"I know what happened to the old one that lived in the house. Without me, you'll never know the truth. The police have already destroyed the evidence and have been doing the same for years. Without me, the body outside the wall and the one inside the house will be blamed on those of you who were there at the time. 249rom there, it only takes a few steps to make you all disappear."

Giuliana's face was determined, but the quiver in her cheek gave away her nerves.

At the mention of the body in the woods, I grew angry.

"Again, your threats aren't motivating me to be helpful, especially since it seems like your husband was the one who killed that man in the woods in the first place."

My tension was rising and I could tell that both Adam and Lorenzo were being affected by it. I tried to calm down, but I also wanted there to be an edge to my voice, so I tried to find a balance.

They looked at each other again before she continued. "Lorenzo didn't kill that man, the Pressors did, and they left him near your property to create suspicion. Lorenzo found the body while out running and told me about it so I could make sure to take the call if one came in."

I wasn't sure whether to believe her, but we didn't have any proof that he had killed the young man, so I backed down a little. "I'm listening, go on."

"If we don't help you, we die. If we do help you, and you don't help us in return, we still die. The choice is really up to you whether you want to help us or not. Without our help, you'll be in danger, but maybe you'll make it out alive. Are you willing to risk the lives of everyone on that gamble, though?"

She had just said the one thing that would make it impossible for me to walk away from the meeting without coming to some deal. I might be willing to risk my life, and I knew Adam would risk his, but I wasn't that cavalier about the lives of the others. Giuliana's lips curved upward slightly; she could tell she'd struck a nerve.

"What do you want from us?" I asked as I locked up my emotional broadcast. I didn't want to give away how I felt about the situation before I had a chance to process their request.

"Lorenzo needs to be on the Council." She didn't waste any time going for the impossible request.

Despite my emotions being locked down, I knew that my face gave away how I felt about the request without me having to say a word. Before I even had a chance to respond, Giuliana continued.

"He doesn't want to represent a pack; he has been alone for too long to go back into the structure of a pack. He would only offer an opinion on rogue Awakened, who have left or been kicked out of their packs."

Her eyes narrowed, and Lorenzo leaned into her side, which seemed to be a comfort for him more than it was for her.

"And what do you want for yourself?"

Her request on behalf of Lorenzo was already more than I could offer without the approval of the rest of the Council. I hoped she had another request that I was able to provide in order to hold them over while I negotiated with the others.

"I want my life to be protected from attack by the Awakened. As a Pressor, I'm…" Giuliana didn't have a chance to finish her request, as soon as the word 'Pressor' left her lips Adam's teeth were bared, and I growled low at her and Lorenzo.

I started to look around for other Pressors, confident that they had somehow surrounded us while we were distracted by the demands of the others. I saw Adam doing the same and using his nose to try to track anyone who might have been close by.

"There's no one out there. That's what I was trying to say. I was a Pressor, and when the Awakened find that out, and they always seem to, I'll be killed. Even being married to one of you doesn't protect me because he doesn't have a pack, so we're both disposable. If the Pressors knew I had helped any Awakened, they would kill me without question. Lorenzo would then be blamed for my death, and if he weren't killed by the Pressors or the Awakened, the human courts would lock him up for sure."

I had to admit that she had a point, but I still didn't know whether I could trust her. I looked at Adam and sent him the mental image to check the woods around us to make sure we were still alone. He loped off quickly but gave a parting growl as a warning before he disappeared into the darkness.

"How can I protect you from attack if you're a Pressor? If you're with the Awakened, won't they put two and two together and come after you? I'm not going to be responsible for bringing a Pressor attack onto the Council because I brought one of them into our protection."

"I think you misunderstood me. I don't need protection from the Pressors, and I will leave it up to you to figure out how to keep the Council safe, with Lorenzo in one of the seats. That is of no concern to me. I want out of this life and away from the killing."

She looked mentally and emotionally exhausted, and Lorenzo leaned into her again, but I could tell that this time it was for her benefit.

"We didn't mean for this to happen," Lorenzo said, pointing back and forth between him and Giuliana. "We fell in love when we were young and didn't know what our families did. When I came of age, I told Giuliana what I was, and when her parents found out, they told the others. The

Pressors her family was aligned with killed my parents and my sister, but I was able to escape. When I wouldn't kill Giuliana in return, the pack forced me out to keep themselves safe. We've been on the run ever since."

Their story made me want to help them, but there was no way for me to know if they were telling the truth or if it was all part of some plan to infiltrate the Council. I knew that The Greek would disagree with me. I expected that Stephen would also feel the risk wasn't worth it and after our fight, Gabriel could honestly go either way. I had no idea what Maeve, Jae, and Kenai would think, but maybe they'd consider an additional Council member if it could lead to finding out what caused Ouriel's death. Adam would back me up, but didn't have a role on the Council, so there was no real benefit there.

As I considered all these racing thoughts, Giuliana and Lorenzo became increasingly nervous. Their eyes darted from side to side, and Lorenzo appeared to be listening for something I couldn't hear. Their nerves caused me to become increasingly anxious since Adam had left to patrol the area, and I was on my own.

"What are you waiting for?" I demanded.

They feigned ignorance and Giuliana spoke up.

"I'm waiting for your answer."

Before I could respond, there was a shrill whistling sound that began to get louder. I had a split-second thought when I assumed it was a signal to Lorenzo before the skin in his right shoulder exploded forward, along with small pieces of bone.

"They found us!" Giuliana yelled, as she pushed Lorenzo to the ground right after another bullet struck his neck. "Get down!"

I realized she was yelling at me even though most of her attention was on Lorenzo. "Who found us?"

"Pressors. They must have followed me here to see what I was doing." She rolled Lorenzo over and began to assess his wounds, which bled profusely. "You, you can heal him. Please do it!" She looked at me, her eyes pleaded, but her face remained an emotionless mask.

"I'm not sure that I can do it on my own. Usually, I have someone with me to help."

When I said it out loud, I realized how much I missed Gabriel and wished he'd been with me at this moment. I left him at home to protect him, but there was no one that I wanted next to me when things were going crazy more than him.

I crawled toward them and started with Lorenzo's neck, which appeared to have the most damage. When I touched the skin there, I could feel the faint pulse under the skin, but each time I did, more blood was being pushed out of the wound. His skin warm from the blood, but underneath I could feel his body heat slipping away. The familiar heat and electric shock that accompanied my healing touches in the past were absent, and I wasn't sure what I could do to make it work.

"Is it working?" Giuliana applied pressure to his shoulder, and still looked around for our attackers. She looked me in the eyes when she was able but then they darted away again quickly as she continued her surveillance of the area.

"I don't think so, no," I said frantically, trying to stop the blood flow with one hand while I searched for a new connection spot with the other. "I told you; I haven't done this on my own before. I don't know how it works; it's just always happened in the past on its own."

As we were talking, I felt Lorenzo's pulse slow even further and eventually stop altogether. I pulled my hands away and watched his neck wound. Blood continued to flow from it, but the speed and volume had decreased so significantly that it didn't seem necessary to keep pressure there any longer.

"I'm sorry Giuliana, I did what I could." I sat back on my feet and mentally called out to Adam, hoping he would somehow know I needed him. When I looked up at Giuliana again, her hand shot out and slapped me hard across the face.

"Avi all'inferno!" After she hit me, tears ran down her face, and she collapsed on top of Lorenzo, whispering something I couldn't understand into his ear. As if they were also in mourning, the insects and other creatures in the woods stopped making noise, and an eerie silence surrounded us. It was broken almost instantly however by the snap of a twig and a deep growl behind us.

Chapter Twenty-Six

I turned slowly toward the sound of the growl to see that Adam had returned. His eyes were locked on Giuliana, and his ears were lying flat against his head. He stalked slowly toward her, his teeth bared, and I realized he must have seen her slap me, but not the events leading up to that.

"It's okay Adam, you can relax," I spoke quietly and smiled to show him I was serious.

He walked quickly to a cluster of bushes and began to change back. When he finished, he walked back out and stood between the two of us.

"What happened?" he demanded.

"Lorenzo was shot, and I tried to heal him, but it didn't work. Giuliana was just upset." I looked down at her, as she continued to weep. "Did you find the shooter?" Worry still hung in my mind at the possibility of getting attacked by the Pressors.

"What shooter?" Adam's face was confused and angry, which didn't make me feel more comfortable.

"The person who shot Lorenzo?" I pointed at his body. "Giuliana thought it might have been the Pressors."

"If it is, we need to get inside, now!" Adam ran toward me and grabbed my arm, pulling me back toward the relative safety of the trees.

"We need to bring them with us!" I refused to be dragged away.

"What?! Why?" He was incredulous, but wouldn't directly disobey me if I made a good point.

"Giuliana may be able to help us, and we can't just leave Lorenzo's body out here to be discovered. We're still too close to the house, and all these deaths in such a short time would bring way too much attention to us."

Adam looked at me as though he was impressed, and nodded. Without letting go of my arm, he leaned down and grabbed onto Giuliana, hauling her up to her feet. I reached down and grabbed onto Lorenzo's undamaged arm but dropped quickly it when the most intense shock I'd ever felt in my life rocked through me. I gasped loudly, and Adam immediately let go of my arm and began shaking his hand.

"What the hell was that?" He looked back and forth between me and Lorenzo.

I looked over, and even Giuliana was rubbing her arm where Adam had grasped it, as though she also felt the shock.

"I'm not sure, I grabbed onto Lorenzo's arm, and he shocked me." My arm was beginning to tingle, and my skin burned, but all of that faded away when out of nowhere, Lorenzo groaned quietly.

We all watched him and held our collective breath, as he made another soft noise followed by a cough.

"Lorenzo!" Giuliana ran to his side and was trying to help him up, unable to see his wounds had begun to bleed again.

"Giuliana, don't move him," I said. My voice was in full command mode, and even though it shouldn't have had any real power over her, she moved her hands away but refused to leave his side. "Adam, help me."

I leaned down and touched Lorenzo again. Just like the first time, there was no shock or heat to indicate that I was doing anything to help. When Adam reached out and touched my shoulder, I could feel the shock travel through my body. It wasn't as strong this time, but I could feel *something* happening. His pulse got stronger, but also forced even more blood from his wounds.

"Adam, hold onto Giuliana again, I think I need more energy."

Without a word, he reached over and placed his hand on her shoulder. The strength of the shock returned and quickly turned into heat that I was able to force into Lorenzo. It healed the damaged tissue faster than I had been able to when it was just Adam and I on our own.

"I think it's working."

Lorenzo groaned again, and Giuliana leaned over him and began to whisper in his ear again. That seemed to quiet him as I continued, making sure to focus on healing from the inside out, to avoid closing the skin before the rest of the wound. When he was completely healed, I let go of him. Giuliana pulled his upper half into her lap and hugged him tightly. Lorenzo wrapped his arms around her as well, and they sat there holding each other.

"Caleb? Adam?" Voices called out for us from the house. They were still inside the wall but sounded like they were getting closer to the boundary.

"We have to go, now." Adam stood and helped me up. My head was swimming, but then my equilibrium stabilized, and I started to walk back toward the house. I heard Giuliana and Lorenzo stand up and begin to follow us, still speaking softly to each other. I couldn't understand what they were saying, but the tone made it seem like it wasn't anything I needed to worry about.

At the gate, I motioned for Giuliana and Lorenzo to wait in the shadows while Adam and I continued alone. Once inside the gate, Gabriel and the rest of the Council converged on us. So much for Maeve keeping them busy.

"Where have you been?" The Greek spoke first, but it was clear that his question was in the minds of everyone in the group, including Gabriel, who refused to meet my gaze.

"Trying to figure out what happened to Ouriel." I kept my tone casual and hoped that it would seem like I didn't feel as guilty as I did. "Someone told me they had information, and I wanted to get to the bottom of things."

The Greek seemed to pale slightly, but I continued as if I hadn't noticed. "If the information didn't turn out to be reliable, I didn't want to bother anyone else with it. When I tried to get the information, we were attacked by Pressors."

This revelation had the desired effect, as the gathering began talking over one another, demanding more information. When I looked at Gabriel, he returned my gaze, but looked away again.

"Since I wasn't able to get the information I needed before being attacked, I brought the sources back with us."

Right on cue, Giuliana and Lorenzo stepped around the corner and onto the property. When they did, The Greek, Jae and Stephen hunched over slightly and began to growl, even though the effect was somewhat diminished by their current vocal chords.

"Stop it, all of you. These are my guests, and will be treated as such until I can get all of the information I need from them."

I walked back toward the house and made sure that Giuliana and Lorenzo walked at the same pace as me while Adam followed close behind. As we made our way toward the front door, The Greek caught up to me and began to match my pace.

"You're making a mistake," he growled at me.

"Thank you for your opinion, but I'm doing what I think is best. If you want to make sure everything is okay, join us and listen to the information they share. Be warned, you may not like what they have to say."

I walked down the hall toward the kitchen. If they were lying to me, and this was all part of some larger plan, I didn't want them to know much about the layout of the house.

The Greek, Maeve, Gabriel, and the rest of the Council sat at the table with Giuliana, Lorenzo and me, while Adam and Jusuf stood, watching over all of us. Since I was the one who started this whole thing, I turned to Giuliana and Lorenzo.

"I'll offer you protection, while I can, from the Awakened gathered here, but I am unwilling to negotiate about the other request until you share all the information you have with us." My eyes would convey my unwillingness to compromise on this point as I waited for their reply.

"What other request?"

"Why do they need protection from us?"

"Who are these people?"

The Council members came alive with questions, each one speaking over the others as they tried to get more information.

"Giuliana and Lorenzo are on the run from the Pressors. Lorenzo's pack kicked him out for not killing Giuliana, and if the Pressors find out that Giuliana has married an Awakened, they will kill her."

I left out the part about Giuliana being a Pressor herself; that didn't need to come up right at this moment. The Council members asked even more questions, but I ignored them this time.

"Do we have a deal?"

Giuliana and Lorenzo looked at each other and then back at me before nodding. "Yes."

"Good. Now, please tell us what information you have about Ouriel's death."

I sat back and took another bite of my banana while I listened.

Giuliana began. "When we came to examine the body, there was no clear indication of what caused his death. There were no obvious wounds, no bruising or other signs of internal damage. There was just red blood all over."

"We already know that, tell us something new," The Greek interrupted.

"Right, sorry," she said, looking around the table at the anxious faces. "The medical examiner discovered burns in his esophagus and stomach lining, which seemed to come from something poisonous or acidic. Whatever he'd ingested, by the time he realized something was wrong, it was too late. Even if he had been able to heal himself, the acid in his stomach would only have made things worse, and the damage would have continued to spread through the rest of his body."

I started to take another bite my banana only to found I'd lost my appetite.

"How would the acid have been introduced to his system?" I worried that the rest of us were also in danger if it was something in the house.

"It would have been in something he ate or drank, and was likely prepared specifically for him." As she shared that information, many of the people around the table let out a sigh of relief.

"It is one of the ways that Pressors have killed Awakened in the past. Prussic acid acts quickly if inhaled or ingested on an empty stomach. But if an adequate dose is mixed with food or drink, it takes longer to get absorbed into the body. It still would have only taken give or take 20 minutes before he would have felt the effects. Like I said, by then, it would have been too late."

" That still doesn't tell us how he would have gotten something with that inside of it. Ouriel never left the house for fear of being recognized by the Pressors, and no one from outside the Council and our companions has come into the house. At least not until his death." Maeve looked at Giuliana critically, as though she had something to hide.

"How do you know it's a common method of Pressor murder?" Maeve pressed on.

Before I was able to stop her, Giuliana responded to the question.

"Because I am one."

All manner of Hell broke loose in the kitchen as a response to the confession. Chairs went flying; everyone was yelling so loudly that it was impossible to understand anything being said. When the teeth and claws came out, Adam jumped in to keep Giuliana and Lorenzo safe from the others.

"How could you bring a Pressor into this house?!" The Greek's voice rose above the rest and his eyes glowed with anger, directed at me.

"I told you that you might not like what they had to say, but it was a risk worth taking. We needed to know what happened to Ouriel, and now we do. The real question is, how did the poison get into whatever it was that Ouriel had? Since the body was discovered outside the walls, the number of occupants inside the house has decreased dramatically."

I motioned around the room and stopped on The Greek for emphasis.

"I think the murderer is one of us. And personally, I don't want to wait around for the next death before trying to get to the bottom of things."

"First Deanna, then the body on the property, and now Ouriel. When is enough going to be enough?" Jae asked the group. "The Pressors have become bolder in their pursuit of us, and I think this--" she nodded her head in my direction "-- is a risk worth taking."

Maeve and Jae sat down, but the others, including Gabriel, left the room in protest. Once they were gone, Giuliana, Lorenzo and I took our seats again, and Adam and Jusuf, who were no longer trying to keep the others back, returned to their original positions around the table. We spoke quietly about the different ways in which something could have come into the house and been given to Ouriel, all of which seemed as plausible as any other.

After an hour of going back and forth, we decided to explore as many possibilities as we could over the next few days. Giuliana assured us that the rest of the food and drinks in the house should be fine because the poison would have dissipated already. No one seemed particularly hungry, and I wasn't going to risk it, so we all went our separate ways for the evening.

"Adam, I'm going to let Giuliana and Lorenzo stay in my room for the evening, would you mind helping me clear some of my stuff out?" I gave him a look that I hoped no one else would notice, and he nodded before walking ahead of us.

Once the three of us were on our own, I turned to them. "Do you need anything before I show you to your room?"

"No, we can make do with what we already have with us," Lorenzo responded.

With a nod, I began to lead them toward the stairs before I spoke again.

"We can discuss the other condition of our agreement tomorrow once the dust has settled from tonight's revelations. For now, please just stay in the room and if you need anything, please let me know, and I will take care of it for you."

We climbed the stairs in silence and when we reached the top and started down the stairs, I stopped at the sight of The Greek and Gabriel standing close to each other and speaking outside Gabriel's room. When he saw us approaching, The Greek said something to Gabriel, scowled at me, and then turned and walked away.

"He's not happy that we're here," Lorenzo said, primarily to himself.

"To be honest, I've never seen him happy, so it's entirely possible that it has very little to do with you," I said, trying to help them feel less uncomfortable.

I smiled a little at Gabriel, but he just watched me walk by, his face free of any emotion.

"You'll be staying in this room here," I said, as I showed them to the room where I had been staying. Fortunately, Adam had understood the look I'd given him and had closed all the doors in the hallway so they couldn't see into any of the other rooms on this floor. They may have provided information about Ouriel's death, but I still didn't trust them completely.

"Thank you for everything. We know it's asking a lot of you to keep us safe, but we appreciate it more than you'll ever know." Giuliana took my hand as she spoke and smiled genuinely at me. Lorenzo shook my hand but didn't add anything to what Giuliana had said. Before they closed the door, they both showed their necks to me again as a sign of submission. When I acknowledged it, they shut the door quietly, and I heard the lock click into place. It seemed like they didn't entirely trust all of us either. I didn't blame them.

I turned to walk toward Adam's room and stopped when Gabriel called out to me.

"Caleb, I'd like to speak with you."

I took a deep breath and prepared myself for what was sure to be anything but pleasant.

"Of course Gabriel, whatever you'd like."

Chapter Twenty-Seven

I followed him into his room and waited while he shut the door after us. I had no idea what he would want to talk about and what he would rather not, so I stayed quiet and let him start the conversation.

"Why did you leave me behind tonight? Does my opinion mean so little to you, that you don't even bother to ask me for it anymore?"

He was angry, but I saw tears in the corners of his eyes.

"No, of course not," I replied. "I didn't want you to get hurt if things went badly during the meeting."

We stared at each other, which felt confrontational, so I sat down on the edge of the bed and waited for him to join me.

"While we were out there, Adam and Lorenzo got shot and Lorenzo almost died." I left out the fact that it seemed to me like he had died and that it was Giuliana that shot Adam. No need to make things worse.

"That's my point; I could have helped heal them if I had been there." As he said it, he seemed to realize that neither man was injured when we got back, and his face scrunched up in anger as he started to yell at me. "You healed them on your own, didn't you?"

I couldn't deny it, so I just stayed quiet and looked down at my hands.

"You don't even need me to help with that now, so what the hell am I doing here

I knew if I interrupted him to disagree that it would only make things worse, so I just accepted his anger.

"I'm so invaluable to you that you've excluded me from conversations that I would have been part of in the past. You don't need me to help you heal people, I can't change into anything else, I probably shouldn't have even awakened when I did…you probably did that for me too."

I hadn't considered it before he said it, but then I remembered that we hadn't changed until he grabbed me. If, like the healing, I needed energy from someone else to do the things I did, it was possible that I helped him awaken early. I didn't say that out loud, of course. I didn't have a death wish.

When I was able to reply, I showed as much sincerity as I could.

"I didn't go without you because I don't value you. I went without you because I didn't want to put you in danger. If something happened, and I died, you could still lead the pack at home, and sit on the Council here. If we both died, what would happen to our pack? They might split apart again, and I would hate to see that."

I wasn't sure how to proceed with the next part, so I looked away as I continued.

"In terms of what we can do, I have no idea why I can do certain things, and why you haven't been able to do them yet. The one thing I do know is that we both awakened early, and no matter the reason, we both got thrown into this situation together. I know it hasn't been easy for you, it hasn't been easy for me either, but having you with me has made everything better. If I didn't have you, I don't know what would have happened to me, but I can assure you that I probably would have died in that alley or somewhere else after being attacked. You're the reason I'm alive. Thinking of you kept me going and gave me the strength to heal when I shouldn't have been able to."

I realized I'd never said that out loud to anyone before and looked up to see how he took the news.

"What do you mean?" He asked, scooting a little closer to me on the bed as his anger slipped away.

"I could feel myself dying that night in the alley, but I thought about you and warmth spread through my body. I thought it was my body shutting down and my brain trying to make me comfortable as it happened. When I woke up in Lorelai's house the next day, I knew something else had taken place."

I reached out and took his hands in my own, rubbing my thumb across his knuckles.

"You don't need me to heal anymore, do you?" He asked. The anger was gone, and I could tell he was just asking to satisfy his curiosity.

"I guess, in certain circumstances, I can do some of it myself. With Lorenzo, I couldn't do anything on my own. It wasn't until Giuliana and Adam were connected to me that anything happened. I don't know what that means, and no one else can tell me how to control this, so I'm not sure what I need to heal people. What I do know is that you have helped me heal people in the past and touching you or thinking about you has saved me. It may not mean much to you, but I think that is something worth being proud of."

I smiled at him and hoped that this would help things get back to normal.

He smiled back, but softly pulled his hands away as he stood up to check his phone that had just alerted him to a waiting text message. When he read the message, his face morphed into a genuine look of happiness that I hadn't seen on him since the previous day, when Giuliana first spoke to us at the wall. He quickly replied and put his phone on silent before placing it back on his bedside table.

"Who was that?" I asked.

"Just a friend from home," he replied as he returned to the end of the bed, a little further away than he had been moments ago. "What do we do now?"

I shook my head, unsure how to respond. "I have no idea. I'm open to suggestions."

"What was the other thing they wanted?" he asked.

"Giuliana and Lorenzo?" I asked.

He nodded his head in response.

"Lorenzo is a rogue, and they want him to have a seat on the Council to represent the other rogue Awakened."

Gabriel's eyes opened wide with surprise. "And you're considering agreeing to that?"

270

His incredulity made me wonder if I had missed some key reasons there weren't any rogues on the Council currently.

"Why not?" I was truly curious and hoped Gabriel might be able to provide some insight into the situation that would help me decide.

"They're rogue for a reason, they refuse to follow pack rules, and cannot be trusted."

The way he said it was almost as if he were reciting something he'd memorized as a child.

"Right, Lorenzo was kicked out of his pack for refusing to kill Giuliana, his wife. I kicked people out of our pack for refusing to allow their children to be trained by Brent and Adam. They all refused to follow pack or alpha instructions, but they did so to protect their families from something. That doesn't make them bad or untrustworthy, does it?"

I hoped that if I used people he knew as an example he would be able to consider them as individuals, and not just generic rogues.

His resolve seemed to wane a little. "I still think you're going to have an incredibly difficult time convincing the rest of the Council that they should share their power with any rogue, let alone one who is married to a Pressor."

He made an excellent point there, and I wondered how I would even bring up the topic. While I considered my options, voices from the house and property began to get louder. Gabriel and I looked at each other confused about what had happened, but as we stood to go to look out the window, the glass shattered. Gabriel jumped, and I covered my face in case any glass went flying into the room.

"What the hell?"

"I'm not sure…" Gabriel started to get closer to the window, but someone pounded on the door to the room, and we both jumped. "Come in," he said.

The Greek opened the door and didn't look pleased to see that I was also inside but pretended like he hadn't noticed.

"You need to leave the room, now!" He yelled at Gabriel and motioned for him to follow him out into the hallway.

As he walked past me, I grabbed Gabriel's arm and stopped him from going any further.

"We'll catch up with you, go on ahead."

The Greek glared at me but ran toward the stairway.

"I still don't trust him," I whispered. "Someone in this house killed Ouriel and probably Deanna, and I don't think we should be alone with any of them right now."

"Caleb," he said, his eyes avoiding mine. "I appreciate your concern, but I think you're too paranoid. We've talked more since the Council meeting, and he seems like a good guy who's just concerned about protecting the people he cares about. He reminds me of you."

Gabriel slipped out of my grasp and rushed toward the door then turned around to look at me again. "Are you coming?"

"Yeah, but I'm going to make sure Giuliana and Lorenzo are okay. I'll meet you downstairs."

With that, Gabriel disappeared down the hall, and I ran to find our guests.

I knocked loudly on my bedroom door. "Giuliana, Lorenzo, are you in there?" I waited a few seconds and then tried the door handle, which was still locked. I knocked again and raised my voice. "It's Caleb, let me in, please."

"Caleb?" Adam was headed down the hall toward me. "What are you still doing up here?"

"I'm trying to find Giuliana and Lorenzo, have you seen them?" I had a bad feeling in my stomach, which got worse as I heard screams and gunshots. Adam ran toward me and kicked the door as hard as he could. The frame splintered, but the door didn't open so he tried it again. This time the door swung open, and we were able to get inside. When we did, I looked around quickly and could tell they weren't inside anymore.

"Caleb, look at the window." Adam pointed to the shards of glass that were all over the floor and the curtain that moved back and forth in the breeze.

"Do you think they broke it to get out of the room?" I asked, unsure why they wouldn't have used the door.

"I don't think so," he said. "It looks like something came through the window from outside ,"he pointed to the the broken glass on the floor. "I guess they could have left through the window if they were able to open it, but I'm not sure why they would have gone outside when we're under attack."

"Whatever the reason, we don't have time to waste, they're not in here anymore and sticking around isn't going to help anything. Let's go!"

We ran out of the room and down the hallway to the stairs. When I got to the landing, I could see that whoever had gotten onto the property made it into the house already.

There were bullet holes in the walls, broken glass on the floor and the scent of gunpowder filled the air.

"Where is everyone?"

"We were able to get the Pressors back outside, but more keep coming," Adam responded as he ran past me, down the stairs and toward the front door. I followed closely, lookingaround for anyone who might still be in the house along the way.

Once outside, the sound of the fight had changed from shouting to growling and the whistling of bullets from guns with silencers. It was hard to tell what was going on in the chaos, but Adam changed and ran toward a group of Pressors who moved around toward the back of the house. I changed quickly, my fear and anger urging me on, and I took off into the fray.

A bullet whipped past my body as I ran toward the nearest Pressor, who looked to be about the same age as Adam but was not quite as large. He aimed again, but before he was able to pull the trigger I launched myself at him, and my front paws landed his chest pushing him backward and making him drop the gun. He refused to give up and grabbed a long knife from a sheathe on his hip. As he tried to stab me with it, I bit down hard on his wrist and winced as the small bones cracked and he yelled in pain. I didn't think he'd be able to do much damage to anyone else, but I grabbed the knife with my mouth anyway and carried it a few hundred yards away before dropping it in a bush.

As I turned around, the whistling of two bullets stopped suddenly, and my hip and back felt like they were on fire. I yelped loudly and looked up to see another Pressor aiming his gun at me. I limped as quickly as I could, to get to safety, but he fired another bullet, which hit my stomach and caused me to collapse from pain. I looked around, my fear helped bring things into intense focus, but the other Awakened were too far away to do anything for me at this point. I watched him get closer and saw the sadistic satisfaction that he seemed to take from the pain he had caused. I tried to focus on healing myself, but I knew I couldn't shift into human form again, and back into a wolf quickly enough to do any good. Without any other options, I did the one thing I was told I should never do; I simply closed the wounds to avoid bleeding out.

Once I stopped bleeding, the Pressor's smile faltered when he tried to figure out what happened. As he did, a loud bang erupted behind him, and he looked down at his chest, where his blood now spread. He turned around to look at the person who had shot him, and before he fell over, he asked them something I didn't understand.

"Zašto?"

"Zašto ne?" In an instant, Giuliana was by my side and stuck her hand out carefully. "Please don't bite me."

Chapter Twenty-Eight

"I'm not going to hurt you, I promise." She spoke in a soothing voice as she approached me with caution. Knowing she'd never seen me in my wolf form, there was no way for her to know that I recognized her. "Are you okay?"

I whined softly and tried to stand up; the pain from the gunshot wounds was intense, and I felt like I might pass out. The fighting continuing around me, I knew I couldn't give up. I forced myself to remain conscious and pushed through the pain to move out of the open. Giuliana looked confused as I struggled to move, and I assumed it was related to the fact that, as far as she could tell, I was healed. Once I was hidden behind some bushes, I tried to focus on healing the internal damage but each time I tried, there was a feeling of pressure, followed immediately by pain. Giuliana continued to watch me struggle until something in the distance caught her eye, and she seemed to forget that I was there.

"I must go. I'm sorry," she said as she took off toward whatever she'd seen.

Once she was gone, I peeked through the bushes and looked for Gabriel and Adam. I saw a black wolf run past, but it was hard to tell, based on the speed, whether it was Gabriel. Adam was nowhere to be seen but may have still been dealing with the Pressors on the other side of the house. I saw another Pressor coming to check on the one Giuliana had shot earlier, and realized I had nowhere to hide, and running away didn't seem feasible at this point. When she got closer to the body, I froze to try to avoid detection, but she looked right at me and without hesitation, shot me.

I felt the pressure of the bullet as it ripped through my body, but the pain was miraculously absent, due to the darkness that swallowed me up at that same moment. I relaxed into it, thinking my body had somehow forced the change to occur to repair the internal damage I had simply covered up. After a few seconds, I realized I was not regaining my senses, which meant something was seriously wrong. In the distance, a faint light caught my attention, which meant that I was at least able to see again; that was a start.

I moved in the direction of the light and realized it was the mirror from my dreams. It was suspended in mid-air and waited for my approach. I walked toward it and hoped that this time there would be an answer instead of confusion. When I was close enough to see my reflection, I realized that I looked a little different than I had the last time I'd had this dream. It was almost as if I could see the power I possessed as a physical manifestation. My eyes appeared brighter and my skin, which I had joked would glow in the dark, seemed to give off a slight radiance. Nothing that would have been noticeable to most people, but it made me hard to ignore in a pitch-black dream.

I could only see my torso in the reflection, so I looked down at the rest of my actual body and realized that the wounds I closed had re-opened and were bleeding again. There was no pain, and it wasn't as grotesque in the dream as I imagined it would have been in real life, so I watched as the little rivulets of red streamed down toward the ground. I could see the one on my stomach in the mirror and got closer to examine it better.

When I did, I was able to see that somehow my tissues were pulling themselves back together, and I heard a pop when a rib that had been broken snapped back into place. I watched the healing take place, in more detail than I ever had before. It was like watching a time-lapse video of a mushroom sprouting. At first, nothing happened, then suddenly it sprung to life and stretched upward toward the sun. The only different was that I watched my wound get smaller, rather than watching it grow.

Once I had healed completely, I looked back up at my face and smiled, but my reflection didn't mirror the emotion on my face. Instead, he stared blankly, examining me. It appeared he were trying to decide what to do next. When I opened my mouth to say something, his opened as well, so I closed mine to listen, and he closed his as well. Frustrated, I started to say something again and stopped when he also looked ready to speak.

"I guess it is just my reflection." I spoke aloud but watched him as his lips formed different shapes. He was saying something else entirely. I stared for a bit longer, until I saw another faint light begin to shine behind me. Turning, I saw that another mirror had appeared, this one larger than the last. The mirror I used disappeared into the darkness, so I had no choice but to walk to the new mirror. The face that stared back at me was the one I'd only ever seen in pictures at Lorelai's house and a few of my previous dreams.

My birth father smiled at me as I approached, but other than that, his movements matched my own. I looked down at my physical body to see that I still looked the same as I always had. When I looked back up, I noticed that his mouth was moving, but I couldn't hear anything he said.

"What did you say?" I asked and hoped he might be able to speak louder. "I can't hear you." I watched his mouth closely, hoping that I could suddenly pick up lip-reading skills, but no matter how hard I concentrated, I could only guess at what he said.

He reached out and touched the mirror as he continued to speak, undeterred by my requests for him to repeat himself or speak louder. I placed my hand on the same part of the mirror as his and when I did, I could finally hear him.

He continued to speak as though I'd been listening the whole time.

"...your own. You have more strength than you give yourself credit for, and I know you'll do great things with it. I'm sorry I couldn't be there to help you through this transition, but when you awaken, you will find that the pack is incredibly supportive, and they will take care of you."

"What do you mean, 'when I awaken'? I've already done it." I was confused by his message, but my question didn't stop him from continuing.

"Your mother and I will always love you. Giving you up is the hardest thing we will ever have to do, but it is what we felt was best considering the circumstances. When you return, you'll be expected to take on a lot of responsibility, but I know you can do it."

He finished speaking and removed his hand from the mirror.

"Wait, I have so many questions for you!" I yelled into the mirror but watched him fade away, and my actual reflection reappear in the spot it should have been all along. I waited to see if something more would happen, but the mirror faded away and left me alone in the darkness again.

I walked into the void for what seemed like hours, and finally found a third mirror that also appeared to be suspended. I couldn't see anything else around it but it was tall enough to allow me to see my entire body in its smooth reflection. I noticed that I had somehow picked up clothing along my journey, which didn't make a lot of sense, but my dreams never seemed to make any sense. When I got closer, the shape of my reflection began to change.

My chest and stomach expanded to give me a more barrel-chested appearance, and my torso and legs shortened, so I had to look down to see my reflection's new face. It was like looking at a younger version of myself, except for my face, which had also begun to change shape. Facial hair sprouted and gradually faded from dark brown to gray and finally stopped when it was white. My laugh lines on my face deepened and became more pronounced, and other expression lines that only existed when I made faces became a permanent fixture in my reflection.

When I stopped looking at the specific details of the reflection, I realized that the face that looked back at me was another that I recognized and was equally surprised to see it in my dream. Standing before me in the mirror was no longer a smaller version of myself, but rather a full-sized version of Ouriel, and he looked a lot better than the last time I'd seen him. When he started to open his mouth, I quickly moved my hand to touch the glass of the mirror. When he pressed his hand against mine, the coldness of the mirror disappeared, and I could feel the heat coming from his palm. It moved up my arm and through the rest of body in slow waves. Despite my fear and confusion, I left my hand on the mirror, not wanting to miss anything he might have to say to me.

"Ouriel, do you know who killed you?" I looked at him expectantly. And when he nodded that he did I felt excitement at being able to stop the killings. "Who was it? Please tell me!" I pleaded with him.

He regarded me for a moment and then pointed directly at me. I was so confused about what he meant that I thought for sure something had happened behind me. When I looked, there was still a vast expanse of nothingness as far as I could see. I looked back in the mirror, thinking perhaps he hadn't understood me.

"No, I need to know who poisoned you. Please, you have to tell me so I can stop them from doing it again."

I spoke slower and louder in case he couldn't hear me from his side of the mirror very well. Still, he continued to point at me calmly, as though he were suggesting I was the killer.

"I don't understand what you mean… Why do you keep pointing at me? What did I do?" I placed my other hand on the glass and watched as his hand followed mine perfectly. When they met, there was a bright light that filled the void completely, and I had to shield my eyes. As I pulled my hands off the mirror, it imploded, and shards of glass rushed away from me into nothingness. The light remained, however, and I was able to see that once again I was alone in the now lit space, which appeared to expand infinitely in every direction.

I reached up to rub my face, but when I felt a full beard, I pulled my hands away and looked down at them. I turned them over a few times, sure that what I had seen was not there, but no matter how hard I tried, the hands never resembled my own. Off to my right, I heard a sound that reminded me of tiny bells ringing and realized that the mirror was reforming itself. Slowly I walked toward it and when the face that looked back at me reflected the fear I felt, I screamed as loud as I could.

* * *

I woke up and realized I was still lying on the ground behind the bush, but the pain that kept me from healing myself was gone, and I felt better than I had in a long time. My heart hammered in my chest, but when I realized it was all a dream, I was able to calm down quickly. I had shifted back to my human self while I was out. I guessed that was what had caused me to heal in my dream.

When I looked through the bushes, I could see that, for the most part, the Pressors seemed to have lost the fight. Many of them appeared to be dead, or had already fled the property. Those that remained were being surrounded by Awakened and would be dealt with soon enough. I felt like it was safe enough to come out from my hiding spot to see if there was anything else I could do. I stood up slowly to make sure I didn't pass out and then stepped into the clearing. I saw Maeve shift nearby and walked up to her to make sure she was okay. She looked in my direction, and her face paled immediately.

"Ouriel? How is that possible?" Her voice was quiet, and she seemed like she didn't believe what she was seeing.

I turned around quickly, afraid that somehow Ouriel had followed me out of my dream. When I saw that there was nothing there, I turned back around to face Maeve and realized she was staring at me.

"Ouriel, how are you alive?" She walked toward me and took my face gently in her hands.

I felt her hands brush against my facial hair, and I started to panic. Somehow the dream had caused me to shift into Ouriel's human form, and I had no idea what to do about it.

"Oh Ouriel, you had me so worried!" Maeve continued. "Where have you been? What happened to you? Why would you let me think you were dead!?" The questions flowed out of her faster than I could respond, so I just waited for her to stop talking before I responded.

"Maeve, I know this is going to be hard to understand, but I am not Ouriel."

She looked confused.

"I'm not sure exactly how it happened, but I woke up in the bushes, and I looked," I motioned to my face. "like this."

"Then who are you?" She asked.

"Caleb."

Her eyes got wide, and she stepped back a little to look at my whole body.

"Caleb, what did you do?" Even though she had said my name, it was clear from her tone that the question was rhetorical, as she continued to examine as much of me as possible. "Well, the first thing we need to do is get you some clothes that fit." She motioned to my body and raised an eyebrow at me.

I realized that when I'd shifted at the beginning of the fight, I hadn't prepared for shifting back afterward, so I had no clothes outside the house. It didn't matter because none of my clothes would fit me if I was in Ouriel's body.

"Can you get something from Ouriel's room for me?" I realized I had never been inside anyone else's room except for Gabriel and Adam's. I didn't even know where the rest of the Council and their various attendants slept.

"Of course! Wait right here, I'll be back as quickly as I can." She changed into her wolf and ran back toward the house, careful to avoid anyone else along the way.

Chapter Twenty-Nine

While she was gone, I ducked behind the same bushes I'd used before and watched as one by one, the wolves in the yard changed back into their human selves. Giuliana had suggested the Pressors might use the police to try to round up the rest of the Awakened. Getting rid of the bodies, Pressor and Awakened alike, was the best possible response to this attack.

Stephen and Kenai moved the bodies of the deceased to the furthest part of the yard from the main entrance. Jae was using a small hose to rinse something off her skin. From what I could see, it appeared to be a combination of blood and something thicker. I didn't look closer. Jusuf helped The Greek clean up broken glass and other debris from the yard. Without Ouriel around, Jusuf must have decided The Greek was the next most important Awakened to look after. Given my suspicions, that made me even more uncomfortable around The Greek. He looked over in my direction as if he felt my stare, but I stayed hidden.

If Maeve was any indication of how the others would react to seeing a fake Ouriel again, I had to make sure to stay away from as many of them as possible. As I had that thought, I heard someone walk up to the other side of the bushes and assumed it was Maeve with my clothing, so I jumped a little when the voice didn't match.

"Caleb, can you please come help me with something?" Adam's voice was strained, but he also sounded exhausted.

I didn't know what to do so I just stayed silent and thought maybe he would go away.

"Caleb, I know you're back there. I can smell you and hear you breathing. C'mon, it'll only take a minute with two of us."

I continued to sit as quietly as I could, but I knew there was no way I would get out of this situation.

It was good to know that I at least still smelled like myself, but that didn't help me feel any better.

"Adam, I want you to promise me you won't react to me when you come around the bush," I spoke quietly, trying not to attract anyone else's attention.

"What's up with your voice?" He asked, ignoring my request as he started to walk back to where I was hiding.

"Stop!" I raised my voice, and he stopped where he was. "Promise me you won't react," I said again, with more urgency.

"Okay fine, I promise," he said as he walked the rest of the way around the bush. "You know, you really need to get over this whole nudity thing…" He trailed off as soon as he saw me and his mouth dropped open.

"I told you not to react!" I whisper-yelled at him. "Get down before someone else sees you!"

He crouched down but kept his distance from me. "What happened?" he asked. "That *is* you, right?" He looked unsure as he continued to stare at me.

"Yes, it's me. I don't know what happened, I just woke up and looked like this." I gestured to my body.

"How the hell did you fall asleep in the middle of an attack?!" That sounded more like Adam.

"It's not like I decided it was a good time for a nap! I got shot three times and couldn't heal in time, so I just closed the skin over the top of it to stop the blood."

He gave me a severe look.

"Then, I got shot again, and I think my body went into shock, or I passed out from the pain. Either way, when I came to again, I had somehow shifted into Ouriel."

"Has anyone else seen you yet? Or am I the first?"

"Maeve saw me when I first woke up because I didn't realize I had changed. Right now, she's getting me some of Ouriel's clothing, so I can get out of here."

I looked back toward the house to see if she had come back outside yet, and then around the yard at the others to make sure no one else was headed our direction.

"Why not just shift back into yourself?" Adam's question was so simple that I couldn't believe I hadn't tried to shift back yet.

I gave him a sheepish look. "I honestly hadn't thought about it. I don't know how I got into this shape, but I hadn't thought that changing back would have been as easy as thinking about my real body."

I concentrated on shifting and imagined my body lengthening and thinning out to return to my actual shape. I could feel the change start to happen, and then there was an extreme amount of pain in my back, and I had to cover my mouth with both hands to muffle my scream.

Adam looked at me with concern evident in his eyes. "What just happened?"

"I don't know. I tried to shift, but something's very wrong with my back." Now that I had stopped trying to change, my back began to relax, and I was able to breathe.

"I don't want to try that again for a little bit. Maybe I just need some time in this body before I have the energy to shift."

"Caleb, you don't need extra energy to shift. Your body can shift as many times a day as it needs to, there's not a rest period required." Adam looked at me as if I should already have known that, and maybe he'd mentioned it at some point and I had forgotten, but that didn't mean I was going to try it.

"Be that as it may, I'm still not trying it again until I get some real rest." I was about to change the subject when Maeve appeared again with some clothing and shifted our attention.

"Oh, Adam," she said. "I see you've gotten a look at Ouriel." She smiled when she said it, but there was a hint of sadness in her eyes.

He just nodded and passed the clothing she had brought to me so I could get dressed. While she'd been inside, Maeve had grabbed some clothes for herself and was dressed again, which meant Adam was the only one who was still missing his clothes.

"I'll be right back," he said and ran toward the house.

"Is everything okay over here?" Maeve asked quietly. "I hope I didn't interrupt anything important."

"Not at all," I assured her. "We were just waiting for you to get back with my clothes." I looked around to make sure Adam wasn't on his way back and then spoke again. "Maeve, do you ever have to take a break between shifting before you're able to do it again?"

"No, I'm easily able to shift as often as needed. Why do you ask?"

"No reason," I replied. "I was just curious." I sat there quietly for a moment and then thought of something else. "Did Ouriel ever have trouble with shifting? Or maybe some chronic back pain you were aware of?"

She considered it for a second before responding, "I don't think he had any issues either. Why are you asking? Did something happen, Caleb?" She crouched down and adopted a motherly look on her face.

"It's just that," I wasn't sure how to explain what the pain felt like. "I tried to shift back into my actual body, and it started out okay. Then it was like something in my spine was stuck. I felt like I was being torn in half."

Not having experienced that feeling personally, I didn't know if that was accurate, but it seemed to explain the level of pain I felt.

"Oh my, that isn't good at all." She rubbed her hand along my arm and smiled sadly at me.

I appreciated her attempt to comfort me, but I still didn't know what had kept me from shifting again, so I just focused on getting dressed. By the time Adam returned, Maeve and I began to talk about how the evening had gone south so fast. According to her, there was no warning about the attack until the Pressors had already gotten inside the walls of the property, something that should have been impossible. What it suggested to me was that Giuliana was right, and someone inside the house was responsible for the deaths of Deanna and Ouriel. That same person could also have made it possible for the Pressors to get inside the walls without being noticed. If I couldn't shift out of this body now, I might as well make the best of things and see who was most upset by the return of the former leader of the Council.

When Adam walked up to the bush, we looked at each other. It turned out that Adam had a similar plan, which involved me pretending to be Ouriel to make things a lot less comfortable for everyone on the property. If he were somehow able to live through the attack and point fingers, no one would be safe. Of course, I had no idea who killed Ouriel, and couldn't point any fingers, but I'd have to deal with that when we got to that point.

Maeve and Adam helped the others to make sure everything was cleaned up in the yard, and then got everyone inside where Maeve would call a Council meeting immediately. That would give me the chance to slip into the house without being noticed, and hopefully give us an opportunity to see everyone react at once. Whoever was guilty would be the most shocked, or at least that was the idea.

I waited silently as everyone filed back into the house and gave them a few minutes to get cleaned up and changed before the meeting. When I was sure no one would be walking around the central part of the house, I ran to the front door as quickly as I could. I listened at the door for a few more minutes, and when there were no sounds of voices or movement I crept into the foyer and toward the Council room.

As I got closer, I could hear everyone as they talked over one another, but finally The Greek spoke over everyone and got them all to settle. Based on what I could hear, it sounded like they were already trying to figure out what caused the security system to fail, but no one was able to offer up any ideas. Since The Greek was the one who posed the question, he was free from having to provide any suggestions and was able to deflect blame as well. I had no idea what I would say when I walked into the room, but I had to figure something out quickly, or I was bound to get caught waiting outside the doors.

"Jusuf, will you escort Giuliana and Lorenzo out of the room, please? We need to discuss a few things without them."

The Greek spoke as though he knew Jusuf would do precisely as he'd requested without any question. I heard the door on the opposite side of the room open and listened as feet shuffled out before the door closed again.

"And will someone please tell me where Caleb is? He's the reason we're in this whole mess in the first place!"

This was the opportunity I needed to make sure I got everyone's reaction at once. I turned the handles and pushed open the doors and walked into the room as though I owned it.

"Actually," I said. "I believe I am the reason we're all in this predicament." I looked around the room quickly and attempted to take in the honest reactions of everyone as they saw who stood before them.

Mouths dropped open, and the Council stared at me in disbelief, The Greek was especially surprised, and I noticed that he'd taken Ouriel's seat at the head of the table. No one said a word, so I took the opportunity to speed the process along.

"I assume you're all surprised to see me, especially since one of you," I looked at The Greek, and then slowly at the rest of the Council. "tried to kill me! Now that I'm back, I think we all need to have a little conversation about what has happened while I've been recovering."

I hoped that the fact that I was wearing his clothing and looked like him would keep them all from noticing that I still smelled like myself.

The Greek stood up then and moved toward me quickly. I looked over at Adam and Maeve, to get one of them to stop him from attacking me. They looked back at me, helpless, as he had already wrapped his arms around my body and squeezed. I waited for the pressure to increase, but it never did, and I realized that tears spilled down his face as he held on to me.

"I'm so glad you're okay, I was devastated when they took you away, I thought we'd lost you for good." He pulled back and wiped his eyes then smiled at me.

For the first time since I arrived in Croatia and met him, he showed me his vulnerable side, and I felt terrible for all the negative thoughts I'd had about him. I felt guilty pretending to be Ouriel to catch him, and when he realized that Ouriel was still gone, he'd be even more heartbroken. I smiled back at him and grabbed his shoulders before I replied.

"I'm sorry for putting you in this situation, and I'm sorry for the pain I've caused. I never meant to hurt any of you."

I looked at the other Council members and realized that none of them looked particularly upset that Ouriel seemed to have returned. Most of them looked happy about it, and I felt like I'd made a colossal mistake. The door on the other side of the room started to open, and I felt another twinge of guilt because I knew I was about to disappoint even more people.

Jusuf walked in, and his eyes went almost immediately to The Greek and me. When he saw me, a flash of something crossed his face so quickly that I couldn't identify it. Then he yelled out something in Croatian that I didn't really understand.

"Demoni, ja ću te ubiti sve!"

When he pulled his gun out and pointed it at me, I got the idea that he wasn't welcoming me home, and I fell to the floor as quickly as I could. Jusuf fired four shots at The Greek and me, three of which hit the wall behind where I had been standing moments before. The fourth hit The Greek in the shoulder as he moved to try to protect me.

I heard a growl, and then something snapped, and the room was silent. When I stood up, Jusuf was on the ground with his neck twisted at an awkward angle, and Lorenzo stood in his place.

"Is everyone okay?" He asked, as he looked around the room.

Everyone nodded and looked as shocked as I felt. The Greek held onto my arm, as if he was trying to steady me, and I realized I was swaying back and forth slightly. He winced as he reached over with his other arm and looked down at the blood that spread across his shirt. He stuck a finger into the wound, and it emerged with a bullet and the sharpened nail he used to dig it out.

"That's better," he said as the damaged skin began to close up. I must have wobbled again from being so close to the action and he turned back to me again. "Ouriel, are you okay?"

"I'm fine, just a little shaken. I think I need to sit down for a moment." I pulled out the nearest chair and began to lower myself into it, but my back went into spasm halfway down. The pain was so intense that I lost my grip and fell the rest of the way into the seat. When I did, I felt a significant pop in my spine, and something dislodged and felt like it was sticking out of the skin on my back.

I cried out in pain and looked at Adam and Maeve. "I think we have a problem."

They jumped up, and Adam pushed The Greek out of the way.

"Caleb what's wrong?"

"Caleb?" The Greek looked from Adam to Maeve and then finally at me.

Adam shrugged a little, looked at me and then responded. "Whoops."

Chapter Thirty

I knew the time had come for me to confess to everyone what had happened, but I was also in so much pain that I could hardly think.

"I'm not actually Ouriel. I'm sorry for tricking you, but I was trying to find out who killed him, and I figured this way would be the quickest. Can we just put all of that on hold? Because I feel like my spine is trying to escape from my body."

Even though they knew it was me, the way the Council reacted was almost as though Ouriel himself were the one in pain. They immediately jumped into action, helped me onto the table, where I laid down on my stomach, so they had access to the bulging disc in my spine.

Maeve leaned over me and said something in Gaelic I didn't understand, and the others seemed to be focused on something specific on my lower back.

"What's happening? Can you tell what happened? Am I going to be okay?" I asked as I started to freak out a little more.

"Just hold still," Kenai said. "I'm going to make an incision so we can get a better look at whatever is sticking out of your back. I'm afraid there isn't any time for painkillers or numbing agents, so you're going to feel everything. Just make sure you don't move."

A cold sweat broke out over my entire body, and my stomach felt like it was tying itself into knots. I had already begun to panic when he told me that there was no anesthetic to help with the pain, knowing that I had to stay perfectly still while he cut into me felt like an impossible request.

"Stephen and Adam, please hold down his legs. Gabriel and Jae, hold his arms steady, and Maeve and The Greek, please keep his torso steady. This is going to be painful for him, and he's going to move a lot. We need to keep him still so that I don't accidentally cut through his spinal cord."

As the last words left his mouth, everyone got into their places, and I felt like I was going to throw up. I could feel the sweat begin to bead up on my forehead, and my cheeks flushed red with heat.

"Isn't there any other way to do this?" I pleaded.

"I'm sorry Caleb, but no, there isn't." Without another word, Kenai took a knife and sliced into the skin along my spine. At first the pain was manageable, and felt more like pressure, followed by a highly uncomfortable burn. It wasn't until he spread the incision open that I began to squirm, and the pain really set it.

"Stop!" I screamed as loud as I could. "Please stop, I can't take it anymore!" I begged for him to leave me alone and for Adam and Gabriel to help me, but the cutting and restraint continued until Kenai hit something with the tip of his knife. I screamed louder than I had ever screamed in my life.

"I think I found the problem." Kenai remained calm despite my screams. "I'm going to try to remove it now, so everyone, hold him as tightly as you can."

"Remove what? Don't I need all of that?" Kenai didn't respond, I could feel him cutting away at the connective tissue, and it felt like he was carving into the muscle along my spine. I was sure that at any moment I would lose feeling in some part of my body. When that didn't happen, I began to hope to lose feeling in some part of my body, because at least then I could focus on something other than the pain. That gave me an idea that I was crazy enough from pain to say out loud.

"Someone bite me, hard!"

"Gladly." No one seemed surprised when The Greek offered to inflict pain on me. He bit down on my shoulder, and I could tell that he had changed his teeth to make them sharper.

I let out a few expletives and screamed again. The new pain pulled my attention away, and I could feel the heat in my face diminishing. I was able to focus on healing just that part of my body, which took my mind off what was happening along my back.

"Thank you!" I said, as the tiny holes in my shoulder closed.

"It was my pleasure," he replied. I believed it.

"Just about done," Kenai said, which brought my attention back to the pain in my back, but it has decreased slightly, or my body had adapted to it somehow.

"Caleb," he asked carefully. "Did you close up unhealed wounds?" Kenai sounded curious, but also like he already knew the answer.

"Yes, I'd been shot too many times for me to heal quickly, so I just closed them. Why?" I asked, afraid I'd done some permanent damage, or would be stuck in this body forever.

"You trapped the bullets in your body, so when you healed, your muscles formed around the bullet. It was pressed up against your spine in between two vertebrae. If I hadn't removed it, you might not have ever been able to shift again."

With a final slice, he removed the bullet and his hands from my back. "I've gotten it out now. You can go ahead and heal."

While everyone continued to hold me in place, I pulled their energy into my body and closed the incision, from the inside this time. I made sure it was completely healed before I focused on shifting back into my normal body. Both felt effortless thanks to the extra boost from five other alphas and Adam. When I finished, I slowly rolled over and looked at everyone, who just stared at me, with wide eyes.

"I just saw it happen, and I still don't believe it." Jae took the seat nearest where she was standing, and the rest of the Council seemed to follow her lead.

"Have you ever seen something like that before?" Stephen asked the group, but no one spoke up.

"Well, there is a first time for everything," Maeve responded, as she helped me off the table. She laughed and patted me gently on the back as I took the seat next to her.

I looked over at Gabriel, and he was focused on anyone else in the room but me, which made me think he had purposely avoided my gaze. I didn't know if there was a way to fix that aspect of our relationship, but I hoped we could.

"I think it's time we moved on to other topics. We know now who killed Ouriel, and I'd guess that Jusuf was also the one who killed Deanna. But does anyone know why he would suddenly turn on Ouriel after so many years?"

"I may have an answer to that question actually," Giuliana said from the door on the opposite side of the room. "If I may," she hesitated and waited for a signal to continue.

"Please tell us what you know," Maeve spoke to her as she would anyone else. It gave me hope that the rest of the Council might be willing to bend the rules for Lorenzo as well.

"Well, just before Lorenzo stopped him, he said 'Demons, I will kill you all.' The Pressors believe the Awakened are demons that have taken over the bodies of people and it's their job to stop them before they spread. I can't say for sure if this was the exact situation, but in other parts of the world, Pressors are taught from a very young age how to blend into Awakened social structures. That's one of the methods they use to infiltrate packs. They either begin to work for the Awakened and become someone they trust or as children they form friendships with Awakened children. This gives them easy access to valuable information through the innocent that their parents can use to attack the pack."

I listened in shock to the lengths Pressors went to to get close to Awakened, just to kill them. I began to question all the relationships I had growing up. Were any of the kids who teased me at school Pressors, who were raised to hate me? And then the worst thought of all popped into my head, what if Megan was only my friend to get close to the pack when they eventually pulled me back into their ranks? She had immediately gone after Adam even though he'd pinned her to a wall the first time they met. She also accepted the whole 'wolf thing' a little easier than I thought she would.

Other situations from the past kept flooding my mind and made me question everything she and I had ever been through together. Fortunately, The Greek said something, and my attention snapped back to the issues at hand.

"It is very likely then that Jusuf was a Pressor all along and was close to Ouriel to deliver key information to the rest of the Pressors in Croatia. When Caleb and Gabriel joined the Council after the death of the female alpha, he must have panicked or been given instructions to take Ouriel out for some reason. Whatever the situation, it is done now."

The Greek was back to his stoic self and acted as though he didn't break down emotionally when he thought Ouriel had returned.

"Now that we have figured that out, I have to bring up another touchy subject that I hope you will all listen to with an open mind."

I nodded to Giuliana who had stepped back to stand next to Lorenzo again and smiled.

"As you may remember, I told Giuliana that we would protect her from attack, but that we would discuss her other request later. The time has come to discuss that request, and I would like to say that I support this idea. Giuliana, can you please tell the rest of the Council what it is that you have asked for?"

She and Lorenzo stepped further into the room and grabbed onto each other's hands before she began.

"Lorenzo does not have a pack because he refused to kill me when the Pressors I was associated with killed his family. As a result, we are both on the run from the Pressors and his pack. If either discover us, we will certainly be killed."

"We have already committed to protecting you from the Awakened here in Croatia, what more do you want from this body?" Stephen spoke up from the other end of the table.
"In order to ensure that we are always as safe from other packs as well, we are requesting that Lorenzo be given a seat on the Council in order to represent other rogue Awakened in the world."

After she had said it, Giuliana held her breath and waited. The silence in the room stretched out for a few seconds and then the opinions of the Council began.

"Giuliana, Lorenzo, I think we need some time to discuss this. Adam, will you please wait outside the chamber with them while we discuss?" Maeve was friendly in her address, and I still wasn't sure how she felt about the situation.

Once they had stepped out of the room and Adam shut the door, the discussion began in earnest. Most of the other alphas didn't want to see a rogue member of the Awakened on the Council because they were not responsible for any specific group of Awakened. There was no way to guarantee that the other rogues would abide by Council rules even with a rogue member.

"What does it change if rogue's follow Council rules?" I asked. "What happens now if they disobey?"

"They're dealt with," The Greek replied.

"Exactly, and that wouldn't change if there were a rogue on the Council or not," I chose not to get into the details regarding what 'dealt with' meant, since I'd already seen Council 'justice' first hand.

He was silent and Jae smirked, but it faded as quickly as it had appeared.

"What benefit is there to adding a rogue if they don't get the others in line?" Kenai asked.

"I'm not sure," I admitted, "but I assume that giving a voice to the voiceless, even if it's not a representative voice, will give us better insight into how we make and enforce Council law."

"You think we're out of touch with the non-pack Awakened?" Stephen asked, his eyes narrowed and teeth bared.

"I think you're all from packs with clear territories, and you've always been in packs, with the support and structure that they provide. But what if, I can in here and cast you out of your packs," I paused to look them all in the eyes, "and no one you know or loved could ever come to your support again?"

"That's not how it works—" Stephen began.

"I don't care how it works, I'm posing a question. What would you do if you suddenly lost everyone and everything that you'd ever known, and now you had no voice or control. And anyone who recognized you for what you were, despised or pitied you for being alone." The thoughts of the family from the party Gabriel and I pulled together, whom I'd forced out popped in my head, and I could feel the emotion of that moment fill my voice as I continued. "If you were ever in that position, and you knew that on the Council, there was someone you could reach out to, wouldn't you try? Wouldn't you want to feel that connection again, even if only for a moment?" I sat back in my seat and let them think it over.

After a few minutes, Jae spoke up. "What do you propose his role might be?"

The rest of the conversation lasted for twenty minutes, with ideas being presented, argued, and finally agreed upon. Once the Council reached their final decision, Giuliana, Lorenzo, and Adam were invited back into the meeting.

The Greek addressed Lorenzo and Giuliana as the official voice of the Council, and I for one was happy to let him do that.

"Based on the issues discussed by the Council about the potential benefits and drawbacks of extending a permanent seat to a rogue member of the Awakened, we have decided that there was not enough benefit to do so."

I looked at Lorenzo's face as The Greek shared the information with him, and though he was obviously very bothered by the decision, he simply nodded before responding.

"I understand your decision, and I appreciate you considering the possibility at all." He turned to Giuliana, who was shaking her head in disbelief and hugged her tightly.

"But," The Greek continued. "I believe I can speak on behalf of the rest of the Council when I say that the help you and Giuliana provided to us during the attacks on this house and this Council were beyond the call of duty for a rogue. We have created a position that is specific to you as an advisor to the Council. It will be your position for as long as you want it, and you will be a special advisor on rogue related issues. Because you do not represent a pack and do not have an actual position on the Council, you have no reason to be the focus of negative attention from any Awakened, pack related or otherwise."

As he finished, The Greek smiled at them. "We hope this is a compromise you can agree to."

When they received the good news, Lorenzo and Giuliana hugged each other again, but this time for a very different reason and the mood in the room became more positive. Ultimately, it was decided that the help they had given during the fight against the Pressors, and the information Giuliana was able to provide as a former Pressor herself, was too valuable to let go. The most extensive debate was the role they would play in the future of the Council, with many still determining how a non-pack affiliated member could be appointed. The idea of the special advisor was presented by Gabriel and ended up being selected as the way to accomplish what they were asking of the Council while still protecting the rules that govern its representatives.

Once they were invited back, Giuliana and Lorenzo sat down at the table while we discussed the next important issue that had to be addressed. Where the Council would be located now that Ouriel had died, and the Pressors had attacked. Attack us in our home once, shame on you. Attack us twice, and we get the hell out of town.

Chapter Thirty-One

Each Council member's home was considered, despite The Greek's early declaration that it had to remain in Europe, and we had to present the potential benefits and risks of relocating to our territory. When it came time for Gabriel and me, I wasn't sure what to say, but I knew I didn't want to have the Council relocate to our part of the world. I looked at Gabriel, and he spoke up for both of us.

"While it would be an honor to host the Council in California, Caleb and I had only recently joined our separate packs into one before leaving to join the rest of you here. We would be bringing the Council into a potentially volatile situation if we suddenly presented our pack with this news as well. As it stands, we have already lost at least three of our members because they refused to follow the new guidelines we put in place."

I watched the way he commanded the room. He may not have liked being an alpha, but it suited him.

"Our homes may be an option for the future, but for now, I think there are more beneficial alternatives somewhere else."

When he finished speaking, he looked over at me and all I could do was smile and nod because the conversation had moved on to Jae. I was incredibly impressed and wouldn't have been able to come up with a reason that good if I'd had hours to prep.

After everyone had presented their territories and made suggestions about what should be done next, we voted and made our official decision. Without Jusuf to continue contact with the Pressors, we hoped the new location, which would be Jae's home in Korea, would be kept secret for a decent amount of time. It also added the bonus protection of providing Giuliana and Lorenzo a new home, well away from their pasts, where they could hopefully live safely. Shortly after the new location was decided, the meeting ended, and we all went our separate ways. With the murders figured out, the Council had no need to remain together for the time being, and Adam, Gabriel and I were allowed to leave when we were ready.

I swung by the kitchen on my way back up to our rooms to grab something to eat since I hadn't eaten anything substantial for dinner, and Gabriel joined me at the table.

"Where's Adam?" I asked, expecting that he would have come in by now.

"I asked him to give us some time to talk. I imagine he's in his room getting packed for our flight home tomorrow." Gabriel looked like he had something on his mind, and from the energy coming off him, I could tell it wasn't anything good.

"Oh, okay, what did you want to talk about?" My stomach knotted up almost instantly, but I tried not to let my tension show.

He took a deep breath and then blurted out. "I think we should break up."

The words hit me like a wall, and all I could do was sit there quietly, replaying what he'd said repeatedly in my mind. I wasn't sure that I heard him correctly, so I kept cycling through it to figure out what I had missed. Each time I did however, I heard the same thing. Gabriel wanted to break up with me.

"Did I do something wrong?" I asked.

"Nothing that you could have helped, no." His assurance wasn't much comfort because he'd said it was my fault. "I just think we got a little carried away. I was supposed to follow you around when we first met, and it was easier to do that if you didn't mind having me there."

It seemed like he was trying to make me feel better somehow but if that was his plan, he'd failed miserably.

"When we had dinner at work that first time and you told me you were gay, I realized that if we started to date, I could find out even more about you than I would have as a friend."

"So all of this was just an act? You never actually liked me at all?" I asked. Anger had begun to creep in as a replacement for my sadness, and my tone was biting.

"It started out like that, yes, but then I really did like you. You were sweet and funny and cute. You still are all those things, but you're also more powerful than I am, and you can do things I can't do. When we awakened together, I thought

310

that it was the Universe telling me that we were meant to be together. But then we got here, and I realized that you were the one who could do everything, and I was just tagging along on your tail."

He laughed a little at the joke he'd made, but his pun had done little to curb my sadness and anger.

"What you're telling me then, is that if you had been able to do all the things I can do, you would have wanted to stay together. But because you can't, it's not worth trying to make things work?" I could feel the tears as they spilled down my face, but I ignored them and stared straight ahead, not looking at Gabriel as he replied.

"That's what I said, but I'm not sure it's exactly what I meant."

"Well, what did you mean then?" I asked as I tried to get my emotions under control.

"I don't know Caleb, this is hard for me too. I don't think I want to be in a relationship right now. It's not you. I just don't want to be with anyone at all."

"Oh my god, did you just use 'It's not you, it's me' to break up with me?" I looked at him this time because I was so angry that I couldn't keep my composure.

"Please keep your voice down, everyone will hear you," he said, as he looked around to see if anyone had walked into the kitchen.

"You know what, Gabriel, you're right, it isn't working out between us. And I agree, it isn't me." I stood up and took my plate of food with me as I walked out of the room and climbed the stairs toward my bedroom. When I got there, I opened the door and saw a somewhat surprised Lorenzo standing in the middle of the room in his pajamas.

"Caleb, are you okay? Did you need something?" He looked at me like I had burst in to tell him something important and then he looked at my plate of food and cocked his head to the side, confused.

In my anger, I had forgotten that I told Lorenzo and Giuliana to use my room, so I backed out quickly.

"Nope, nothing's going on, I'm so sorry to walk in on you. Have a good night!" I closed the door as I crossed the threshold and practically ran to Adam's room, where I knocked on the door and waited.

When he opened it, he was on the phone but motioned me into the room.

"Right, I understand," he said into the phone and then waited. "If that's how you feel, that's fine," he waited again while the other person responded. "Okay…okay…don't worry about it, I'll be fine."

Based on the side of the conversation I could hear, I imagined the other side wasn't going so well.

"All right Megan, goodbye." My ears pricked up at the mention of Megan's name, but I simply ate my food in silence and watched as he ended the call and then sat on the corner of his bed.

At the mention of her name, I remembered my suspicions from earlier.

"Adam, do you think there's any way that Megan is a Pressor?"

"She's not, I already investigated her history. She and her family check out. They are who they say they are. Why do you ask?"

I felt a little silly for bringing it up now but was glad to hear that my best friend wasn't out to kill me, or just my friend to make her job of keeping tabs on me easier.

"Just checking." I finished all the chips that I'd piled on my plate to fill the silence, but when Adam still said nothing, I finally blurted out what had happened downstairs.

"Gabriel and I just broke up." I figured I would start so he could prepare for what was sure to be the most awkward flight home in the world.

"You did? I'm sorry to hear that. What happened?" He attempted to sound surprised, but it seemed like maybe I had missed some signs of trouble that he'd picked up already.

"Long story, I won't bore you. He basically said the Universe wasn't giving him a sign that we were meant to be, and he didn't want to date anyone right now." I used air quotes as I spoke, and sounded a little snarky, even for me, but I didn't care.

"What did you say?"

"I agreed with him, then said I wasn't the problem. And I came up here, where I walked in on Lorenzo as he was about to get in bed, and then your phone call. It's been a great ending to the evening, let me tell you."

I took a bite of the sandwich I'd made and sat on the other corner of the bed.

"What did Megan have to say?" I didn't want to pry, but I knew I would hear it from her. I'm sure he realized that as well, so giving him a chance to share his side seemed like the right thing to do.

"Not much really, I called to let her know we were coming home tomorrow and that I should be able to see her in a couple days. She told me it wasn't working out because I was so distant all the time."

That, unfortunately, sounded like something she would say. Megan approached all her breakups as the victim regardless of the reality of that claim. She was the innocent bystander who was taken advantage of, left behind, or smothered by an overly eager guy. In fact, she had probably already found someone else and just didn't want to admit it. Absence did not make her heart grow fonder; it made her lust for others grow stronger.

"I'm sorry that she did that to you. You know it was bound to happen eventually though, right? That's just how she operates." I finished up my sandwich and put the plate on the nightstand.

"It's okay, I would have ended things eventually anyway, I'm not really interested in a human mate." He looked over and gave me a small smile and then changed the subject. "In other news, I also happened to call Lorelai and Brent to let them know we'd be coming home tomorrow so one of them would be able to pick us up at the airport."

"Oh, good thinking, I hadn't gotten that far along in my planning yet. What did they have to say?"

"Lorelai just asked what had happened, and I told her about all the major events that happened over the past few days. She wants you to call her when you have some time to talk."

I had expected she'd want to speak with me about things even though Adam had already told her everything. I planned to do it in the morning. We had a long flight tomorrow and for some reason, watching movies and cuddling didn't feel like a possibility.

"How about Brent?" I asked as I started to fold my dirty clothes to make packing easier.

"Well, that's where things get interesting. As I'm sure you remember, Brent and Tanya started dating."

"Right, how's that going? Did something happen?" I thought maybe they had broken up as well. I was still surprised they had even started to date in the first place.

"Well," Adam continued. "I asked Brent how everything was going, and he told me they're getting married." Adam's face lit up, and he looked happier than I had seen him in a while.

"Wait, what? Married? When did that happen?"

"Apparently he asked her as a joke last night, and she said yes." He started laughing when he said it. "I think he's too scared of her to back out now, but I also like that she keeps him in line. Plus, it will give you a chance to officiate the wedding, and that is something I can't wait to see!"

I realized that at least some of his happiness had been in anticipation of this moment when he knew I'd start to panic.

"Why do I have to do it? What do I even do? What if I mess something up?" I pictured all the things that could go wrong and how I could ruin their ceremony. Adam continued to laugh at me and jumped out of the way when I threw some jeans at him. "I hate you so much right now."

"It isn't a big deal. You'll be fine. And just think, now the pack will have a great reason to stay together even though you and Gabriel split up."

He tossed my jeans back to my side of the bed, and I folded them again.

"You do make a good point I suppose. I hadn't thought about what would happen if we weren't together. Do you think the pack would have split apart?" I asked, worried that maybe I'd been too harsh on Gabriel, and should have tried to work through things rather than getting upset and walking away.

"I have no idea, but you don't have to worry now because we're all about to be bound by marriage, and that will solidify everyone's commitment to a single pack. And it's not like they're going to be getting married tomorrow or anything. You'll have months to prepare for it."

Adam loved to freak me out, but he was always there when I needed him, and he calmed me down just as often, so that was a good balance to have.

"Thank you for saying that, I appreciate it." I smiled at him, and he smiled back.

"No problem. Now, are you packing tonight or in the morning, because I'm exhausted, and I'd like to go to sleep."

"I'm going to finish up tonight, but I'll be quiet, so go to bed if you're tired."

"Okay, good night, Caleb," he said as he pulled some of the covers back on the bed and climbed in.

"Good night, Adam." I packed up as quickly as possible and then climbed into bed myself and was asleep almost as soon as my head touched the pillow.

* * *

Adam and Gabriel were ready to go early the following day, so we threw our luggage in the trunk of the car and went back inside to say our goodbyes. We started with Kenai, Stephen, and The Greek, but since we knew we would see them again, it was more a discussion about the future than it was an actual goodbye. Afterward, The Greek pulled me aside and thanked me for what I'd done for the Council. I was surprised at his change of heart, but I decided to take whatever I could get. I gave him a hug, which he didn't return, but didn't pull away from either.

Then we said goodbye to Jae and Maeve, who were doing their best to get things in order for the move. They stopped when they saw us and pulled Gabriel and me into tight hugs, and then switched. They felt almost like family, despite the short amount of time we'd known each other. I was excited to get back home, but I also looked forward to the opportunity to visit Jae's home and see Maeve and the others again in the future. When I turned around from hugging Jae, Giuliana swept me up in another hug.

"Thank you so much for everything you've done for us Caleb! We couldn't have survived for very much longer without the help of the Council." Giuliana tried to keep the emotion out of her voice but failed miserably.

"I'm just glad everything worked out, and you did a lot for us as well. You and Lorenzo both saved my life, so we are more than even now. And I'm excited to see what will happen now that the Council has a rogue offering input."

I smiled at Lorenzo, who stood quietly next to Giuliana, and took my hand in both of his once she released me and grabbed onto Adam.

"Thank you for everything." He showed his neck to me as a sign of submission, but I just chuckled and told him he didn't have to do that for me anymore.

He smiled when he looked back at me. "I'll try to remember that."

"Make sure you do." I laughed. "Well, we'd better get going. It is an incredibly long flight back to California!"

Adam and Gabriel finished their goodbyes, and we all walked back out to the car and back toward our regular lives.

Epilogue
~Fifteen Months Later~

I sat on the edge of the bed as I mentally ran through everything I had to make sure to say during the wedding, when there was a knock on the door. I got up and opened it and had to backpedal out of the door as Megan forced her way into my room.

"Oh my god, I have to pee so badly!" She ran to the bathroom and slammed the door behind her.

"Nice to see you too," I said through the door.

"Shut up, I think my bladder was ten seconds from exploding, and then who would you have had to keep you entertained during the festivities?"

I didn't like to admit it, but she had a point. I hadn't thought about what today would be like with Gabriel by my side, but not as my boyfriend, until it was too late to do anything about it. I knew it was for the best, but even that knowledge didn't make things any easier. I had to change the subject, or I was liable to lose my cool before the wedding even started.

"I just assumed you'd have a date already, or that you'd be on the prowl for someone new."

The toilet flushed, and Megan appeared again, washed her hands, and flung droplets of water in my face. "That is an excellent point. I can't let you hang all over me tonight. It might give the men at the party the wrong idea."

"Oh, believe me, none of them would be fooled by me being on your arm. Your eyes betray your inner sexual beast, and they'd know I wasn't keeping you from releasing her."

"And don't you forget it baby!" She kissed my cheek and then rubbed away the lipstick that was left behind. "In reality though, I'm glad you asked me to come today. I was afraid I'd never see you again because of what happened between Adam and me." She'd moved on while we were still in Croatia, a few times, I was pretty sure, but never confirmed. Adam had been disappointed but not surprised and wasn't upset, as far as I could tell. But I didn't share that with her and risk bruising her ego.

"As if we could have kept you away if we had tried," I laughed. "Adam made it very clear that your relationship shouldn't get in the way of our friendship. He knows how important you are to me."

We smiled at each other.

"Ditto."

"Can I just say I think you're crazy for leaving him? I mean, damn!" I shook my hand like it'd been burned, and she laughed.

"He's great and all, but I'm looking for absolute perfection. Plus, he was gone for a long time," she said, as she fixed her makeup in the mirror.

"Perfection, or a challenge?" I asked.

"Is there a difference?" She replied, an evil twinkle in her eyes.

"For you, apparently not. I happen to like the idea of not having to fight with someone to keep things interesting."

I grabbed my vest off the chair in the corner of the room and buttoned it up. I looked at myself in the mirror, evaluated my appearance and hoped I looked official enough for the ceremony.

"Yes," she agreed. "But without the fighting, there isn't a reason for make-up sex, and without that, what's the point of being in a relationship?"

She laughed and fixed the back of my collar, smoothing it down and giving me her approval.

"Looking good! Maybe I won't be the only one to land a man tonight."

"Yeah right! You know you'll find someone before I ever have a chance." I smiled at her before shooing her out of the room. "Speaking of which, you'd better go scope out your next conquest!"

"Good point, thanks for looking out for me!" She laughed as she walked out of the room and left me to finish getting ready.

I thought about what she'd said about fighting being an essential part of a relationship and wondered if she was right. Was it possible that relationships were supposed to be that much work? Gabriel and I had never fought about anything until the very end, we didn't always agree, and we didn't always want the same things, but we never really fought. Maybe that was why things hadn't worked out. There weren't enough reasons to keep us together to make our relationship worth fighting for.

In the months since we returned from Europe, Gabriel had avoided me as much as possible, but still attended all the pack functions as was required by our role. He seemed happier now and more relaxed as an alpha, which was due in part to the fact that once he turned 18, he was able to shift into other forms.

One day he sent me a picture of a deer with the message, *Hey, look what I can do!*

He'd finally gotten what he wanted and felt like he was worthy of the position he held.

I shook my head and tried to clear my thoughts away. I didn't have time for that now. I had a wedding to officiate, and I wasn't confident that I knew what the hell I was doing even after months of studying.

There was a knock at the door, and I assumed Megan had forgotten something, so I started to look around for a stray phone or something shiny she might have left behind. When I opened the door, I stopped breathing.

"Can I come in?"

I nodded silently and moved out of the way as Gabriel walked into the room.

"I thought you were…"

"I know, I was supposed to be, I just felt like I should…"

"Oh right, of course, you should. Why wouldn't you?"

Our conversation felt incredibly awkward and based on Gabriel's refusal to look me in the eyes, it seemed like I wasn't the only one who thought it.

"It's nice to see you again," I said, as I did my best to smile. I felt like an idiot for not having something better to say, but it was too late now.

"Thank you. It's nice to see you too," he offered. "You look great!" His smile seemed genuine, and he finally met my eyes. I felt myself getting drawn back into the safety of his smile and the warmth of his eyes.

"Thank you, so do you," I replied lamely. I turned away and picked my jacket up off the chair, pulled it on and buttoned the top button. "So…" I started.

"Caleb, I just…" he said at the same time.

"Sorry, go ahead." I hoped listening to him would help me figure out what I wanted to say.

"I just wanted to let you know that I brought someone with me tonight," he said quietly, his eyes searched mine for a reaction. "A date, I guess."

I could feel the blood drain from my face as my heart sunk into my stomach. I struggled to breathe normally and was surprised to feel my mouth spread into what I hoped was a natural looking smile.

"Oh? Great! That's great!" I lied.

"Really?" He took a small step closer to me, his eyes narrowed, and his nose twitched subtly, like he was trying to tell if I'd lied or not.

"Yeah, of course." I took a deep breath and let it out as a cough. "I'm glad you found someone new," I took another deep breath so it wouldn't seem like I was gasping for air. "And so quickly." I smiled again and when I exhaled it sounded a little like a laugh. I wondered if I had perhaps lost my grip on reality and had slipped into a manic state.

"Hey Caleb," Adam popped his head in the door, and when he saw Gabriel, he stopped. "I'm sorry, I didn't realize anyone else was in here."

"It's okay. I was just heading out to take my place," Gabriel said as he turned to leave. He smiled and walked out of the room, nodding at Adam as he passed by.

"Are you okay?" Adam asked. He stepped into the room and shut the door behind him.

I looked up at him and fought the tears that burned my eyes.

"I've been better." I closed my eyes tight and felt the tears streak down my face, leaving wet trails on my cheeks as they did. "But I'll be fine. I have to be. Brent and Tanya are getting married today." I tried to infuse excitement into my voice.

"If it's any consolation, I've seen the guy Gabriel brought to the wedding, and you're much better looking." He winked at me as he said it, and I cracked a smile.

"Of course I am," I said, and wiped my tears away. "I mean, look at me! I'm the whole package! Who wouldn't want all of this?"

I laughed, but even the joke compliment to myself helped to lift my spirits. I looked in the mirror again and saw, for the first time, the man I could become, and I liked what I saw.

"Damn right!" Adam replied, patting me on the back. "Here, I have something for you from Lorelai."

He walked over and grabbed my left arm, pulled the jacket sleeve up and exposed my shirt cuff. He pulled a cufflink out of his pocket and pushed it through the buttonhole, then repeated the same process on the other side. When he released my right arm, I raised it closer to my face to examine the addition and smiled at what I saw.

I stared at the silver cufflinks with my initials on them.

"Thank you." I caught his eyes and saw something there I hadn't noticed before, but it was gone before I could identify what it was.

"No need to thank me, like I said, they were a gift from Lorelai." He looked down at his watch and then reached around me and placed his hand flat on my back as he led me to the door. "Ready?"

"As I'll ever be," I replied.

"You'd better be, we're about to be late!" Adam pushed me out the door and toward the rest of the pack.

I considered trying to stall but realized that today wasn't about me, and no one would remember if I made a small mistake if the outcome was the same. Adam steered me through the house and into the backyard, where everyone, except for Brent and Tanya, waited. I looked around for Lorelai and Megan in the crowd. Megan was near the back next to a guy I'd seen before but didn't know, which seemed an excellent way to start. At least he was someone from the pack. On the other hand, Lorelai was near the front of the crowd with the rest of the pack elders, and she smiled brightly when our eyes met.

"Good luck!" Adam whispered as he pushed me toward the platform at the front of the crowd.

"Gee, thanks," I mumbled under my breath, but I looked back at Lorelai and focused on her face to stay calm. I walked over to Gabriel, and we began our path to the front of the group. Each row stood as we passed, then kneeled and exposed their necks to us. Lorelai and the pack council were the last to do so, and the first to return to their seats once we had taken our places on the platform.

Gabriel and I read from pages of the book Lorelai had given to me about the history of our traditions. It included information about the ceremony itself, and a few other events that had taken place over the previous week. When that was finished, Brent and Tanya walked to their positions in front of us, where they also kneeled and exposed their necks. I took a deep breath and let it out before I kneeled next to each and bit down on their exposed flesh.

"Marked by me, marked by thee," I said loud enough for the entire pack to hear.

Gabriel followed me and made his mark next to mine.

Brent leaned forward as Tanya exposed the other side of her neck to him and bit down, his teeth sharpened enough to draw blood. When it came, he licked her wound clean and then moved back to his knees, exposing his neck to her. Tanya repeated the action, opening minor wounds on Brent's neck and then licking them clean.

I turned to Brent and gestured toward Tanya as I continued.

"Brent, provide the gift of flesh to prove your ability to care for your mate."

Adam stepped forward with the hindquarter of what appeared to be a small pig and handed it to Brent, who took it before setting it at Tanya's feet.

"For all my life I pledge to hunt with you and for you. To provide for you when you cannot provide for yourself and to care for you when you cannot care for yourself. With this gift of flesh, my oath is sealed."

Gabriel turned toward Tanya and then repeated the directions.

"Tanya, provide the gift of flesh to prove your ability to care for your mate."

Tanya's attendant stepped forward with an entire sheep, which she passed easily to Tanya, who lifted it as though it weighed nothing, then laid it gently at Brent's feet.

"For all my life I pledge to hunt with you and for you. To provide for you when you cannot provide for yourself and to care for you when you cannot care for yourself. With this gift of flesh, my oath is sealed."

Brent's mouth dropped open at the animal's size and almost caused me to lose my composure. I had to bite my cheek to keep myself from laughing.

"Tanya and Brent, you have entered this space of your own will and sealed your union with blood and flesh in front of all those gathered. By the old laws of the Awakened, we pronounce you mated for life."

The crowd erupted into applause, and Tanya stepped forward, wrapped Brent up in a tight hug and lifted him off his feet while he laughed happily. The pack rushed in to congratulate them, and there was a massive crush of bodies. Fortunately, I was on the edge, so I stepped back from the crowd and observed everyone's happiness and excitement from outside the fray. For the first time, the whole pack seemed to be one, and I was surprised that Tanya and Brent would be the reason everyone came together. I wasn't going to question it though. I was just happy that it had happened without any real trouble.

Adam joined me on the platform and looked into the mass of bodies that still waited for the chance to congratulate the newly mated pair. "You did a great job!"

I looked at him and smiled. "I did, didn't I? I'll be honest though if I had been forced to lick blood off their necks, there might never be another mated pair in this pack."

We both laughed, and I continued, "Kind of makes me glad to be single."

I wasn't sure I meant it, but I had started to believe that being in a relationship right now wasn't all it was cracked up to be.

"Are you sure about that?" Adam leaned down and pressed his lips against mine, his tongue licking playfully at my lips, which parted in surprise allowing him access to the rest of my mouth. His tongue slipped in and tangled with mine before he broke off the kiss. "You're right, that was horrible." He looked me in the eyes, his smile broad and cocky.

When I finally regained the ability to speak, I looked at him carefully, "You know, for a straight guy, you sure do like to kiss guys a lot."

He laughed. "Who said I was straight?"

"What do you mean!?"

"You assumed I was straight because I dated Megan, and there wasn't a reason to correct you, but you never asked." He leaned down and kissed me again, and I could feel a weight around my heart loosen slightly as warmth spread through my body.

He moved back and when I opened my eyes, he was staring at them, and smiling at me. Suddenly, the craving for an extra-large pizza ripped through my body. When I realized what happened I looked incredulously at him.

"You asshole!"

His laughter rocked his whole body and the vibrations from it shook the air around us, which was increased by my laughter.

"What?" he asked innocently. "I'm hungry, aren't you?"

I punched him in the shoulder.

"Of course I am," I said.

As our laughter subsided, I knew I would be okay and that I'd figure everything out eventually. Until then, I was happy to have the support of the people in my life and the comfort of knowing they'd always be there for me.

The End.

330

Thank You!

I have had so much fun with the story of Caleb, Gabriel, Adam, and the others and while this is the end of the series for now, these characters continue to live in my head and I have not ruled out the possibility of something happening with them in the future. For now, I am focusing on other projects and stories about new characters, new small towns, and new relationship woes.

When I began writing Awakened, I wanted it to be a metaphor for the coming out process that so many have to go through, but I didn't want to write about a gay character who struggled with that aspect of his life. Coming out is not a one-time thing, every time we meet someone new, we come out. Every time we change jobs, or take a new class, or move to a new area, we come out all over again. I hope that Awakened helped put that situation into perspective.

Challenged, was meant to demonstrate that first love isn't always forever, and that's okay, because you can still learn a lot, and grow as an individual or couple through that experience of love and loss. Who knows, maybe someone better has been waiting for their chance all along.

About the Author

Kenneth Creech is an award-winning author who currently lives outside Houston, Texas. *Awakened* and *Challenged* are his first and second novels, respectively. He has also contributed to the 2023 Independent Press Award's selection for best Anthology, *Queer for the New Year*. The 2001 non-fiction book *Coming Out Young and Faithful*. To find out more about Kenneth, his current and future projects, and more about his writing process, visit him at:

www.kennethcreech.com

You can also follow Kenneth on his various social media platforms here:

https://linktr.ee/kbcreech_

www.ingramcontent.com/pod-product-compliance
Lightning Source LLC
Chambersburg PA
CBHW010334010826
48970CB00014B/2696

9 798986 880129